Not Exactly the Girl You'd Bring Home

Sunshine and Specter Paranormal Agency #0

Dan Ackerman

Supposed Crimes LLC • Matthews, North Carolina

Published in the United States.

ISBN: 978-1-952150-34-0

Covert Art by Vincent Pesce

www.supposedcrimes.com

This book is typeset in Goudy Old Style.

For David

Late May, 1914

Hiram sat in his study, a blanket pulled across his lap and a wool coat pulled over his shoulders. He had started a fire in the grate but the heat from it had not yet filled up the room. Within an hour he would be perfectly warm, or, as warm as he would ever get in this city. Even after nearly a century in Canada, he still yearned for the heat of his native Georgia.

But he had a life here in Canada. Or he'd had a life here. His niece had passed away a few years ago, comfortable and happy in her own bed with her dog at her feet. Her mother and grandmother were long gone. The dog had died, too.

He put his thoughts of Ellen aside and picked up the stack of papers he'd brought to review. After half an hour, he'd shrugged off the wool coat and rolled up his sleeves to avoid ink stains, though it had been somewhat of a struggle with the use of only one hand. After so many years without the hand, he had mastered many things, but some acts would never come easily.

A slippery voice said, "Hello, Hiram."

He gasped and started, his head jerking up. He managed to stop himself from spilling ink everywhere.

Standing before his desk was an impossibly tall man with spindly limbs. A man that Hiram recognized right away.

"What?" Hiram asked. He hated the nervous whisper his voice

had become when faced with the Devil for the second time in his life.

"I have a job for you," the Devil said. "Good thing I didn't let you go to waste."

Just after his twenty-sixth birthday, Hiram had suffered a fatal injury and the Devil had saved him, granting him an unnaturally long youth in the process. Hiram had not asked to be saved or to stay young, and now he suspected he knew why Satan had done what he'd done.

"No, I..."

"Hiram, I'm not asking." Satan took a basket from the floor and set it on Hiram's desk.

Hiram made himself peek inside and found an infant nestled within, swaddled in blankets. He'd expected something awful, a severed head or pile of entrails. He blinked a few times, trying to reconcile his expectation with reality.

Then fear settled in his stomach. How had the Devil acquired this child? Had he done something awful to the baby's parents? Would he do something hideous to the poor little thing?

"His name is Felix. He is in terrible danger," the Devil told him.

"Why?" Hiram asked. He couldn't take his eyes away from the too-small baby.

As he gazed into the basket, the Devil mumbled, "It's the small matter of his parentage."

Hiram didn't know what that meant. He looked over the child again, searching for signs of anything untoward. "I don't follow."

"He's my son."

"And his mother?"

"Human." Satan's fingers combed his hair behind his ear, then skimmed over his shirt. He cleared his throat. "She's...She's passed, unfortunately."

Hiram finally looked at the Devil. He didn't know the Devil well, nor did he want to, and he didn't know if the Lord of Hell experienced the same feelings as humans did, but he looked guilty. "How did she die?"

"Oh, poor Mercy. She was the victim of, well, I suppose we must call it an honor killing. Due to my presence in her life, I'm afraid. Her family wishes the child dead as well," Lucifer explained. He made a face and offered, "Moralists."

Hiram wrinkled his nose. Moralist involvement never boded

well. Their pro-human tendencies could skew toward terrible violence if given the opportunity. "Why bring him here? Surely, it's within your abilities to manage Moralists. They're only human."

"The child has another pursuer."

Hiram sighed and ran a hand through his curls. He didn't want to know, but he didn't know how else to proceed, so he asked, "Who else?"

"An angel."

"What?" Hiram knew a great deal about unnatural creatures and the workings of their community. He was, by some right, part of it, given his marriage to a fallen angel and his status as a mage. He had never heard of Heaven concerning itself with such affairs. "I'm not aware of any of your other children being hunted by angels."

Satan reached his hand into the basket and with long fingers, gently extracted the child's left arm. He turned it to show a birthmark on the forearm.

Hiram could not quite make out any particular shape. It looked like a smudge more than anything, ordinary and pale brown.

"He is…or, well, I suspect that he is an antichrist. There have been three born so far but none have lived long enough to walk." Satan released the child's arm and the babe snuggled further into the blankets.

"He's *what?*" Hiram demanded.

"It's a potential, not a promise. He has no more innate capacity for evil than any of my other children and well, I could go on about what the nature of an antichrist even *is*…But that's not the point."

Hiram leaned in to take a closer look.

The baby stirred.

"What is the point?"

"That he's just a little baby and he needs someone to protect him."

"I…I don't think this is entirely an appropriate course of action," Hiram said. He had been an uncle, but what the Devil implied now…Hiram couldn't fathom keeping a demon, let alone the antichrist, as a ward.

"I know that a mage of your caliber would be able to protect him," the Devil said. It was a statement of fact with no intent to flatter.

Phaedrus, wearing a long velvet robe in a shade of deep brown that complimented the jade of their skin and the fawn of their hair, entered the room with a steaming mug in their hand. "Darling, I..." They frowned when they saw their king. "I knew it."

"Knew what?" the Devil asked mildly.

"That you were saving him for something. I knew it," they said, scowling. "Pretending like you kept him young for me."

"Phaedrus," Satan said.

"You might as well get out. Whatever it is you're after, I'm not about to let you weasel your way into some deal or another with him."

"Let me?" the Devil asked, almost smiling with one eyebrow raised.

"Yes, *let you*, Lucifer. You might be king down there, but this is my house and that's my husband."

"I can't believe you married a Reinhart. God, the things they've done!" Satan tutted.

Hiram's face heated. He wanted to argue, but he knew the ugly things his family had done in the New World and couldn't fathom what they'd been like as aristocrats in Europe.

"We aren't all in love with you. You can only push our loyalties so far before they break," Phaedrus warned.

"Don't you even want to know I've come to *ask* of you?" Lucifer's eyes drifted toward the basket.

Phaedrus peered into the basket and crossed their arms. They sighed and looked up at their king. "Yours?"

The Devil nodded. "Yes."

"And I expect you're trying to pawn the poor thing off on the two of us?"

"I am not a fit parent."

Phaedrus sighed, some of the irritation going out of their tone. "You can't blame yourself about Elisa."

"I can."

The demon rolled their eyes.

Not quite begging but certainly insistent, Lucifer said, "Please."

Phaedrus looked the Devil over. "Maybe you shouldn't be having babies if you won't take care of them."

"Yes, well, these things happen. I did feel quite foolish," the Devil said with a shrug. "The only one born in quite some time. I've been much more careful."

Phaedrus sighed and looked at the baby again.

"His name is Felix," Satan said, looking down at the child with a softness in his face that unnerved Hiram.

Phaedrus, on the other hand, seemed to respond to that softness and put a hand on the Devil's arm. "What happened with Elisa aside, you should raise your son. I know you want to."

Satan shook his head. "No. I can't. I'm not fit."

Phaedrus rubbed their king's arm. "It wasn't your fault."

"Please," Lucifer said.

Phaedrus gave the Devil a sad smile.

Hiram asked, "Phaedrus, are you...complicit in this venture?"

"We'll need to find a nurse," the creature said.

"Yes, that much I surmised on my own. That's not what I'm asking."

Phaedrus held his gaze. "I don't see much in the way of courses of action. Would you send him away?"

Hiram would have sent the Devil away a thousand times, but the baby presented a different scenario altogether. Whatever this infant was or would become, it was just a tiny, helpless thing now. "I don't know anything about babies."

Phaedrus smiled at him. They blinked a few times and Hiram thought he saw the shine of tears in their eyes. "You'd be a good father, darling, you haven't got to worry about that."

A father!

Hiram hadn't thought of it that way. A guardian was one thing but a father! He looked between the two fallen angels, then back at the baby. Neither of them had even been babies or children, they had never needed to grow up or been helpless or small. If Hiram sent the Devil away, and he thought he could, where would he take the baby? Who else could keep him safe? Without any arrogance, Hiram knew he numbered among a small number of mages who could have accomplished such a daunting feat.

"We..." He looked at Phaedrus. "We could be parents."

Phaedrus nodded. They wiped beneath their eyes, then sniffled and turned back to their king. They nodded to him as well. "Consider him safe. Hiram is uncommonly good at his craft."

"You'll need to ward the babe from prying eyes. Human and divine," Satan suggested. "Right now, I can shield him but when I'm gone, that will fade."

Hiram looked down into the basket. "An angel?"

Satan nodded. He reached out to touch the infant's cheek.

"I'll get started on the wards," Hiram said, heading to his bookshelf and resigning himself to the fact that his students' papers wouldn't be graded that night. A strange sort of shock settled over him. He was in no way prepared to care for a child, but he could cast the wards. He would focus on that.

"Would it...you wouldn't mind if I came to visit, would you?" the Devil asked.

Hiram glanced over, his lips pursed. "You don't seem to have any problem dropping by whenever you please." Already, he disliked the idea of Satan visiting his son.

Well. Their son, he supposed.

Not an hour ago and his greatest concern had been grading papers. Now he had a son.

"Hiram, it will be a great debt I owe you. The both of you. I repay my debts."

The mage hummed a non-answer and turned back to the bookshelf. He needed to cast these wards, focus on something other than the enormity of what had just happened.

"Of course, you can visit," Phaedrus said. They reached into the basket and picked up the sleeping babe, then cradled him against their chest.

Hiram almost started crying at the sight of that. He hadn't expected any of this, not ever. He didn't know what he'd thought his life would be like, but this wasn't it. It wasn't that he didn't feel ready for fatherhood. At his age, it would have been a ridiculous concern. He'd never thought it would be accessible to him.

Phaedrus asked, "When was he born?"

"April fifteenth."

"Not even two months!" Phaedrus exclaimed softly. "And he's so *small*."

"He came too early. Junius, though, he...he said he would be well. You know, hearty stock and all."

"Felix what?"

"Hmm?" the Devil asked.

"What's the rest of his name?"

"Felix James Specter."

"Felix James Specter," Phaedrus repeated.

"Keep him safe," the Devil pleaded, putting a hand on the baby. "Please. I fail my children, all of them, and I know...Phaedrus, I know that you won't fail him."

"No need to be maudlin," the demon chided.

"And what about me!" Hiram demanded from the bookshelf. "Do you think I will?"

"Of course not, Hiram, of course not," the Devil said. "Thank you."

Hiram pulled down a handful of books, balancing them carefully in his handless arm, and set them on his desk. "This will take me a few hours. Phaedrus, love, maybe you should see if you can find a nurse."

"At this hour?" the demon asked, then looked at their king. "What have you been feeding him?"

"Uh. If I said blood, would that be a bad answer?" Satan said.

"A terrible one," Phaedrus said.

"Then I didn't."

Hiram could not tell if the Devil was being serious.

"Darling, I'll be back as quick as I can," the demon said and returned Felix to the basket. "I think Dorothy's mother is nursing still. Or maybe it was Mildred's? I'm not sure. I'll be home soon enough."

"Thank you," Hiram said without looking up. "Love you."

"You, too, dear," Phaedrus said and gave the mage a pat on the arm and a tender kiss on the cheek. "I do love you so, Hiram," they reminded warmly before they left.

LATE EARLY SUMMER, 1920

FELIX HATED Lionel Sullivan. He was seven years old, but big for his age, and possessed a shrewd nastiness that only showed its face when adults were not about. During classes, he would pinch the other students when the teacher's back was turned. To the adults themselves, he was sweet, educated, and polite. He brought in gifts for them and always raised his hand with the right answer.

The worst thing that Lionel did, worse than pinching Felix and pulling Mildred's hair, was when he cornered Charlie, a boy the same age as Felix, outside the bathrooms and pushed him around, knocking him to the floor and hissing nasty things. Charlie could never tell his parents because his parents did not know that he snuck into the school bathrooms every morning before class and changed out of his dress and into a suit that he borrowed from Felix.

Charlie refused to tell anyone, even Felix's parents, who ran the school they all attended.

"They'll tell my parents," Charlie said.

"So?" Felix demanded.

"*Don't tell,*" Charlie insisted.

Felix sighed. "Bibi would help."

"We're going to be late," Charlie said and walked away.

Felix followed behind, wishing to shed the jacket of his suit, and wondering how long it would take before Charlie got caught for sure. So far, none of the teachers had questioned anything, but that was because Felix had tampered with Charlie's enrollment records.

He had thought his handwriting would never pass as an adult's, but then he had seen the shaky writing of the other parents who sent their children to the Academy for Young Learners, a branch of the Reinhart-Queen University of Arcane Magics and Sciences. The Academy was a highly charitable branch of the University. Almost half of the students attended on scholarships.

A handful of students of middling economic status attended, but for the most part, the other half of the school came from mage families. Those children would go on to take classes at the University when they completed their studies at the Academy. Some would even join the school's staff as adults.

Felix settled into his desk next to Charlie's, trying to figure out what to do about Lionel. He had no good answer. He knew someday he would come into his own magic, different from the arcane magic taught at the University, but not for years.

He could not tell his parents without betraying Charlie.

He fiddled with the amulet around his neck until his teacher, Ms. Perkins, cleared her throat and fixed her eyes on him.

He looked around the class and saw that every other student had their primers on their desk. He hurried to take his out.

The school year would be over soon and that meant that Lionel wouldn't be able to bother them unless he went out of his way to do so.

After school, Charlie waited for the other students to leave and then ducked into the bathroom. He slunk back out in a pretty dress of pale blue cotton, his shoulders hunched. He held out a ribbon to Felix and said, "I can't get it back in right."

Felix fixed the matching ribbon into Charlie's short strawberry-blond hair. He looked miserable.

"Bibi wears dresses, too," Felix said.

Charlie scowled.

"They're not a girl either. It's just clothes."

Charlie said, "I'll see you tomorrow."

Felix nodded, walked him out, and then sat on the stairs of the school's entrance for a while.

"Why the long face?"

Felix looked up to see one of his parents, a fallen angel with jade skin and hair that they had recently cut short. It still jarred him to see them with short hair, but long hair had started to fall out of fashion for everyone after the war. "Nothing, Bibi."

"Nonsense." The creature sat beside him. They smelled of violets and had for as long as Felix could remember.

"I can't tell you."

"You can tell me anything."

"It's a secret."

"A secret?" the creature asked, raising their eyebrows. "Not like Jangles, I hope."

"No. It isn't my secret," Felix said.

"Oh, that's grave indeed," they said, and Felix didn't get the sense that Bibi was being facetious. They put an arm around Felix and pulled him close, leaving a kiss on the top of his head, then smoothing down his pale hair. "Your father left early to go to the post office. He should be home by now."

Felix nodded.

"Or did you want to sit and brood some more?"

"No."

Bibi stood and held out a hand to Felix, who took it and giggled when the creature unexpectedly scooped him up into their arms. They set him back down after a moment and they walked home hand in hand.

The house they lived in had been bought long ago, for a larger family. Felix had never met them, but he had seen their portraits, daguerreotypes kept on his father's desk, of his father's niece, Ellen, and her mother and grandmother, all dark-skinned women with the same strong features.

Jangles, a gangly, half-grown cat, leapt down from a bookshelf and wound around their feet, mewling sweetly.

Felix had found the tortoiseshell kitten a few months ago and had unsuccessfully tried to hide the creature in his room to avoid the disappointment of being told he couldn't keep her.

His father had taken to the cat immediately.

Felix had felt foolish for trying to hide it. He reached down to pet her and she arched against his hand, purring.

"Phaedrus?" a voice called from upstairs.

"Hiram, darling?" Bibi called back up.

"Just making sure," he said.

Bibi smiled and headed for the kitchen. A few minutes later, Felix's father joined the two of them, giving his spouse and child each a kiss.

"How was school?" he asked.

"Fine."

"Hm."

Felix shrugged. "I'm ready for summer."

"That makes two of us," his father said. "The end of the term is always a terror."

"Oh!" Bibi cried.

"What?" his father asked.

"Oh, that woman. That *awful* Caldwell woman. She cornered me this morning and absolutely *insists* that she needs to speak with you."

His father sighed. "I'll make time tomorrow. Felix, will you do me a favor?"

"What, Papa?"

"Can you get me a pen and paper from upstairs? I have to write myself a note."

Felix nodded and scurried upstairs, enjoying the sound of his shoes on the hardwood stairs as he ran. He grabbed a piece of paper and doubled back for a pencil, then rushed back downstairs.

"Thank you," Papa said and gave his arm a pat.

After a few hours at home, with his parents making dinner and the cat settled onto his lap as he read, Felix nearly forgot to worry about Charlie and Lionel.

LATE ON Saturday, Felix saw Charlie at the market with his parents. He tugged his hand out of Papa's to wave.

Charlie waved back and his mother, a petite woman who shared his coloring, took notice and came over.

Felix didn't believe that Mr. and Mrs. Banks thought very highly of his own parents, but he also knew that they had financial struggles that would have been worsened if they'd had to pay for Charlie's schooling. Public school was an option, but they wanted their child to do better than that.

"Doctor Queen," Mrs. Banks said.

Bibi glanced over. "Hello, Mrs. Banks. How are things?"

"Just grabbing some things for dinner."

While their parents spoke, Charlie and Felix hung back. "You should ask if you can come over for dinner," Felix told him.

Charlie shook his head. "Aunt Ruth is coming over."

Felix nodded. "Maybe tomorrow?"

Charlie shrugged. "I don't know."

Felix scrunched his face up for a second, trying to think things through, then tugged on Bibi's sleeve.

"What, dear?" Bibi asked, looking down.

"Can Charlie come over tomorrow?"

"I have a meeting with my publisher at noon," they said. "But afterward would be fine. Does that work alright for you, Mrs.

Banks?"

Mrs. Banks hesitated. She glanced down at Felix and he could see the worry on her face. Worry about his parents or maybe worry about Felix himself; his dark red, almost black, eyes and stark white skin marked him clearly as the Devil's child to those who knew enough to look. People outside the Community thought Felix sickly.

"We can come by to pick her up," Bibi offered. "My meeting shouldn't take more than an hour."

"I suppose," Mrs. Banks said. "I can't think of any reason why not." She added a smile to show that her statement had not been meant to offend. She put a hand on her child's shoulder. "Anyway, we've got to be going. More shopping to do."

Bibi nodded and Felix waved goodbye to Charlie.

"Glum little thing," Bibi remarked after they had gone.

Felix said nothing. He said nothing for the rest of their shopping trip, not unless Bibi pried it out of him.

At home, he stared down at the blank piece of paper he had taken out and set on the coffee table. He had a crayon gripped between his fingers but put it down after a minute and sighed.

Jangles watched from her perch on the couch, her large greenish-yellow eyes fixed not on him but on the paper he had. He reached out a hand and she butted it against it, then placed a paw on his wrist.

He crumpled the paper and tossed it across the room. She bolted after it and pounced on the ball. He watched for a minute, then took another piece of paper and drew the cat. Besides the cat, he drew Papa and Bibi. Bibi was harder to draw because their clothes were so full of folds and drapes. Papa dressed in a suit almost always and usually in dark colors. He stared down at the picture.

Jangles came back over, the ball in her mouth.

He reached out and took it, then tossed it again. A few more tosses and she would mangle it beyond use.

His father wandered down from upstairs, ink stains on the cuff of his left sleeve. Even though he kept the sleeve on his left arm permanently pinned up, he used his stump to hold papers as he wrote on them and invariably stained his shirt. Bibi frequently suggested that he get rid of the left sleeve altogether, no matter how ridiculous it would look.

As he walked by, Papa kicked the ball away from the cat and

sent her loping after it. He set a pile of envelopes on the table by the front door then looked over to Felix. He didn't say anything, but it was a look of suspicion, the same look he'd had when Felix had been sneaking scraps of meat into his bedroom.

Felix picked up his drawing and his crayons, tucked them under his arm, and went to his room. He needed to persuade Charlie that his parents could help.

Or he needed to get rid of Lionel, but he had no idea how to do that.

On Sunday, he and Charlie played checkers and Charlie flatly refused to discuss what to do about Lionel. When Felix suggested that they should tell his parents, Charlie knocked the checkerboard off the table.

"My parents aren't *like yours*," Charlie snapped.

Felix looked down at the pieces scattered on the floor. Nobody's parents were like his. No one else in the entire school had a parent like Bibi and none of the parents had a child like Felix, either. He was the only unnatural creature that attended the Academy.

"They won't understand," Charlie said, "They'll be mad and they'll make me wear dresses and they *won't* let me be friends with you anymore."

Felix looked up. "Why not?"

"Because!"

Felix knelt to pick up the checkers, picking them up in fistfuls and dropping them back into their box. Charlie knelt as well, scooping the checkers on his side into a pile and then scooping them up.

Once everything had been picked back up, Charlie sat back, the short skirt of his dress pushed up to show the checked panties that matched his outfit.

Felix looked away when he realized he'd been staring.

Charlie noticed, too, yanking down the hem.

It was normal, really. All the girls wore dresses like that, short ones that were meant to let the matching undergarments peek out. It only felt odd because it was Charlie, because Charlie hated dresses.

"Do you want to wear something else?" Felix offered.

Charlie shook his head. "Your parents will tell."

Felix sighed, stood, and offered his hand to Charlie. The other boy took it and Felix pulled him upright.

His father walked by and glanced into the room. "Are you two doing alright in here?"

"We got tired of checkers," Felix said.

"Why don't you get the chalk? It's a nice day, you should play outside."

Felix nodded, then said, "Charlie doesn't want to get h-her dress dirty. Mrs. Banks would be angry."

Papa glanced over Charlie, then suggested, "You have play clothes you can lend her, don't you?"

Felix nodded.

His father came into the room and sorted through his closet, finally taking out knickers and an old shirt. He handed them to Felix and gave his hair an affectionate ruffle.

Papa wandered away again after that, likely he had more work to do. The school ate up a lot of his time, especially because he was overseeing several students' end-of-term projects. In the summer, things would be different.

Felix held out the clothes to Charlie with a grin.

At first, he scowled, but eventually snatched the clothes out of Felix's hand and changed. Once he'd changed his clothes, a smile started to grow on his face.

Felix grabbed him by the hand and tugged him downstairs.

"Don't go too far," Papa called when they started rummaging through the closet for the chalk.

"We won't!" Felix shouted back. He emerged from the closet with a small, dented tin bucket full of chalk bits and a jump rope.

Outside, he and Charlie played several rounds of hopscotch and had a contest to see who could jump rope more times in a row. Charlie won by several dozen jumps.

Bibi came out after a few hours and said to Charlie, "I told your mother I'd have you home by five. Go on up and get changed."

Once Charlie had gone, Bibi muttered, "Who knows what she thinks we'd do to the kid..."

Felix looked up from putting all the chalk back into the bucket.

"Oh, I forget about your hearing, love," Bibi said, "I didn't mean for you to hear that."

Felix shrugged. He heard most things people said, even whispers in other rooms or shouts from two houses over.

Bibi knelt beside Felix. "You know we've got a good family, don't you?"

"Yes."

"And that we love you."

"Yes." He put his arms around Bibi's neck and said, "I love you too."

Bibi gave him a squeeze and rubbed his back. "That's my boy." They kissed Felix on the temple, then released him.

Charlie reappeared in his original outfit. Bibi and Felix walked him home and Mrs. Banks didn't invite them in when they returned Charlie.

Instead, she said, "I hope she was good."

"An angel," Bibi said. "She's welcome anytime."

Mrs. Banks nodded, took Charlie by the hand, and said, "It's nearly time for dinner, go wash up and set the table."

During their walk back home, Felix asked, "Bibi, how did you know you weren't a boy?"

"Oh, hmmm...I don't know. It took a while to figure out."

They walked together for a few more feet.

"It was just this sort of feeling..." Bibi paused to think, their grip tightening a little on Felix's hand. They continued, "It's hard to understand if you've never felt it. It's...disorienting and you get this nervous sort of feeling about things. Nervous that someone will call you 'sir' and things like that. Uncomfortable when they happen, or angry. Or embarrassed. Things that don't make most people feel that way."

"Oh."

"It's more than that, too, and it's different for everyone."

Felix nodded.

"Why do you ask, love?" they asked.

"I don't know. Just wondering."

"There's no wrong way to be yourself, Felix."

Felix looked up, frowning for a second. "Oh. No. Bibi, it's not about me."

Bibi nodded.

A moment later, Felix said, "Imagine if we took all our last names to make one big one."

Bibi laughed. "Goodness, no thank you!"

They spent the rest of the walk home trading combinations of their last names, each one more ridiculous than the last.

LATE THE LAST DAY OF SCHOOL

A BUZZ floated through the entire school, not just through the students, but through the teachers as well. Everyone was ready for summer vacation. In the halls, children traded vacation plans and promised to get together over the summer.

When the last class was dismissed, the pupils streamed out, one single-minded mass thinking of cold drinks and unoccupied days full of sun and laughter.

Except for Charlie and Felix. They had lingered behind, waiting for everyone else to leave, as they did every day. Felix waited outside the bathroom, leaning against the wall. Eventually, Charlie came out, Felix's borrowed clothes folded up and looped with a belt. He handed the clothes back.

His hazel eyes were red-rimmed and he still had a little bit of snot dribbling from his nose. He sniffed and wiped his nose on his sleeve.

"You can still come to play," Felix offered.

Charlie shook his head. "I'm going away for the summer. To stay with my cousins in Nova Scotia."

"Oh."

Felix heard footsteps approaching but thought nothing of it. One of the teachers, he assumed, but he should have known the gait was too light to be an adult's. He didn't realize his mistake until someone gave him a hard push from behind.

He stumbled, dropping the clothes Charlie had handed to him.

Lionel said, "Coupla freaks." He reached out and yanked the ribbon out of Charlie's hair. "I knew something was squirrelly about you. Knew you weren't right."

"Quit it," Felix said.

Lionel barely glanced his way. Instead, he stepped towards Charlie, grabbing his hair again, this time dragging the small boy closer.

Charlie squirmed, grabbing on to his own hair and trying to pull back.

"Figured you for faggots, maybe," Lionel said, pulling so hard that Charlie had to stand on his toes.

Felix kicked Lionel, hard, as hard as he could, in the knee.

The older boy buckled, dragging Charlie with him.

Felix kicked him again, then grabbed on to his arm. He sunk his teeth into the meat of Lionel's arm, making him cry out and release Charlie.

Lionel grabbed Felix by the front of his shirt and Felix felt the chain around his neck snap. The amulet slithered down his chest and fell out of the bottom of his shirt where it had come untucked.

"Charlie, go home!" Felix insisted.

Charlie stared for a minute.

"Go!" Felix said again and this time Charlie took off running, not looking back.

Lionel tossed Felix and he landed hard on his side. The bigger boy gave him a kick in the ribs, then headed after Charlie.

Felix pushed himself up, one arm wrapped around his side. He wanted to stay on the floor and he wanted badly to curl up and have a cry, but he knew that Lionel would catch up to Charlie.

He ran outside, down the front stairs, and saw Lionel looking around to see which way Charlie had gone. Felix jumped onto the older boy's back, causing him to stumble to one side.

Lionel grabbed him by the arm and pulled him off, but Felix latched on to his arm.

Felix had never thrown a punch before in his life but now seemed like a good enough time. He balled up his fist and swung, hitting Lionel in the cheek. It sent jolts of pain he hadn't expected through his hand.

"Boys! Now, hey, boys!" one of the teachers called from a window, not sounding too concerned.

Lionel took ahold of Felix's shirt again and hit him in the mouth. Lionel seemed to have considerably more practice at punching.

"Boys!" a different teacher called, this one nearby.

Felix glanced over to see Ms. Perkins coming down the front stairs. He jabbed his fingers into Lionel's eyes and was dropped to the ground, rolling his ankle when he landed.

Lionel raised his hand for another blow but then stopped, eyes wide and his mouth going slack. His eyes stared at something behind Felix, something taller and apparently worrisome.

Felix turned and expected to see Mr. Durand, the only teacher in the school that everyone walked carefully around. Instead, he saw something else. A man, but not a man at all; it looked like a creature made all of sunlight. It had a warm, shimmering tan and golden curls, but Felix had never seen anything like it before and he had certainly never been stared at with such cold distaste.

The man, or thing, or whatever it was, had orangey-yellow eyes and a greenish-silver blade gripped in one hand.

Behind him, he heard Lionel running away.

It took him by the left wrist and peeled back the sleeve of his shirt to show his birthmark, a pale brown squiggle about three inches long.

Felix tried to pull his arm back, but the creature held firm, its grip uncomfortably tight. It hurt where it held Felix.

Once it had seen the mark, it raised the blade and plunged it toward Felix's chest.

The blade missed its mark, biting into Felix's shoulder instead, and only because his father had come out of the school and shoved his hand into the creature's face. His father chanted, arcane words that Felix didn't understand, and, with a blast of heat and light, the creature vanished.

The blade hurt more coming out than going in; going in had felt almost like nothing, like a strong static zap, but on the way out it felt warm, and then very hot.

His father's hand pulled open his shirt, checking for something. Then he wrapped his arm around Felix and lifted him up, hurrying into the school.

Something skittered when his father kicked it. He set Felix down so he could snatch up the amulet; he tied the broken chain around Felix's neck.

Felix could not think of why his father would do this. It seemed more important to do something about the blood. There was a lot of blood, staining his shirt bright red and his jacket dark.

"Papa."

"I know, love, I know, don't worry," his father said.

He pulled off Felix's shirt and jacket, struggling a little with just one hand, his face going pale as he looked down.

"Papa?"

"You'll be fine, just…"

His father wadded up the shirt and pressed it to Felix's shoulder.

"Not so bad, Felix, it's not so bad. I…God help me, I'm not a doctor, but I think it's just flesh."

Tears burned down Felix's face.

His father took his hand and pressed it against the shirt. "Hold this, as tight as you can."

Felix held the shirt in place, sniffling.

His father used his arm to push down painfully hard against the wound in Felix's shoulder, murmuring apologies and reassurances.

"You're hurting my fingers."

"I'm sorry, it has to be tight."

Teachers began to crowd around.

His father shouted for them to get back, to go for a doctor.

Felix grabbed on to his father's sleeve and pressed his face into his shirt. He began to weep.

His father wrapped an arm around him, holding him close.

A doctor arrived with a large, leather bag, followed shortly by Bibi. The doctor cleaned his wound, stitched it shut, and bandaged his shoulder with almost no fussing. He informed Felix's parents that he had suffered a flesh wound and had been very lucky to do so.

Bibi talked to him through the whole thing, insisting that Felix answer questions about his school day.

Felix didn't understand why Bibi wanted to know about his day so badly, but he answered every question.

"It could have been much worse," the doctor said.

"Shh, don't give the poor thing a fright!" Bibi said. They reached out to touch Felix's hair, then placed one hand on his cheek. "Let's get you home, love, and into bed. Hiram, darling, come along."

Bibi wrapped their jacket around him, picked him up, and carried him home as though he were made of feathers. Felix always forgot how strong they were, even though he had seen them lift his father off his feet with ease.

They helped him change into pajamas and tucked him into bed. His parents did not ask what happened and, though Bibi disappeared for a few minutes and came back with a mug of tea, they did not leave his side after that.

"Here, this will help," Bibi told him, "Tastes terrible, but it will help."

Felix sipped from the mug and couldn't help but make a face. He drifted off into a hazy sleep before he could ask his father what that creature had been.

The following day, he woke to find his parents still in his room, both of them on the floor. Bibi had their back against the wall and Papa had curled up in their lap, his brown curls mussed terribly.

He pushed himself up using one arm, the other held stiff for fear of making it hurt worse. "Bibi?"

They opened their eyes and Felix wondered if they had been asleep at all.

"Felix, love."

Felix looked around, a familiar but usually absent smell in the room. "He was here."

"Who?"

"My father."

Bibi shook their head. "No, I don't think so."

"I can smell him."

"Maybe he's on his way," Bibi said. "Love, what happened? How did your amulet come off?"

"Lionel broke it when he grabbed me."

"Lionel?"

"A boy in my class."

"You were fighting?" Bibi asked, their eyebrows shooting up.

Papa stirred, then sat up. A red mark across his face showed the texture of his spouse's trousers. "Hmm?"

Bibi asked, "What were you fighting about?"

Felix looked down at his hands. "Lionel picks on Charlie. And he picks on me. He picks on everyone."

"Why didn't you tell us?" Papa asked.

"Charlie doesn't want me to."

"Is this your secret? The one you're keeping for a friend?" Bibi asked.

Felix nodded.

"Why doesn't she want you to tell?"

Felix shook his head. "He'll be mad if I tell."

"Who?" Bibi asked, his brows knit.

Felix realized he had misspoken. Charlie was a boy, but most people didn't know that and it was his worst fear that an adult would find out.

"Felix, who will be mad?" Papa asked. "You won't be in trouble."

"Charlie will," Felix said, tears coming to his eyes again. "Charlie thinks you'll tell his parents."

His father stared. "The same Charlie you had over to play?"

Felix nodded.

"Is...Charlie...uh, Felix..." Papa said. "Is Charlie a boy?"

Felix said, "I'm not supposed to tell."

"Goodness, I wouldn't tell either if I had his mother," Bibi muttered. "Tell Charlie his secret's safe with us."

"We'll see about that Lionel boy, too," Papa said.

Felix reached up to touch the amulet around his neck. "I didn't mean to take it off."

"I know, Felix, of course, you didn't," Papa said. "We'll fix it. Don't worry."

"What was that man?"

"An angel," his father said.

Felix turned his eyes towards Bibi.

"No, dear, not like me," Bibi said, "Or, well, yes, like me, but this angel still works for Heaven."

"It didn't smell like you."

"Well, this one wears a lot of perfume," said a voice from the foot of Felix's bed.

They all looked over to see a tall, lanky woman dressed all in black, this form hardly distinguishable from the form his father usually took. Felix asked questions about the Devil's changing shape when he'd been younger, but had only gotten the same kind of waxing, philosophical answers about the uselessness of bodies that Bibi gave.

"I hear you had a kerfuffle, little one," said the Devil. His voice, and his face, never changed.

"My amulet broke."

"I will stay until your father fashions you a more secure one," the Devil said. "As long as no one objects."

"No, stay, of course," Bibi said.

Papa stood.

Bibi followed suit. "I'll make something to eat. I'm sure you're hungry," they offered.

"Starving," said the Devil, smiling a wide, terrifying smile.

Papa rolled his eyes and shook his head, walking out of the room.

Bibi gave Felix one last pat on the face and left as well.

The Devil took a seat at the foot of Felix's bed.

Jangles jumped up right away to join him.

"I'm sorry such rotten circumstances brought me by," the Devil said, regarding Felix with her, or his, red-gold eyes. The Devil didn't seem to care what labels people put on which form. "I suppose it can't all be birthdays and Christmases."

Felix gave a small smile. He was never sure what to do around this father.

"Any more than that and I think I would draw too much attention to you."

"I know." Felix smoothed the blankets over his leg and studied the Devil.

He had stared for too long because the Devil met his eyes and asked, "What?"

"When...when you have this body—"

"It's the same body I always have," Satan told him.

Felix sighed. "But when it looks this way, are you...are you still my father? Should you be my mother?"

"Things like that have never meant much to me," the Devil said, "You may think of me however it pleases you." The Devil ran a hand along the cat's back and she purred, kneading into the bedspread. "Lovely cat. Is she new?"

"I found her a few months ago," Felix said, "She was hiding under Mildred's porch and she wouldn't come out for anyone."

"We do well with animals," the Devil said. "What's her name?"

"Jangles," he said.

His father grinned, nicely this time. "How's school?"

"Today was the last day."

"Oh, wonderful. Do you have...plans for the summer? That's something that they do here, right? Summer holidays."

"We aren't going anywhere I don't think," Felix said. "Papa's busy all year, he likes to stay home for the holidays."

"Homebody, he is," the Devil said. "I knew they would be good parents."

The Devil continued to stroke Jangles.

Felix watched. It took him a little while to work up the nerve to ask, "Why did that angel come? Why did it hurt me?"

"Oh, that one is a miserable, misguided creature," the Devil said with a disinterested wave of one spindly hand. "But if I get rid of that one, surely another will be sent."

"By God?"

"Goodness, Felix, I don't know, it's not like He keeps me up to date on things," Satan said, "An archangel could be sending them. But don't fret. Hiram and Phaedrus will keep you well protected."

"Why do they want to hurt me?"

The Devil sighed and ran his fingers through his long, black hair. Long hands, long fingers, and long hair. Everything about him seemed to stretch on and on. He made Felix think of eternity, of the sky on a cloudless day. He began to braid his hair and said, "Because of what you are."

The Devil reached out his hand to touch Felix's arm, turning it upside down to show his birthmark. He turned Felix's arm back over and gave his hand a pat.

"These are things we can discuss when you're older. Your parents would be angry with me if I told you too much."

"Oh."

"But it's really not something to worry about. Just keep your amulet on and focus on your schooling."

Felix nodded.

"Do you promise?"

"Yes."

"That's a good boy," he said. "Have you read the book I gave you?"

"No, it's too hard."

The Devil nodded. "I worried it might be. It's one of my favorites."

Felix reached into his bedside table and pulled out a hardcover copy of *The Hobbit*. He ran his fingers over the scrawny dragon on the cover. He flipped through the first few pages. "The date inside is wrong."

"Hmm? Oh, no, this book hasn't come out yet. It won't be out for some years," he said. He held out a hand and Felix gave him the book. "Would you like me to read it to you?"

Felix nodded.

The Devil opened to the first page, clearing his throat and then starting to read in a smooth, mild voice.

Felix scooted closer and closer.

He didn't see his father often and didn't know how he should feel about him. Sometimes he wished he could see him more. Sometimes he wished he never visited at all. Wishing the Devil would never visit made Felix feel guilty. He could tell the Devil cared about him, even if he was strange and sort of uncomfortable to be around.

Not uncomfortable like when Mrs. Banks yelled at Charlie, but uncomfortable like watching a skinny stray sniff through the garbage.

Felix curled up against Lucifer and held on to his hand.

LATE APRIL 1927

FELIX, ON his thirteenth birthday, had received a gift from the Devil along with a note apologizing for his absence, saying that he would visit when he could. The note had ended rather ominously with the postscript 'I'll be sending someone along to help.'

He had shown the note to his parents and Bibi had said, "I'm sure he means about the magic."

Felix hadn't thought much about his inborn magic in some time; he already knew more arcane runes than most of the underclassmen at the University. He had spent the past six years peering over his father's shoulder, reading his books, and offering to help correct the student's coursework. His parents allowed him to dabble but insisted that his other studies had to come first. He wasn't sure why, since his father had been learning magic since he could read, but chalked it up to some kind of superior adult judgment.

On a raw Thursday afternoon in the spring, someone knocked on the door.

Felix threw the crumpled paper ball for Jangles one more time then went to answer it, expecting Charlie. Instead, he found a short, black-haired man with a scar across his face; it started high on his cheek and angled down across his upper lip, passing close to his nose.

"Our father sent me," the man said.

Felix stared. The man, with his dark red eyes, was clearly of the same bloodline as Felix and it jarred him to think that this man was his brother.

"You are Felix, aren't you?" the man asked.

He nodded.

"Nicholas." The man offered his hand.

Felix hesitated to shake it. The man's skin was as white as his own, though it lacked the translucence that Felix's had. No veins showed in his wrists or around his eyes as they did for Felix. He wanted to call for his parents, but they had gone out.

The man drew his hand back after a few seconds, unperturbed. "He did tell you I was coming, didn't he?" Nicholas asked. "He says you're coming into your magic soon."

"I...my parents aren't home, I can't let you in," Felix said, feeling stupid and callow. He wasn't as brave as he pretended.

Nicholas nodded understandingly and even smiled a little, showing sharp teeth. "That's fine. I can stop by again later. Or I've taken a room at the Hudson, I can be reached there."

Felix nodded.

The man took a step back like he was going to leave.

Felix blurted, "Did he come to see you?"

"Our father?"

He gave a short nod.

"No. A letter."

"Oh."

"He gets busy, he's got a whole realm to deal with, you know," Nicholas offered.

"I know."

"I'll see you around," the man said. He gave a wave and turned, walking down the steps into the wet, cold afternoon. As he walked away, he pulled his wool coat tighter around himself.

Felix peered up and down the street; Charlie was supposed to be coming by. It wasn't that they had made plans together, just that Charlie came by every day unless he was particularly ill or had plans with his family that he couldn't avoid. Charlie hadn't mentioned any previous commitments when they'd seen each other at school.

Jangles came over to the door and peered down the street too, then looked up at Felix as if to say, 'might as well wait where it's warm'. She turned around and went back inside.

He closed the door and returned to the couch, picking up a book he'd pilfered from the university library without either of his parents knowing. They had never forbidden him from reading on any topic, but when he had brought home books on angels for several weeks in a row, they had exchanged looks and he had heard them whispering about it later.

After that he had kept the books out of their sight, not wanting to worry either of them. They wouldn't be home until after five, so he still had an hour or so to read uninterrupted.

He couldn't focus for long though, still wondering where Charlie could have gotten to. Eventually, he stuffed his book into his hiding spot behind the couch, left a note for his parents, then grabbed his jacket and headed over to Charlie's house.

He knocked on the door and a woman he knew to be Charlie's aunt answered. She frowned down at him.

"Is Charlie round?" he asked.

"Charlie?"

"Charlotte," he clarified, "Sorry." Apparently, his extended family hadn't picked up the name; initially, his older sister had taken to it as cute and modish, a good name for a girl in the age of flappers. It had stuck after that.

"I'll get her." She closed the door in his face.

A few minutes later, Charlie appeared, stepping out onto the stoop so they could talk with a hair more privacy.

"My cousin brought her baby over," he said, "I couldn't get out."

"Sure."

"Maybe tomorrow," he said. "I'd invite you in but...it's miserable anyways, the baby won't stop crying."

Mr. Banks opened the door and said, "Charlie, what's...Oh, Felix. Hello."

"Hi, Mr. Banks," he said.

From within he heard a baby not just crying but screaming in misery. He glanced at Charlie and something compelled him to say, "I can fix it."

"What?" Mr. Banks said.

A weird tingle grew in his chest; it was static-y and uncomfortable, instead of warm and pleasant like the tingle that had started to come over him when he noticed a pretty girl. "The baby, I can calm her down."

"Uh, no, thank you, Felix, that's alright," Mr. Banks said.

Charlie gave him a funny look.

Charlie's father said, "Maybe you ought to run home."

Felix nodded. He clenched his hands. "See you tomorrow?" he asked Charlie.

"Yeah."

Felix backed down the steps and shoved his hands into his jacket pockets. Once home, he struggled to hang up his jacket, fumbling when he was usually sure of his movements. He paced for a while, tapping his palms against the sides of his legs.

His parents came home about a quarter of an hour later and found him sitting on the couch, his leg bobbing with nervous energy.

Bibi frowned immediately. They came to sit beside him and put a hand to his forehead.

"I'm not sick," Felix said.

"I know, love, you don't get sick," they said. "Which is what worries me."

"Bibi, I'm fine."

Papa came over and sat on his other side.

"It's...I think. I just...I went to Charlie's and the baby was crying—"

"What baby?" Papa asked.

"His cousin or something. I don't know. It was...god, it was *screaming* and I knew that I could...that if they'd let me, I could help," Felix explained, halting and anxious.

"Oh," his parents said in mutual understanding.

He asked, "What?"

"That was your first call to magic," Bibi said.

That jogged Felix's memory. "Oh! A man came by. He said my father sent him. Our father, he said."

"Another demon?" Papa asked.

He nodded. "He's staying at a hotel in town. The Hudson?"

His parents looked at each other.

"I suppose we can look into it," Papa said.

Bibi agreed, "It would be best, considering that my king can lack judgment sometimes."

Felix started to tap his hands against his thighs again.

"Dear, you've got to let it out," Bibi said, putting a hand on Felix's shoulder.

"How?"

"I believe you need to focus on something you want to

happen," Papa advised. "It really isn't like arcane magic at all. Instead of using specific runes to call forth the magic you need, it's a matter of will and tapping into the natural magical reserve that lives within your body."

Felix couldn't think of anything to do with the energy that buzzed just beneath his skin. He glanced around the room and saw one of the cat's toys knocked under the curio cabinet. He squeezed his eyes shut for a second and imagined the small, knit mouse sliding out from beneath.

He reached a hand out and tried to focus.

His parents watched, calm and patient.

Papa put a hand on his back.

At first, nothing happened. He tried to bring back the feeling of need he'd felt when he'd heard the baby crying; it had been a terrible sound and he had needed it to stop. The mouse skittered forward just a little and after that, with a grin, Felix coaxed it all the way out in jerks and leaps.

Jangles pounced before it had stopped moving.

Felix made the thing pull out of her grip.

The cat loped after the mouse and attacked again.

Papa wrapped an arm around him and squeezed him close.

Bibi gave his hair a ruffle, a grin on their face. A moment later, though, their grin faltered.

"What?" Felix asked, his brow knitting.

"No, it's...you're growing up so fast," they said. They pulled him into their embrace and gave him a tight hug. "Christ, it's going to kill me!"

"Phaedrus!" Papa scolded. "You're going to worry him, saying things like that."

Bibi let him go and touched his face, a few tears rolling down their cheeks. "This isn't like me, I don't know what's gotten into me, I'm sorry, love," they said, drying their eyes with their sleeve. They stood and walked away, heading towards the bathroom.

Felix heard them whisper a series of swears under their breath as they went. He couldn't help but crack a grin. Papa never swore and Bibi only swore when they thought no one was listening because bad language always left their spouse scandalized.

LATE FRIDAY, after school, Charlie came home with him. He didn't bother to change between the school and Felix's house, leaving his dress in his backpack for when he had to go home. As they walked, Charlie asked him to clarify what had happened the day before.

"So, he just showed up?" Charlie asked.

"Well, my father sent him."

"Uh. Hiram or...?"

"No, the other one," he said.

"The Devil," Charlie whispered. He had an odd fascination with Felix's parentage; not in any obsessive, worshipful way, but because he found it extraordinary.

"Yes, that one. Because I guess, uh, they call it 'coming into my magic' and I guess it happened."

"Cause you moved the mouse?"

Felix nodded.

"You've got to show me," Charlie said.

He'd been insisting all day but Felix had been shy about using magic around people who weren't prepared for it since he'd made a teacher faint by showing off the runes he knew.

"I said I would!"

The other boy pressed a hand to his stomach and said, "I feel awful."

"Maybe you should go home," Felix suggested.

"And hear that baby cry some more! No, thanks." As they came up to Felix's house and walked up the steps, he said, "Can't get you sick anyway, if it's something nasty."

Once inside, the boys put their backpacks beside the couch and Felix collapsed on to the cushions. He called, "Bibi?" but got no answer. "Papa?"

The house remained silent. They never left him home alone for more than an hour or so at a time, so he knew they'd be back well before dinner.

He glanced over at Charlie, who hadn't sat but had taken a weirdly hesitant step toward the bathroom.

"What?" Felix asked. "Are you going to be sick?"

Charlie shook his head but headed towards the bathroom anyway.

Felix settled into the couch and picked his nails for a minute, ready to await Charlie's return.

"Felix?" he heard Charlie call.

He sat up.

"Uh...Felix?" he called, more panicked.

Felix approached the bathroom door and asked, "Uh, what, Charlie?"

"Can you come in?" he asked.

Not liking the waver in his friend's voice, Felix turned the knob and let himself into the bathroom. He found Charlie standing there with no shorts or underwear and with, more surprisingly, blood on his thighs and hands.

"The towels are all white," he said. "I didn't want to ruin them."

"Are you...uh. Is that...?" Felix stared for a minute. He knew what this was. He'd read texts on anatomy, he knew about menstrual cycles, but he had forgotten it would ever happen to Charlie. "Oh, Charlie, I haven't got anything to give you! One of those...those belts!"

He'd seen the advertisements for things like that in the ladies' catalogs that Bibi brought home from time to time.

Charlie bit his lip. "It's not going to stop."

"Uh...wait, hang on," he said and hurried to the linen closet. They had old dishtowels there, ones that weren't nasty enough to be rags, but not quite up to Bibi's standards to be on display.

He grabbed a few and brought them back to Charlie. "Uh. I

guess...wash up? I'll find you something to wear."

Charlie nodded, looking down at the towels in his hands.

"I can go to the store," Felix said. He took a step back but didn't feel right leaving him there. He moved closer and put a hand on the other boy's shoulder.

"Don't go," Charlie said.

Felix nodded, "Okay. We can wait. It'll be fine. Bibi and Papa will be home soon and they'll know what to do."

"Yeah."

Felix pulled back and turned on the sink, checking to make sure the water came out warm. He took one of the old towels and dampened it, then handed it back to Charlie.

"Besides," Felix said, "It's just a little blood. I'm sure Papa knows a spell for getting out bloodstains."

Charlie started to dab at his thighs.

Felix tried to think of what to do to stop the blood from getting all over. Having Charlie sit in the tub until an adult came home seemed like a bad solution, but without something to stop the flow, leaving the bathroom felt foolish, too.

He headed back to the linen closet and found a few towels and grabbed his bathrobe from his room.

Once Charlie had cleaned up, they worked together to jerry-rig the towels into a sort of sanitary belt held in place by diaper pins left over from Felix's infancy. A few times Felix had to bite back a hysterical giggle.

"This is awful," Charlie said.

"They'll be home soon." Felix gathered up all the dirtied towels and the clothes that Charlie had discarded and tossed them in the tub. "You should, uh, the shirt has to go, too."

Charlie looked down to see bloodstains on the hem and sleeves. He sighed and unbuttoned the shirt, placing it in the tub and then taking the robe Felix held out. "Thanks." He washed his hands and lingered by the sink.

"Charlie..."

The other boy turned around, eyes red-rimmed.

Felix grabbed on to him, wrapping him up in a hug. He had nothing to say and neither did Charlie, who hugged him back just as tight. Felix took his hand and brought him out to the living room. He folded up a bath towel on the couch and gestured for Charlie to sit.

He settled awkwardly on to the towel and let out a sigh.

Felix patted him on the back.

After a few quiet minutes, Charlie said, "Emma's been teasing me for months."

Felix waited.

"I don't know what's worse, that or my mom pointing out that, ugh, that my breasts are starting to grow!"

"Well, I mean...all the girls make their chests flat now anyways. You can just use one of those things. A what, a bandeau?"

"Do you read all of Bibi's fashion magazines?"

He shrugged. "Not all of them."

Teasing, Charlie suggested, "Or do you just look at the ads for ladies' undergarments?"

"No," he said, though his interests had strayed to that section lately.

Charlie looked down at his hands. "I always...I don't know, I sort of figured that I would like girls. Boys are supposed to like girls."

"Papa doesn't."

"Normal boys," he amended.

Felix shrugged. "You never know. Papa thought he only liked men until he met Bibi. Sometimes..." He tried to think of what his father always said. "Sometimes you don't know what you want until you see it."

"I don't know."

Felix wanted to have the right thing to say. For years, he'd noticed the sideways glances people gave his family when they went out together; people mistook Bibi for his mother and if they began to suspect otherwise, their attitudes soured. Conversations ended abruptly. Parents had taken their children out of the Academy. It was worse when Bibi wore trousers instead of something ladylike. It made the incongruity of their family more obvious.

"You're my best friend, Charlie. That's all that matters to me," he said. "Do you want to play checkers?"

"Sure."

Felix gave his friend's shoulder a pat and jogged upstairs to get the game. He set it up on couch cushion between them. They played for a while, Charlie making faces every so often and often pressing his hand to his stomach.

Finally, Felix's parents returned and he jumped right up when he saw them, upsetting the checkerboard enough that some of the pieces slid onto the floor.

The first thing Papa said was, "Why is Charlie wearing your bathrobe?"

"He...uh, he got blood on his clothes and we didn't have one of those belts."

His father stared.

With bright red cheeks, Charlie whispered, "I got my period."

"Ahh, right," Papa said. He glanced at his spouse. "Love, would you run to the store?"

"Of course, anything else while I'm out?"

Papa glanced at the boys, who shook their heads. "No."

Bibi put a hand on Papa's shoulder, left a kiss on his cheek, and then walked back out the door.

"Are you doing well, Charlie?" Papa asked.

Charlie shrugged.

"Is your stomach bothering you?"

"Sort of."

"I can help with that, at least," he said and headed off into the kitchen.

Felix knelt to pick up the game pieces that had fallen. He tossed them back into the box and Papa poked his head back out. "Oh, Felix, we stopped by the Hudson to speak with that man. Nicholas."

"Oh?"

"He's coming by tomorrow morning at eleven."

"Why?"

"Because your father sent him," Papa said.

Felix wrinkled his nose. Papa didn't trust the Devil.

"I know. Bibi seems to think it's important," he said. "And I must admit, he does care about you very much, Felix."

"But what is he supposed to do? That other demon?"

"It's my understanding that at your age many of your kind undergo changes that can be unsettling to some."

"Like the teeth?" he asked. Some of his teeth, after they'd fallen out, had come back in pointed and sharp.

"And the sleeping. Or, rather, the lack of sleeping."

Felix shrugged.

Charlie tapped him on the back. "Can I watch?"

"What?"

"When that man comes, can I watch you do magic?"

Felix glanced at his father, who said, "I don't see why not."

The kettle began to scream.

Papa went back to the kitchen, then returned to the living room with a mug in his hand. He handed it to Charlie and said, "It should help with the cramps."

He turned back to the kitchen then returned with another mug, which he handed to Felix. "Cocoa," he said, "Miserable, raw day."

"You have the best dad," Charlie whispered.

Felix smiled. He couldn't argue.

Bibi returned and they helped get Charlie situated with the belt.

Felix provided a change of clothes and Charlie stayed for dinner. Around the table, everyone traded stories about their day, laughing. When the time came for Charlie to go home, Felix felt the lack of his presence in a way that seemed to get heavier each day.

LATE SATURDAY, at just after ten-thirty, someone knocked on the door and Felix set aside his book to open it. He expected Charlie but again found the strange man instead.

"Your parents said to come by. I'm a little early, I think. Or late. Am I late?" he asked.

"No. Early."

The man nodded.

Felix stepped back. "You can come in."

He entered the house and looked around, his eyes gliding over the tasteful furniture and finally settling on the cat.

"I used my magic fine," Felix said.

The man did not seem to notice.

"Uh, mister? Mister...Nicholas, was it?"

"Just Nicholas will do," he said.

Felix nodded; there were no adults he addressed by their first name, but there was something about this man that didn't feel quite like an adult. He had no childlike qualities, but more of an air of the impossibly old.

"I said I used my magic. It wasn't a lot of trouble, I don't think I'll need a lot of help or anything like that," Felix said.

"Still, when the Devil asks..." Nicholas said. "He wants me to keep an eye on you, I think."

"Keep an eye on me?"

"The change can be a trial for some," he said, "It's when our kind start to go sour."

Felix frowned. "What do you mean?"

"There are just some of our kin that...hmm..." Nicholas trailed off and gave Felix a hard look. "How old are you?"

"Thirteen."

"Old enough to know, then," he said, "Our kind have reputation for being rough, sordid. Generally immoral scoundrels known for thievery and brawling. And other things. Lewd ones."

"Oh."

"I think it has more to do with circumstance than lineage," he said, "Not so many of our kind have very stable families. But still, he worries."

"Our father?"

Nicholas nodded. "He worries a lot."

Felix didn't know what to say. He shifted from one foot to another, then called, "Papa? He's here. That Nicholas fellow."

His father came downstairs and offered his hand to Nicholas. Standing next to each other, the two men seemed bizarrely proportioned; his father stood nearly a foot taller than the other man. "Thank you for coming by."

"No trouble," the demon said as he shook hands. "I think it would be good to see what the lad can do and set up...a..." He trailed off, then came to a moment later. "Schedule. Sorry! English is *not* my first language and I'm just too old to remember everything these days."

"Perfectly fine. I have to say, I don't know too much about this sort of magic. The University in Triviai holds those secrets dear."

"Well, after the civil war..." Nicholas said and Felix thought it was meant to be an explanation because his father nodded. "Anyways, come on, lad, show me what you can do."

"Uh. Like what?"

Nicholas glanced around the room, then fished a handful of coins out of his pocket. He went over and set them down on the coffee table. "Stack them," he said, "Or lift them, at least, if you can."

Felix approached the coins, aware of the other two watching him. Arcane magic generally wasn't used for parlor tricks like this. At least, not anymore it wasn't. He'd seen old books in his father's library about magic for entertaining and maybe somewhere, among the flappers and lounge lizards, there was a mage who still did such things, but arcane academia had taken a serious turn in the last few decades.

A rune came to mind, one he knew as part of a spell for construction work, and he uttered it, sending the coins hovering an inch or so above the table.

He glanced at the adults.

His father had a silly grin on his face.

Nicholas frowned. "Rune magic," the demon accused.

The coins clattered back on to the table.

"Not quite," said his father.

"What do you mean?" asked Nicholas.

"*Ool* is an inert rune, it wouldn't do anything on its own," Papa said. "Most runes are inert, actually, and without an animation rune to set things in motion, they're just words."

"Oh," Nicholas said, his brow furrowed.

Papa continued in what Felix recognized as his teacher voice, "It's actually the animation words that can make arcane spells so dangerous. Obviously, if your grammar and word order are wrong, the spell won't work properly and could even have a poor result, but it's really the improper pairing of inert and animation runes that makes the catastrophic type of reactions of which people are so wary..."

Papa seemed to realize that he had gone on too long and stopped. Felix had seen him speak like that for minutes straight, with Bibi staring dreamily at him the whole time, a small, fond smile on their face.

"Demons don't use rune magic," Nicholas said, "Inert or otherwise."

"There's nothing stopping him, really," Papa said. "I knew a mage once who trained his parrot to use a spell for...hmm, what was it? I think it was to open his cage door."

Nicholas sighed. "Yes, but..." He glanced at Felix. "Without any of that arcane stuff, go ahead. Try again."

Felix turned back to the coffee table and crouched beside it, eyeing the coins. He tried to recall the feeling he'd had before and the way his parents had grinned when he'd moved the cat toy.

His fingers hovered near the coins and one of them began to wiggle; he drew back his hand, afraid to touch it. He coaxed the coin up and settled it on top of another. It took about a minute to stack all the coins.

When he looked back, Nicholas had his arms crossed.

"Did I do it wrong?" he asked.

"No," the demon said.

Felix stood.

"Just thinking," Nicholas clarified, his face softening. "Thinking of my boy at this age. Centuries ago..."

"Oh," Felix said, "Uh...was he good at magic?"

"No, he hated it. Still does."

Felix glanced at his father. "Um."

Nicholas waved his hand as if to shoo away a fly. "But we aren't talking about him. Have you got a candle?"

Felix nodded and headed to the kitchen. While he sifted through the drawers, he heard Papa ask, "What's your son's name?"

"Ashley," the demon answered.

Papa hesitated, studied the demon's face, then asked, "Surely not...not Ashley Stauton?"

"The same," Nicholas said.

With a lighter tone, Papa asked, "Oh, how's he been?"

Felix returned to see Nicholas looking puzzled.

"I sent over these caramels with my Christmas card, I wasn't sure if he'd like them or not," Papa said. "Or if they'd survived the trip intact."

"Um. I, uh, I'm not sure. He lives over there, you know, and we've taken up residence in the States," Nicholas said. "I'll, you know...You sent him caramels?"

"Yes. He's been inviting me to come over and I keep putting it off, I was so hesitant to leave the school and then there was Ellen's health..."

"To go where?" Felix asked.

"To Triviai," his father said.

"You *know* Ashley?" Nicholas asked. "I mean to say, as friends?"

"Well, maybe not so close as friends but I am very fond of him," Papa said. "And I do have my suspicions he puts pressure on the University there when I request to borrow books because I've heard they're very finicky about loaning them out and I haven't been denied yet."

Nicholas smiled. "Good to know the lad made a friend. Gods help me, he's terrible at it."

Felix wrinkled his nose, looking between the two men. He'd thought the demon had come for him, not to find out about his father's friends. He held out the candle to the man and said, "You wanted this."

"Yes, lovely, thank you," Nicholas said and took the candle. He waved his fingers over it and a flame sprung up. He pinched it out a moment later and said, "You think you can do that?"

Felix shrugged.

"Conjuring is more difficult than moving things," the demon said. He handed the candle back to Felix, who stared down at the slightly softened wax.

Someone knocked at the door and Felix knew it must be Charlie. He went over and opened the door.

"What's the candle for?" Charlie asked immediately.

"I'm supposed to light it."

"Uh. Well, alright," he said, stepping inside and taking notice of Nicholas. He turned to Felix and asked, "That's him?"

Felix nodded.

Charlie grinned.

Felix closed the door and said to Nicholas, "This is Charlie. Charlie, this is Nicholas...my, um, my father sent him." He didn't know if he should introduce the older demon as his brother.

Charlie put out his hand for the demon to shake, something that seemed to catch him off guard briefly. Probably because Charlie hadn't changed yet and walked with a distinctly male stride that didn't quite lend itself to cloche hats and middy blouses. "Charlie Banks, nice to meet you."

Nicholas shook the boy's hand. "Nicholas Lundberg."

Charlie said to Felix, "I'm going to change. Don't start without me."

He hurried upstairs after that and Felix knew he would help himself to whatever he wanted from Felix's wardrobe. His newest clothes he didn't have to worry about since they were too big for the smaller boy, but everything else was fair game.

When Charlie returned in boy's clothes, Nicholas said, "Ah," in a mild way that indicated understanding. He turned his eyes to Felix and said, "On with it, then," with a gesture to the candle he still held.

Felix set down the candle and sat on the couch to stare at it. Charlie stood off to the side, his hazel eyes wide with anticipation. It would have been terrible to disappoint Charlie, who loved magic but had no mind for runes, or much that had to do with academics.

He turned his thoughts from his friend to the candle, contemplating the wick. Without warning, the entire thing went with a sudden blast of heat, the wax catching fire. Felix flinched and

Papa called out a spell to extinguish the candle.

Nicholas laughed. "Not much for finesse."

"Sorry," Felix said to his father.

Papa waved a hand. "I should have expected as much. Maybe we ought to have our lessons at the school."

Nicholas shrugged. "Sure."

"Do I really need lessons?" Felix asked. His time outside of school was valuable to him; he had his own interests to pursue.

"It's a bit of practice, lad. Control."

Felix frowned.

"Aye, I know, you think you can control it now, but you haven't been angry yet. Or scared. You'll want it well managed when that happens," the older demon continued.

He hadn't thought of that. Felix generally went about life in a state of calm or of mild annoyance with his classmates, many of whom had little interest in school, but he had, on occasion, gotten into scuffles with the other boys. Once he'd gotten into a shouting match with Mildred over something, some fact that they'd both been sure about, but he couldn't remember what exactly.

His hand went up to touch his shoulder, right where he'd been wounded by the angel. Sometimes still in the middle of the night, if he heard scratching at the window or if Jangles knocked something over, his heart would race, his ears would fill up with ringing and he would be brought back to that moment. Sometimes it happened even if he saw someone with curls in that particular shade of blond on the street; the mistake would send him grabbing for one of his parents' hands, his breathing shallow.

It would be good, he decided, to be able to control himself in such moments.

"When?"

"I've no schedule to keep," Nicholas said.

"We'll have to work around the school schedule," Papa said. "I've got a copy upstairs, why don't you come up to my study?"

Nicholas nodded and followed Papa upstairs.

Once alone, Charlie gave Felix a push. "That's something else, you know. No words at all!" he said.

Felix nodded.

"You get the easy end of things," he said, his tone light, "All I get is blood and these awful *lumps*."

"How is that going?"

"My mother is just about having a conniption," he admitted.

"All grown up and that nonsense." He rolled his eyes and shook his head.

"Oh!" Felix said and gestured for Charlie to come into the kitchen. "Papa wrote down the recipe for that tea...it's here somewhere." He looked around on the kitchen table, checking under the newspaper and finally finding it held down by the saltshaker.

He handed it over to Charlie, who glanced it over. "It's rubbish, you know."

Felix asked, "What the recipe?"

"No, all of this!"

Felix didn't know what to say. "Maybe...um. I don't know, I'll go to the library, maybe there's something that can help," he offered, feeling entirely useless. "I...you know, there's got to be something."

Charlie shrugged, not looking at Felix.

"Do you ever think..." he began but knew what Charlie would say. He would never tell his parents.

"Think what?"

Felix asked, "About what you want to do for a job?"

"What?"

"When you grow up."

He shrugged. "I don't know. I'm useless at school. Besides, I'm just supposed to..."

"Hm?"

"Get married, have a bunch of babies," he said as though the words had a bad taste.

Felix felt stupid for having broached the topic. He didn't know what the adult world would be like for Charlie.

He went over to the cabinet and took out a Whitman's Sampler that a student's parent had given to his father. He pulled off the top and set the box on the table, peering at the lid to determine what he wanted. Someone, he suspected Bibi, had picked through it already, but there were some good ones left.

He held one out to Charlie, who asked, "What kind?"

"Uh, one of the ones with nuts."

Charlie shook his head and came over, finally picking one after a lengthy consultation with the box. Felix ate the one he'd taken out, which had started to melt a little between his fingers. He licked the chocolate from his fingers tips and reached for another.

"You should come live here."

Charlie paused his chewing and looked at Felix. "You know they wouldn't let me."

"I know but...I don't know, I wish you didn't have to go home."

In a voice that Felix barely heard, he said, "Me too."

Several minutes later, Nicholas and Papa returned from Papa's study; his father called him out of the kitchen and Felix knew it was because he had to say goodbye. After that, Papa joined them in picking through the sampler.

LATE FELIX'S bedroom shared a wall with his father's study on one side and his parents' bedroom on the other. Sometimes he heard sounds coming from either side, quiet conversations, or laughter; occasionally, he heard other sounds, ones that he had just begun to understand to be the sounds of more intimate things. Tonight, however, he heard something that made his belly twist.

He heard his father crying, muffled and tired-sounding. More weeping than bawling. He set aside his copy of *Black Mask* and sat up a little straighter.

Before he could decide what to do, he heard Bibi go into the study and ask, "Hiram, love?"

His father sniffled.

"Darling, what's wrong?"

In a voice thick with mucus, Papa said, "I'm so *tired*, Phaedrus."

Bibi sighed. "And I expect you don't mean that you need to sleep."

"No. I don't, I'm sorry."

"Come here," they said and Felix assumed that they had gone to Papa's side and taken him into their arms. "You were never meant for this, Hiram, you can't take it personally."

"How do you do it?"

"I'm made of different stuff," Bibi said mildly.

Papa let out a shaky, wet breath.

Felix sat on his bed, his stomach cold. Bibi was a fallen angel, ever-youthful by design, and Felix, son of the first fallen angel, would live eternally because of his father's blood. Papa, on the other hand, was human and humans were not meant to live forever.

"Why did he do this?" Papa asked.

"Because he knew he'd need you for something," Bibi said. "He...collects people, collects favors. You're an extraordinary mage, Hiram, he knew you'd be good for something."

Papa protested, "There are other mages!"

"There are no mages like you, Hiram, it's why I love you so," Bibi said, their voice tender. "What other mage would raise Felix as a son and not keep him as an experiment?"

"A decent one."

"And no decent mage has the power to keep him safe," Bibi pointed out. "They're all greedy, hungry things. You know they'd be searching for some way to use the boy to their advantage. Here, blow your nose."

Felix heard his father blow his nose and then sigh tremendously.

"And I'm sure I'm somewhat to blame for this," Bibi said. "He is...bizarrely sentimental at times; he does terribly with loss, it's why he's so distant. He must have thought I'd want you to be mine forever."

Papa made a sound of acknowledgment.

"And I do...or I would, if forever wouldn't be so hard on you," Bibi said. "I love you, Hiram, more than I thought I could. You and the boy, both. I'd be lost without either of you."

Papa sniffled.

"Come to bed, dear."

"I suppose."

Felix heard them leaving the study and settling into bed. Bibi said, "I'll be right back," to their husband and then, before Felix realized what they were doing, came into Felix's room to find him sitting on his bed.

"I imagined you were awake," they said from the doorway.

Felix shrugged.

"And if you were awake, I know you heard."

"No, I...it isn't...it doesn't matter," Felix said.

"Your father—"

"Bibi, please," Felix said. He didn't want to hear anymore.

"We love you, Felix, no matter how it was that you came to us," Bibi said.

Felix nodded.

"I'd tell you to go to sleep, but I know it'd be useless."

A quiet moment seemed to stretch forever until Felix made himself ask the question he couldn't get from his mind. "Bibi, is Papa going to be alright?"

"I should think so," Bibi said. "He might need gentle handling, but that is for me to worry about."

Felix nodded.

"Anything else?"

"I love you, Bibi."

"And I love you, Felix," they said. They crossed the room and kissed his hair. "Go back to your reading and no more worrying about your father."

Felix nodded.

Bibi gave him one more kiss and a quick hug, then left.

Felix picked up *Black Mask* and found where he'd left off but couldn't do more than stare at the pages. After another hour or so, he drifted off to sleep and woke in the morning with Jangles curled next to him and his book on the floor.

He nestled further into his bed, pulling the blankets close. After about half an hour, his father came in, sat on the edge of his bed, and gave his arm a gentle shake. "Felix, time to get up."

For as long as he could remember, his father had woken him up in that way.

"Is it Monday?" he asked.

"Already, I know," his father said.

He sat up and studied his father's face. A close-cropped beard did something to hide his youth, but Papa would never look older than his mid-twenties. Even Bibi looked older than that. He put his arms around his father, squeezing him tight.

Papa put an arm around him and returned the embrace. "You still have to go to school."

Every morning, they walked to the school together, arriving long before the other students and often before the other teachers. Some days Bibi walked with them. Felix remembered the days when he had clung to his father's hand and hurried to keep up with Papa's long legs.

"I'm sorry." The words slipped out.

"For what?" his father asked.

"That he did this to you."

Papa looked down at him, puzzled until realization spread across his face. "You overheard."

"I didn't mean to."

"What he did has nothing to do with you."

Felix frowned.

"We crossed paths and he would have found a use for me one way or another," he said.

"But—"

"And if our paths hadn't crossed, I would be dead. Not from old age, either, I would have died when I was barely twenty-six."

"Oh."

"No matter what else comes of this...youth, I am glad to be your father," Papa said, his voice cracking a little. "Don't ever be sorry for that."

Felix hugged his father again.

"It is time for school, though, we don't want to be late," Papa said after a moment.

He couldn't stop himself from rolling his eyes, not irritated but amused. Papa hated to be late for anything, even things he didn't want to go to. He pulled back from the embrace and went to wash up.

When he came downstairs for breakfast, he found Bibi already eating and his father preparing another omelet.

Once at school, he sat in his father's office reading his pulp magazine and waiting for Charlie. He would trudge up the stairs, let himself into the office and take out the change of clothes kept for him there.

Today, however, Charlie didn't trudge. He shuffled into the room and Felix sat up straighter, surprised to see the other boy's eyes red-rimmed and his nose running.

"What happened?"

"My father got a promotion."

Felix glanced at his father, not sure why this would be a problem.

"A really good one!" he said, wiping his nose on his wrist.

Papa set down his book and came around to the front of the desk, handing Charlie a handkerchief. "Where do they want to send you?"

"To the convent school my cousins go to," he said.

Felix stared, his grip on his pulp going slack. "In Nova Scotia?"

Charlie nodded.

His book fell from his hand. "That's all the way on the other side of Quebec!"

Charlie blew his nose.

Felix looked to his father in desperation. A scholarship had kept Charlie at the Academy for years, even though his parents no longer qualified.

Charlie said, "It's a *girls' school.*"

"But they'll let you finish the year, won't they?" Felix asked.

The other boy couldn't answer; he buried his face in his hands and began to cry, his shoulders shaking. Papa put a hand on the boy's back.

"Papa, he's got to at least finish the year! No one goes to a new school in April."

"I'll find out what I can," Papa said. "Charlie, come have a seat." He walked the boy over to a chair and crouched beside it. "You'll get through this, Charlie, whatever comes."

He shook his head.

"You will," Papa promised.

"I can't go to a girls' school," Charlie said, the word hard to hear through his sniffles. "I can't!"

"You should tell your parents," Felix said.

"I can't."

"But—"

"Felix, they'd lock me up," he said, "You should hear the things they say about your parents."

"I..."

"I think Charlie's right," Papa said. "Until he's older, it might be, um, unsafe to let his parents know."

"If they find out you've been letting me..." Charlie trailed off, "letting me dress how I want, they'll never let me near you in a million years."

Felix heard footsteps; the teachers had started to arrive. He heard Ms. Perkins making demure advances toward Mr. Lowe and he heard Mr. Lowe trying to extract himself from the conversation, stammering and mixing up his words. He was nervous around women and as such had to be restricted to teaching in the Academy, though his teaching style worked better for older students.

"You should get changed," Felix said.

"What's the point?" Charlie asked but stood and stomped over to get his clothes anyway. He went into the bathroom adjacent to

Papa's office.

"What do we do?" Felix asked his father.

"I'm afraid there's little we can do," Papa said.

"There has to be something," he said, "Charlie can come live with us."

"No."

"But—"

"It's not a matter of what I want, Felix," Papa said, his voice soft, "Without consent from his parents, it's kidnapping."

"Charlie wouldn't..."

"No, but imagine what Mr. and Mrs. Banks would think if their daughter, on the brink of becoming a woman, came to live with us without their permission and suddenly started dressing in boy's clothes. Imagine the police becoming involved, finding out what you are, what Bibi is...and mixing a pretty, young human like Charlie into the situation."

Felix fidgeted. He did not like the worried tone in his father's voice.

"I don't want to frighten you, love, but there are laws that don't look favorably on families like ours."

Felix sighed.

"People don't like us, but as long as we don't do anything to draw too much attention, they'll leave us alone. We have the advantage of the school's good standing and public charity but..." Papa sighed. "I shouldn't be telling you any of this."

Felix shook his head. "No, you're right. I...it was a stupid idea."

"Wanting to help is never stupid."

His hand reached for the amulet around his neck; he began to fidget with it. Papa was right, he was always right. Charlie could not be part of their family; he didn't know if it was worse than the hushed, anxious way his father had spoken.

He tightened his grip on the amulet and the edges bit into his palm.

Charlie returned from the bathroom, his face wet no longer with tears but with water from the sink.

Felix picked up his book and set it on his father's desk. To Charlie, he said, "I'm staying after to practice today."

The other boy raised an eyebrow, moody but interested. "To practice what?"

"Magic."

His face rearranged a little. "Oh."

"You should stay and watch."

Charlie nodded, still out of sorts from the prospect of being sent to a girls' school but now at least distracted. He had chattered continuously about not just Felix's magic, but the demon since their first meeting.

Throughout the day, Charlie's mood remained stormy but when classes were over, they waited together for Nicholas in an unused classroom. Charlie sat on the teacher's desk, his heels tapping against the side of the desk. Felix wandered the room, going from window to window. He spied Nicholas walking down the street towards the school, his gate smooth and jaunty.

"So...does he *feel* like your brother?"

"What?"

"Nicholas. He's your brother, isn't he?"

Felix shrugged. "I think so. I mean...I don't know him; he doesn't feel like anything."

"You think so?"

Felix shrugged again.

"You don't even have brothers, what would you know anyway?"

"You're like a brother."

"If I was your brother, we'd be mean to each other. Emma's always got something to say," Charlie told him.

Felix looked away from the window. "Maybe Emma just isn't very nice."

"None of them are. They've always got something to say about someone else."

"So does Bibi."

"Bibi's different."

There was no argument for that. Bibi was different, even from the other fallen angels, as far as Felix had been able to gather.

Nicholas came into the classroom. "Hello, lads, how've we been?"

"You're his brother, aren't you?" Charlie asked.

Nicholas glanced at Felix, a little wild-eyed; Nicholas almost always seemed confused. "I did mention, didn't I? Half-brothers, really, but what difference does it make?"

Charlie asked, "You have any kids?"

"Two."

"Boys or girls?"

"Uh. One of each, I think." He paused. "Yes. One of each."

"Did the Devil come to visit you on *your* birthday?"

"Charlie!" Felix hissed.

"No," Nicholas answered. "But I wasn't any little lordling or anything, no one wrote down when I was born. If they had, wouldn't have done me any good, anyway, I wouldn't have been able to read it."

"When were you born?"

"Did I come to teach magic or to tell you my life story?" he asked. The question seemed like it could have been entirely innocent; he might not have known why he was there.

"Magic," Felix supplied.

"Thought so. Let's get to it."

NICHOLAS STAYED through the rest of the school year.

So did Charlie.

Felix pretended that the next school year would never come. He pretended all through June and July, and right up until the middle of August.

Charlie came over less and less in August, busy with packing and getting new uniforms, and because he and Felix had started fighting over stupid things when he did come over.

Felix knew they were stupid even while they were fighting.

He thought Charlie knew it, too.

He sat out on the front steps, staring at the street, occasionally tossing a pebble, or poking at the dirt with a stick.

Papa came to sit beside him. He didn't say anything for a while.

Felix fiddled with his magic, setting little tufts of grass on fire, or making orbs of light, or flicking rocks around.

Nicholas had gone home at the end of the school year and without his magic lessons, Felix found himself playing with his power more often.

It wanted to be used.

He liked using it.

Learning to use his magic had been like learning to walk. He didn't think he could ever stop.

He set light to the end of a stick and then snuffed it out in the dirt.

"Be careful."

"I am."

Papa eyed the various scorched patches of grass. "Not a nice look for the lawn."

Felix sighed. He closed his eyes and concentrated, then peaked one open. He grinned at Papa.

He'd grown the grass back.

Papa looked unnerved.

It wasn't the magic. Papa loved magic. He knew almost everything about it, or, at least, everything people had discovered so far.

It was how fast Felix had picked it up.

Felix had overheard him telling Bibi.

"Charlie's leaving tomorrow, isn't he?"

Felix shrugged.

"When were you going to say goodbye?"

Felix shoved the stick deeper into the dirt. "I wasn't."

"Charlie's your best friend."

Felix huffed.

"You'll regret not going over," Papa warned.

"That's what Bibi said."

"Bibi knows a lot more than I do."

Felix scowled up at his father. "Charlie's parents hate us."

Papa didn't say anything.

It was nearly impossible to pick a fight with either of his parents. "Shouting never fixes anything," they both said and both of them had the years to back up that statement.

Felix still tried sometimes. This time, he said, "They hate us because you and Bibi are freaks."

Papa sighed.

"They wouldn't want to send Charlie away if *you* weren't such queers." Even saying it made Felix's stomach hurt, but he glared at his father as he said it.

"You might be right," Papa said. He didn't look hurt. He looked tired. "But you know, if Bibi and I weren't so queer, you probably wouldn't be friends with Charlie."

Felix scowled at his father.

"I know you haven't got a lot of friends, Felix, and I know a lot of that is because of how different our family looks to other people.

Charlie going away is going to be hard on you."

"It's your fault," Felix sulked. His throat hurt.

"It will be hard for Charlie, too. Maybe harder. He's leaving behind the only friend who knows who he is."

Felix sniffled. He rubbed his nose with the back of his wrist. He threw the stick. He rubbed his eyes, hard.

"You should say goodbye."

"I don't want to."

"It's the right thing to do."

"I don't want to!" Felix shouted. His voice cracked. His face flushed and then he was crying.

Papa put an arm around him and rubbed his back.

Felix wrapped his arms around his father and sobbed. "It's not fair."

"I know."

When Felix finished crying, Papa sent him inside to wash his face.

After that, he walked him over to say goodbye to Charlie.

Mr. and Mrs. Banks didn't look thrilled to see him.

They looked less pleased when Felix gave Charlie a long hug goodbye.

Felix insisted, "I'm sorry I shouted at you."

"I'm sorry, too," Charlie said. "I'm gonna miss you."

Felix squeezed him harder. "I'll write. I promise."

"Charlotte still has some packing to do," Mr. Banks reminded.

"Quite a bit," Mrs. Banks agreed.

Felix couldn't make himself let go of Charlie.

"Charlotte," her mother called. "Come along."

"I'll really, really miss you," Felix insisted.

Papa put a hand on Felix's shoulder.

"Charlotte." Mrs. Banks sounded angry now.

They pulled apart.

Felix had shed a few more tears.

Charlie's eyes had gone red, and he had snot on his face.

Felix handed him a handkerchief.

Charlie blew his nose. "I'll write, too."

"Good luck at school," Papa said to the boy. "You've been a delightful pupil. I'm sure you'll do well at your new school."

"Thank you, Mr. Reinhart. I'll...I'll really miss the Academy," Charlie said.

They stood around awkwardly for a minute before Charlie's

parents called him one last time.

"God, I'm just saying goodbye!" Charlie shouted at his parents. "Why do you want to ruin my life!"

He didn't wait for an answer. He ran inside and slammed the door.

Papa smoothed his shirt. "The Academy will always have room for—"

"No," Mr. Banks said. He added a stiff, "Thank you."

"Mmm." Papa put his hand on Felix's shoulder.

They took the long way home and stopped at a malted shop on the way home.

It didn't fix how Felix felt.

He played with the straw in his drink. "Papa?"

"Hmm?"

"I shouldn't have yelled at you."

"I imagine not."

Felix scowled. He jammed his straw into the bottom of his drink. He sighed. "It's not your fault, it's *their* fault. Charlie's parents."

"Trying to blame people never gets us anywhere."

"But it is their fault!"

"Their actions are their own, of course," Papa agreed. "They are closed-minded, but no one is born that way. And no one changes their mind by getting yelled at."

"So what am I supposed to do?"

"Be yourself. Don't apologize for it, not ever. Fight for your space in the world. Fighting with individuals doesn't do as much as taking on the larger institutions that influence those individuals."

"So just let people call us names?"

"There's a difference between yelling at people and letting them walk all over you. You'll figure out what works best for you." Papa rubbed Felix's arm.

Felix huffed.

"Are you ready to head home?"

Felix sighed but got up. He knew he was too old for it, but he held Papa's hand and leaned against his arm on the walk home.

THE LAST few weeks of summer dragged by.

He kept good on his promise to write to Charlie.

They exchanged letters weekly, if not more frequently.

Writing letters to Charlie and studying magic became his only real hobbies. Well, and devouring his pulps. Reading them kept him sane, saner than trying to write to someone thousands of miles away or trying to master all the magics he could.

He also figured out a handful of good hiding places in his room. His parents still got cagey if he brought up angels, so he'd avoided the topic altogether with them.

Maybe they thought it would traumatize him, talking about the thing that had almost killed him, or maybe the attack had done a number on their nerves.

He didn't know what he'd do if someone hurt Papa or Bibi.

He glanced up from his magazine.

Papa had a pile of midterms in front of him.

"Bibi says sitting like that is what makes your back hurt," he reminded his father.

Papa straightened up. He looked at the clock.

Felix shouldn't have said anything.

"You should be in class."

Felix sighed. "I don't want to go."

Papa frowned at him. "Go."

"Fulton's an idiot."

"Felix James!" Papa scolded. "Go to class."

Felix threw his magazine on the floor. "Not my fault you hired an idiot." He stomped out before Papa could say anything else.

He walked into class without explaining himself and flipped open his book to a random page, then sat with his arms crossed.

He'd read the whole text already. He didn't see the point in sitting here and listening to some overgrown child explain it to him.

Fulton couldn't be more than five or six years older than his pupils. His hands shook most of the time and he stuttered his way through most of his lessons.

When Fulton called on him, Felix offered the most scathing answers he could. Always technically correct but designed to embarrass the asker.

Two days later, Papa called him to his office at the end of the day. He pointed to a desk with several sheets of paper and a pen. "Write a letter to Fulton apologizing for your behavior."

"What?" Felix wrinkled his nose.

"Being my son doesn't give you carte blanche to disrespect my staff. In fact, you should be setting an example for your peers."

Felix snorted. "I'm not apologizing."

"It will be waiting for you."

Felix turned and left.

A few days later, before he left for school, he asked Bibi, "Can I have a quarter?"

"No."

Felix opened his mouth. He had no idea what to say. His parents had denied his requests for things before, but never so coolly or without explanation. "Why not?" he demanded.

"Your father asked you to do something. Have you done it?"

Felix scowled. He turned and stormed out of the kitchen.

Jangles scampered out of his way and up the stairs.

He didn't stop by his father's office that morning.

He thought about cutting class.

He went anyway and sulked through the class.

He spent most of the weekend in his room, not talking to his parents.

It took about a week for him to get sick of reading old magazines. Thursday night, he scribbled out a quick letter and brought it downstairs.

He shoved it toward his father. "Here."

His father took it and looked over it. "This is neither sincere nor well-written and is addressed to me. I have no need for it." He returned the letter.

Felix balled it up and threw it into the garbage.

He stormed back upstairs.

It took him a day to decide to put any effort into his letter.

He wrote a few drafts and presented the final to his father on Monday morning.

Papa read it, then handed it back. "Sit down."

Felix sat in the chair across from Papa's desk. He folded his hands in his laps, his palms sweaty.

"Do you know what an apology means?"

"It means I'm sorry."

"No."

Felix's stomach flipped.

"An apology means that you won't repeat your offense."

Felix rubbed his palms on his trousers.

"I know you've been lonely without Charlie, and I know you're a smart young man, and that Fulton has his flaws as an instructor. He's a nervous man and it's not your business to know why. It's your business to act like a gentleman toward everyone, regardless of whether you benefit from that relationship."

Felix sniffed.

"Do you understand that?"

"Yes."

"If you bring this letter to Fulton, you're making him a promise. I didn't raise you to break promises."

"I understand."

Papa folded the letter shut and sealed it with wax. He handed it back to Felix. "Come back upstairs once you've delivered this."

Felix nodded. He took the letter.

He found Fulton in his classroom, preparing for the day's lessons. He knocked gently on the doorframe. "Sir?"

Fulton looked up. His eyes widened at the sight of Felix. He cleared his throat and straightened up.

"This is for you." Felix offered the letter. "I." He swallowed. "I was rude. I'm sorry. I'll...uh. I'll do better."

Fulton turned the letter over. He looked like he thought it would burst into flame.

"You're, uh. You're new this year. Right?"

"Yes. I. I. I relocated from the States over the summer."

"Did you teach there, too?"

Fulton let out a nervous laugh. "I hardly teach here!"

"Oh, no, it's...It's not that bad."

"That's kind of you." Fulton set the letter on his desk. "I. My mother. My mother was a teacher. She worked here for a while before she got married. She wrote to Dr. Queen and they arranged this position for me. Professor Reinhart said he'd give me a year to see if it worked out."

Felix didn't know what to say. A teacher had never addressed him like this before. Not exactly as an equal, but as something close. "What'd you do before?"

"I wrote plays."

That made sense. Fulton had a better knack for teaching literature.

"Plays? What kind?"

Fulton blushed. "Oh, I can't say."

Felix almost rolled his eyes. "No offense, sir, but you've met my parents."

"My...I had a friend, a good friend, but he, uh. He passed away. I haven't..." Fulton looked him over. "I shouldn't be telling you this. You're a just kid."

Felix tilted up his chin. "I'm thirteen. Really, almost fourteen!" he insisted.

"I haven't written since Daniel passed away. My. My mother thought a change of scenery might help my nerves."

Felix felt bad. A snotty pupil wouldn't help his nerves. He was about to ask where he'd lived and what he'd written, but the other students started to come into class.

"My father said to go see him."

"Of course."

Felix went to his father.

Papa handed him a stack of papers. "These need to be graded by the end of the day."

Felix looked them over. The midterms for an intro to runes class. He frowned.

Papa handed him another stack. "And these, too."

Felix sat.

He spent the day grading papers.

It absolutely bored him out of his mind to reread variations on the same thing over and over again.

He didn't know if he was supposed to learn something from

the experience or if boredom was meant as a punishment.

He handed the stack to his father at the end of the day. "They should be all right."

"I expect they are."

Felix could hear the students as they hurried out of the building.

The Academy ran on a different schedule than the University.

"May I be excused?"

"Of course."

Felix went back to Fulton's room. He asked, "Where did you live?"

Fulton's head jerked up. He blinked a few times before he answered, "Chicago."

"Have you read *The Jungle?*" Felix asked.

Fulton looked taken aback. "Have you?"

Felix shrugged. "I'm an advanced reader. That's what Bibi always says. Burroughs was born in Chicago."

"You like pulps?"

"I'd eat 'em for breakfast if I could."

Fulton smiled. "I. I appreciate your apology."

"I was being rotten. You didn't deserve it. What did you write? Just plays...?"

"Plays mainly, yeah. Short stories here and there."

Felix nodded. He rubbed his arm. "I. I really am sorry. I'll...I'll see you tomorrow."

Fulton gave him a nod.

Felix headed home.

He found Bibi reading on the couch. He curled up next to them.

Bibi put an arm around him and started to read out loud.

Felix helped them make dinner.

He laid low until Christmas break. He raised his hand and gave helpful answers when Fulton called on him.

Charlie came home for Christmas. As soon as he could get away from his family, he came to visit.

Felix threw his arms around him as soon as he opened the door and saw him there. He dragged him inside and squeezed.

"My ribs, Felix!" Charlie said, but he said it with a laugh.

Felix dragged him over to the Christmas tree. He shoved presents into his arms. "You have to open them!"

"Felix!" Bibi scolded with a chuckle. "Let him inside for a

second."

Felix nodded. He stepped back. He put his hands in his pockets. "Do, uh, do you want to change?"

Charlie glanced down. "I can't stay for long."

"Oh. Well. Come open your presents."

Charlie shook his head. "I can't take anything back with me. My parents think I'm visiting Mildred."

Felix frowned. "I...Well. Will you open them anyway?"

Charlie nodded. He looked older like he'd gotten five years older in one term. He wasn't any taller, but he just looked...tired.

He sat on the couch.

Felix handed him the gifts one at a time.

Books, candy, a fountain pen.

He thanked Felix and hugged him.

"We can mail them to you at school," Papa offered. He handed Charlie a hot cocoa. "How are your studies?"

Charlie listlessly rattled off information about his classes.

Bibi asked if he'd made any friends.

"Not really."

"That takes time, making new friends. You'll get there. Do you get along with the girls at least?"

"They're not so bad. Most of the are nice, anyway. A few who aren't." Charlie shrugged.

"Doesn't it always play out like that?" Bibi said. "Look for the nice ones."

Charlie nodded.

Bibi put a hand on his shoulder. "It's not easy but you'll get through it. You will."

Charlie shrugged.

Bibi pulled Charlie in for a hug. "Don't worry, love, you will. You're a strong boy, and you'll make it. Even when it feels like you won't."

Charlie grabbed onto Bibi.

Felix felt stupid.

He walked Charlie most of the way home. He stopped before Charlie's parents would be able to see him.

Charlie sighed. "My parents think you're sweet on me."

Felix laughed. Then he covered his mouth. "Sorry! Sorry, I am, but that's ridiculous."

"That's why they don't want me to see you anymore. If we were both boys—"

"We are both boys."

Charlie rolled his eyes. "Yeah, well, if I wasn't a boy you could knock up, it'd be different, I bet."

Felix made a face. He didn't want anything to do with getting people pregnant. He didn't even like to think about kissing or holding hands too much. It made him feel sweaty. "Well, just tell them I'm not sweet on you."

"I tried. They, uh…They didn't believe me. They keep telling me I'm a young lady now, that I need to be careful. Watch out for my reputation."

"I'm sorry."

Charlie sighed. "Don't you dare stop writing me letters."

"I won't."

"Promise," Felix swore.

"They're the only thing keeping me sane, I swear."

Felix hugged him again. "Maybe…Maybe ask if I can come over instead of you coming to my house. I'll be extra polite and everything."

"I'll ask."

Felix watched him walk until he rounded a corner.

He went home and curled up in bed, not sleeping, but angry and restless and hollow all at once.

Before Charlie went back to school, Felix got to go over once.

They played board games under the scrutiny of Mrs. Banks.

Her fingers moved in an untraceable pattern, turning out crocheted lace, and her eyes never left Felix.

It made the hairs on the back of his neck prickle.

The whole time he did his best to act like nothing more than a friend. He didn't think it changed Charlie's parents' opinions, but he didn't know what else to do.

He made careful note of each of the other children their age that Mrs. Banks mentioned.

When school started back up again, Felix made an effort to be friendly with Mildred and a few other girls that Mrs. Banks seemed to like much better than him. If they couldn't spend time alone, they could at least hang out in a group.

Summer would be an awful bore if Felix couldn't spend it with Charlie.

MAY 1928

"THERE'S A letter for you," Bibi called from the kitchen as Felix came inside.

Felix bolted over to the table and snatched the letter. He saw Charlie's name on the return address and ripped the envelope open.

Charlie hadn't written in a while.

When Felix read the first line, he understood why. The next three lines didn't bring any better news.

He shoved the letter in his pocket and hurried into the kitchen.

Bibi sat at the table, an empty plate and a newspaper in front of them. They glanced up, then did a doubletake. "What's that face for?"

"Charlie isn't coming home for the summer. He's going to Nova Scotia."

Bibi sighed and set down their book. "To stay with his cousins?" they guessed.

"What am I supposed to do?"

"Keep writing."

"Bibi, it isn't fair!"

"No," they agreed.

Tears dribbled down his cheeks. "Bibi!"

"Charlie is not my son. I don't know what you want me to do."

"I want you to help. He can't stay with his cousins! They're all *girls*."

Bibi sighed. "Spending time with girls isn't the worst fate a boy could ask for. A summer in Nova Scotia isn't so bad either."

Felix didn't understand why Bibi didn't want to help. Of all the people in the world, Bibi should have wanted to help. They should have understood what summer in Nova Scotia meant for Charlie. "What's wrong with you!"

Bibi tucked a lock of hair behind their ear. "Felix, how old am I?"

"I don't know."

"A guess."

"Very old?" Felix guessed.

"Very old," Bibi confirmed. "Old enough to know that what you want me to do will not end well."

"We have to help."

"You help Charlie by giving him hope."

Felix shook his head. "It's not enough."

"No, it's not. But it's the most we can do."

Felix slammed his hand on the table. "Bibi!"

Bibi wrapped his hands around Felix's upper arms. They pulled him in close. "Do you think I've never tried to help a boy like Charlie before?"

Felix tried to step back.

Bibi didn't let go. "Charlie is a wonderful boy and he's a good friend to you, but he is not my son. You will always be more important to me than him."

"Bibi," Felix whispered.

They'd never done anything like this before. They had never looked scared before, not like this, not even when that angel had attacked him.

Felix tried to step back again.

"Even if a hundred other boys have to suffer for it, I'll keep you safe."

Felix started to cry.

Bibi dragged him into a hug. When they spoke, their voice sounded thick and wet. "I'm sorry, Felix. I'm sorry we can't help your friend and I'm...I'm sorry I spoke to you like that, but I'll never let anything happen to you."

Felix wrapped his arms around Bibi. He buried his face against their chest and cried, not able to help himself, angry and embarrassed. "It's not fair!"

"I know."

Felix stomped his foot and screamed, "It's not fair!"

"I know," Bibi said. They tightened their arms around him.

Felix pushed himself out of their arms and stormed upstairs. He curled up in bed, too angry to care that he could hear Bibi crying downstairs, too angry to care that they were probably right.

He stayed in his room all night, even after Papa came and called him to dinner.

He heard his parents fighting in the living room.

They never fought. Oh, they bickered and argued, but Felix had never heard them shout at each other like this.

He couldn't even tell what they were fighting over.

He covered his ears until they stopped.

In the middle of the night, he went into their room. He had to make sure they'd gone to bed together.

He heard from his classmates about fathers who slept on couches and parents who fought all the time.

Papa rolled over then sat up with a start. He put a hand over his heart. "Felix!" he scolded softly. "What are you doing?"

"What were you fighting about?"

"Something stupid."

"Was it my fault?"

Papa shook his head. "No."

Bibi pulled the blankets over their shoulders. "Hiram?" they asked groggily.

"It's only Felix."

Bibi rolled over. They patted the bed. "Come here."

Felix went. He sidled between the two of them.

He was fourteen now, too old for this.

The other boys would make fun of him.

Probably the girls too.

"What are you doing up in the middle of the night?" Bibi asked.

"I'm always up."

Bibi huffed, then smiled. "That's going to get you in trouble someday I bet. Being up all night."

"In trouble?" Felix asked.

"The sort of trouble young men tend to get into in the middle of the night," Bibi confirmed. They wrapped an arm around him and kissed his hair. "But you're not a young man yet. So, stay out of trouble for a little while longer."

Papa pulled a blanket up from the foot of the bed.

"If it was stupid, why did you fight about it?" Felix asked.

"People fight about stupid things all the time," Papa said.

"Not you."

Bibi assured, "Even us."

"What did you fight about?"

"Oh, you don't really want to know," Bibi said.

Felix glanced at his father.

Papa smiled. "I was *staring* too much."

Bibi reached over and smacked Papa's arm. "Hiram, you're a beast."

Papa grinned.

Felix didn't know what else to say. He hunkered down between his parents and pulled the blankets up to his chin. He felt little again.

They both fell back asleep and he lay awake, not angry anymore but feeling bad for them. They were just scared. He knew the world could be scary and he knew it wasn't always nice to people like Papa and Bibi.

They were scared just like Charlie was scared.

Someone had to look out for them.

Might as well be him.

He fell asleep knowing what he needed to do, if not necessarily how to do it.

He kept writing his letters to Charlie, for one, and got the address for his aunt and uncle's house. He saved up his pocket money penny by penny, going for the whole rest of the spring without buying a single treat or magazine.

He worked a few jobs around the neighborhood and the university, helping with chores or research, or sometimes grading papers, as long as he promised not to tell his father.

He kept writing and saving until finally, in the middle of the night in July, he packed a bag, snuck out his bedroom window, and headed to the train station.

He'd snuck out once a week for the past few months, just to make sure he wouldn't get caught tonight. He'd memorized the walk to the train station, memorized the stops and trains he would need to take.

He'd never left Pickering on his own before.

His hand shook as he handed over the money for his ticket.

Nothing would go wrong. People took train rides all the time.

Boys his age went out on their own all the time. He was fourteen, old enough to take a train ride on his own.

Bibi and Papa treated him like a little kid sometimes.

They just worried about him, he knew. Most teenagers didn't have an angel that wanted them dead.

His fingers found the amulet. He never took it off, never even *thought* about taking it off. The angel could only find him if he took it off. With it on, he and that angel could be in the same room and the angel's eyes would slide right over him.

Not many others boarded the train with him, late as it was.

Days later, when he arrived in Wolfville, it took him a while to find Charlie's aunt and uncle's house.

People pointed him in the right direction without too many questions when he asked about Robert Banks, though they ended up pointing him toward the general store.

He ended up following Charlie's uncle home at night.

He hung back, keeping to the shadows, and doing his best to stay unnoticed.

He almost got sick when he saw Charlie.

The first time in months.

He sat out on the lawn with his cousins, all of them on a blanket beneath a tree. His cousins looked over a magazine together.

Charlie had a magazine too, but he just flipped back and forth between a few pages.

Felix stayed at the end of the driveway.

No one could see him.

He made himself scarce and waited till late that night, until all the lights had gone off and no one made a peep. He circled around the house a few times to make sure he didn't hear anything.

He unlocked the front door with an enchanted key. It crumbled apart once it turned. He wiped his hands on his pants.

He tiptoed through the house, checking the rooms until he found Charlie.

He wondered, briefly, if this was what murderers felt like.

Bibi would blame the pulps he read for that.

He covered Charlie's mouth and shook him awake.

Charlie tried to push up away, then froze when he saw Felix. His eyes widened.

"Get dressed. Meet me outside."

Charlie frowned. He pushed Felix's hand down. "What are you doing here?" he whispered. He wrapped his arms around Felix and pulled him close.

"I came to help."

"My uncle's going to kill you."

Felix shook his head. "Come outside."

Charlie sighed. "Fine."

Felix went to wait outside.

Charlie reappeared in the dress he'd worn earlier that day. He'd even put on a cloche hat and stockings.

Maybe it was better. If they were caught together and Charlie was only half-dressed, it would look ten times worse.

They walked in silence to the end of the drive, out of sight of the house.

"What are you doing here?"

"I..." Felix realized he'd never asked Charlie what he wanted. "I missed you."

Charlie gave a crooked smile. "I miss you, too. And not that I'm not happy to see you but..."

"I got kind of worried."

Charlie rubbed his nose.

"You don't write back as much. And when you do...You don't sound happy."

"I figure..." Charlie sighed. "I'm not happy, Felix. I'm...I'm in sort of an awful state most days."

Felix looked him over.

The other boy had grown a few inches since Christmas, almost as tall as Felix, and looked like he hadn't slept in weeks.

"Your parents don't know you're here."

Felix tilted up his chin. "No. They couldn't help. They're...They're scared of what people would do. If we helped, you know, helped the way you really need."

"You just come to visit?"

Felix shook his head. He took off his backpack and pulled out all the money he'd saved, and some that he'd stolen.

He'd never really stolen anything before, not once he'd understood that things could belong to people. Once as a little boy, he'd taken a candy without paying, but Papa had explained things to him.

He'd filched quite a bit from his parents over the past months, a dollar here and there.

He knew he shouldn't steal, but not helping was worse.

He handed the envelope to Charlie. "This is enough to get you to Triviai, and a little extra."

Charlie frowned. He handed the envelope back. "What for?"

"Papa gets all these academic papers from the university there. The first university of magic in Europe. They're pioneers in medical magic. There are people there, at the University of Triviai, that can do magic, the kind of magic you need."

"Need?" Charlie asked.

"They can change people's bodies. You can look how you want, stop...stop your cycle if you don't want it, make your chest flat..." Felix trailed off. "Other things."

Charlie took a step back.

"It isn't cheap, but, but you know, there's...there's work you can do over there, there are jobs and you can save up. And then, then you can home and we can...You know, your parents won't make you wear dresses or say you can't be friends with boys, and they won't send you to a girl's school! You can come back to the Academy and..."

"Felix."

Felix grabbed him by the arms. "And if your parents don't let you come home, you can live with us! Or we'll find a place together, I don't care what Bibi and Papa say, you're my best friend and I'm not standing around and reading your *miserable fucking letters anymore.*"

"So you came here to tell me to run away from home to another continent so maybe someday I can have a different body."

"If it would make you happy."

"If it would make me happy," Charlie repeated dryly.

"Or, you know, less miserable."

Charlie shook his head.

"Cause you seem miserable, Charlie. And I don't figure it's gonna get better."

"Figure you're right."

Felix pulled a sheaf of papers out of his bag. "This is everything you need to know to get there."

"My parents weren't kidding when they said demons go crazy."

Felix's answer stuck in his throat. Charlie had never called him a demon before, at least, not to his face. "I guess it's sort of nuts."

Charlie smiled at him. He gave him a push. "Are you serious

about this? That's a lot of cash you're trying to give me."

"Dead serious, Charlie."

Charlie threw his arms around Felix and squeezed the air out of him. "You really mean it."

"You're my best friend." He hugged Charlie back.

Charlie pulled back. "I...Can...Let me go get some stuff, okay? I'll be right back!" He took off toward the house.

About fifteen minutes later, Charlie returned with a bag.

They went to the train station, but before they bought tickets, Felix pulled Charlie into the bathroom.

"Here, switch clothes with me," Felix said.

"What?"

"I tried to bring you an extra set of my old clothes, but you know, you grew!" Felix said.

"You don't want to wear a dress."

Felix shrugged. "When people look for you, they'll look for a girl. And you've got to go a lot further than I do. Safer to go looking like a boy. And, uh." Felix grinned. "Someone tries to give me trouble, I'll put his eyes out."

Charlie snorted.

"Oh! Did I show you what I can do now!" Felix flicked his wrist and sent a dart of glass hurtling toward the wall.

It stuck in the wall.

Charlie pulled it out of the wall and turned it around in his fingers. "Neat."

Felix stripped off his jacket and handed it over.

Ten minutes later, Charlie had put on Felix's clothes and Felix was checking his stocking seams.

"You seem kinda good at that," Charlie pointed out.

"Watched Bibi do it."

"Not anything you want to tell me?"

Felix glanced over.

Charlie looked so at home in a suit. Relaxed. He shrugged. "Maybe that's why we're friends."

"We're friends cause we like each other not cause I like to wear dresses."

"So you do like to wear dresses?"

"I don't know, I just put it on." He put his hands on his hips and gave them a swish. "What do you think, am I pretty?"

Charlie put the cloche hat on Felix's head and squashed it down a little bit. "You've got gams for days, that's for sure."

Felix fixed the hat. He studied himself in the mirror. He was thin and he hadn't hit puberty hard enough that his Adam's apple showed yet. He didn't even have peach fuzz. He looked like a weedy twelve-year-old girl, but he looked like a girl.

"What are your parents going to think when you come home in a dress?"

Felix looked at his shoes, Charlie's shoes, which pinched his toes a little. "They'll probably figure out where I went pretty quick. They'll probably be mad. I'll probably get grounded. Or who knows what. I've never run away from home before."

"There was that time you hid under Mildred's porch."

Felix snorted. He gave the envelope of cash to Charlie, and the packet of instructions to get to Triviai. "Write to me. Let me know you're okay."

"I will."

They had to go on separate trains.

Felix's train took him back to Pickering, and Charlie's would bring him to a port where he could book passage to Europe.

Felix kept it together until about halfway home, where he broke down crying at the train station waiting for his next train.

"Miss?"

He looked up to see an older gentleman standing in front of him.

"Are you lost?"

He shook his head. "No."

"Is there something I can do to help?"

Felix shook his head. "No. Just. My brother moved away. He won't be home for a long time."

"Ah. That is hard. Where did he go?"

"Europe. For, uh. For school."

"Do you mind if I sit?"

"Not at all," Felix said.

It was actually kind of a relief to talk to someone. He'd kept to himself this whole trip and he hadn't even spent very long with Charlie. He'd needed to get out of town before his aunt and uncle realized he was missing.

The police would probably look all over for him.

He talked with the gentleman until his train arrived.

He got back to Pickering late in the evening.

He stepped inside and found his parents in the living room.

They looked terrible.

And he'd done that to them.

Quietly, he said, "I left a note."

He hadn't given a lot of detail, just said that he'd be home soon and had to take care of something.

At the sight of him, Bibi pressed a hand to their mouth.

Papa looked faint.

"Where the fuck have you been!" Bibi demanded.

Felix's stomach flipped. Bibi had never sworn at him before.

The fallen angel swept across the room, their eyes blazing, and all the scarier for their moon-silver color.

Papa stood more slowly like he was weak.

"I had to go," Felix insisted.

Bibi grabbed him, hard, almost too hard.

"Don't! Don't yell at me, I had to help, I *had to*," Felix insisted. He pulled away from Bibi but what he really wanted to do was hug them.

He'd never been away from home for so long.

"Why are you wearing a dress?" Papa asked. He stood beside them and looked like he'd seen something much worse than Felix in a dress. He had circles under his eyes. His lips had gone dry and had cracked in a few places.

Felix shrugged.

"No, don't answer," Bibi asked. "Go upstairs and get rid of it. Get rid of *everything* that might get you in trouble. Do you understand?"

Felix nodded. He took his hat off. He looked at his father, then back at Bibi. "Am I in a lot of trouble?"

"No," Papa answered.

"Yes," Bibi said at the same time.

"No," Papa said more firmly. "Absolutely not. You're not in trouble."

Bibi crossed their arms.

Papa put his arms around Felix and hugged him. "You scared me."

"I had to help."

"Felix, I thought something awful had happened to you," Papa said.

"I left a note, I said I was coming home."

Papa sniffled. "You're just a boy, Felix, just...Anything could have happened. People do *awful* things to children on their own."

"I'm not a child."

"You're *my* child," Papa insisted.

Felix squeezed him hard.

"Go upstairs," Bibi said. "Get rid of everything."

Felix went.

He burned the clothes and hid all the letters he'd gotten from Charlie with his books about angels. He came back downstairs when he had. He walked past Papa on the couch and found Bibi in the kitchen.

Bibi handed him a dinner plate. "You've got to be hungry."

Felix sat at the table. "Is Papa sick?"

"Your father is over a hundred years old and he is human. He was never meant for this life. You can't do things to his nerves like that. Or to mine! You scared us. And..." Bibi sighed. They sat across from him. "Charlie's parents are going to think the absolute worst. They're going to think he's dead."

Felix picked at his dinner. "I had to help. Charlie...He can't live like this."

Bibi sighed. They leaned back in their chair. They studied Felix for a while.

"Are you mad?"

"Livid."

"I'm sorry."

Their face softened a little. "I forget. You young things, how much more urgent things are for you, how important everything feels. I'm so...I'm so old that waiting a few years didn't seem like anything at all. It feels like yesterday I could hold you in my arms. But those years, they must feel like forever to you."

"I'd rather get in trouble than lose my friend."

Bibi inhaled and let out a heavy sigh. "Don't say things like that."

"That's what you meant, though. When you said you'd rather have other boys suffering than have something happen to me. I read his letters, Bibi. They weren't right, the things he was saying."

They said, "Eat your dinner."

"I'm not stupid, Bibi, I made sure no one saw me there."

"I know you're not stupid. That's another thing that's going to get you in trouble: being too smart for your own good."

"I'm sorry I worried you. I'm not sorry I went."

Bibi put a hand over his. "I'm terribly upset with you, but...But I'm also proud. You're a good boy, Felix. You really are."

Felix grinned. "So I'm not in trouble?"

"You stole money and ran away from home, of course, you're in trouble."

Being in trouble amounted to extra chores to make up for what he'd stolen, although Felix knew he'd taken a lot more than they were making him pay back.

His parents didn't let him out of their sight for a few days. For a week or so, they barely let him leave the house on his own. After a month, it was like nothing happened.

In August, Felix received a letter. He recognized the handwriting, but not the signature. He asked Bibi about it, who advised him to write back 'Dear Oscar' instead of 'Dear Charlie' and didn't dwell on it too much beyond that.

JUNE 4, 1940
Tuesday

FELIX CHECKED himself in the mirror, tugged at his waistcoat, then grinned at his reflection. He grabbed his hat and jacket and stopped by Papa's office.

"I'm heading out," he told his father.

Papa looked up. "Where to?"

"Just out with Oscar."

"On a Tuesday?"

Felix shrugged.

"You need money?"

Felix rolled his eyes. "No, Papa."

Papa reached for his pocket anyway.

"Papa, I have a job! Stop, put it away. I'll see you in the morning."

"Have fun."

Felix kissed his father on the cheek and headed downstairs.

"And where are you off to on a weeknight?" Bibi asked as he walked through the living room.

"Weeknight? Bibi, the semester's over! Can't a fellow have some fun once in a while?" Felix asked.

"Your father says you didn't sign up for any classes next

semester."

Felix glanced around, not sure where this conversation had come from. "No. I thought I might take some time off from school. I don't know what else I'd do with another Bachelor's. Or another Master's. Two of each seems like enough for now."

"Hmm."

Felix put a hand on his hip. "What?"

"No, nothing, just hmm. What are your plans for the future?"

"Bibi, can't we talk about this some other time?"

"You said that last time I asked."

Felix came to sit next to Bibi. "How about you tell me what you're worried about and I'll tell you it's nonsense."

"You and Kathleen—"

"Oh, no, Bibi, not about Kathleen again," Felix groaned. He sunk lower in his seat and leaned on Bibi's arm. "That was *months* ago."

"She was your first girlfriend."

"No, she was not."

"First girl you went steady with. Two years you went around with her and suddenly, it's all over, you're not going back to school, you turned down that job at the Michaels' workshop," Bibi listed.

"Listen, Kathleen wanted something I wasn't ready for. You know, she kept asking about getting married and it wasn't fair to lead her along like that. And you know, school, I've been in school forever. And, honestly, Bibi, if I had taken the job with Michaels, then you should have been worried!"

"Exactly."

Felix straightened up. "Come again?"

"You haven't made any terrible choices in months, I'm starting to worry what you're getting up to going out all these nights," Bibi said, sounding perfectly serious. It didn't last.

Felix smiled.

Bibi cracked a grin. "Don't do anything foolish."

"Bibi, you know I've got to do something foolish every once in a while. I'd absolutely burst if I didn't."

Bibi shook their head. "Be safe, at least, whoever it is you're seeing."

"Oh! Bibi, for shame. I'm a gentleman. And it's not me going after anyone. Oscar's got a fellow, you know, or. He hopes he has."

"Oscar has terrible taste."

"So you know I have to tag along and make sure he doesn't get up to anything stupid."

Bibi asked, "Who is it this time?"

"Ah, this crooner down at the Bell."

"Can he sing?"

Felix waggled his hand. "Voice is alright. Forgets the words a lot, though, if you ask me. Anyway, I'm...I'm not so sure this fellow even leans Oscar's way."

Bibi patted Felix's arm. "Be good. Do you need money?"

"No." Felix kissed Bibi's cheek. "Love you. Don't wait up."

He met up with Oscar and Soon-hee outside the Bell.

Oscar had come back from Triviai with Soon-hee and even three years later, Felix didn't know how he felt about her.

Jealous, for one. He had enough self-awareness to recognize that. He hated that his friend had come home with a new best friend, someone with whom he'd spent the better part of a decade.

They had a lot of inside jokes.

Felix tried to be nice. Tonight, he smiled and said, "You look lovely, Soon-hee."

She smiled back. "Thank you."

"Is that a new dress?"

She glanced down. "No."

He could have sworn he'd never seen the dark green dress before. Maybe he just hadn't seen her enough to know all her dresses. He shrugged.

Oscar insisted on getting seats as close to the stage as they could.

Felix wanted to tell him it was hopeless. He didn't think this singer would go for Oscar and even if he did, Felix wasn't certain he'd turn out to be a nice guy.

Not that he knew anything in particular about Rich Phillips, but he knew a lot about Oscar's taste in guys.

He pulled out the chair for Oscar and Soon-hee, though not too much later he caught Soon-hee giving him a poisonous look.

He worried about his drink instead of about her. He didn't want to get involved. Once his thoughts about someone got sour, they tended to stay that way, and they tended to find their way from his mind to his lips.

Phillips had a good backing band, though, so even if he made up half the words, Felix didn't mind coming.

He elbowed Oscar. "You want to dance?"

It was that kind of place; they could get away with it.

Oscar raised an eyebrow.

"Yeah, yeah, I know, Phillips. But, uh. You know, he can see the dance floor. He might notice you."

"Notice me dancing with someone else," Oscar pointed out.

Felix rolled his eyes. "Sometimes that's the best way to get someone's attention."

Oscar rested his chin on his hand and directed his eyes toward the stage. "I'd rather listen."

"Soon-hee?" Felix asked.

She shook her head. "No. Thank you."

Felix sighed, sat back in his chair, and scanned the room. Ultimately, he stayed seated.

When Phillips came off the stage and another singer took his place, Oscar went to hang around the bar. Phillips always went there after for a drink. Oscar had even spoken to him a handful of times over the past few months of this infatuation.

"Sort of sad, really," Felix mentioned to Soon-hee.

She ignored him.

Phillips walked away from the bar with a girl.

Oscar slunk back over to their table, unnoticed again.

Felix poked him in the side. "Come back to the house."

"Ah, no, I just want to go home."

"You should stop by before they head out. Papa loves when you visit."

Oscar shrugged. "Maybe."

"Oh, stop being so miserable, Oscar. He doesn't mean anything to you, he's just some boy who can sing. When are you going to get your head on right about this?" Felix asked.

Oscar scowled at him.

"All these stupid boys who probably don't even remember your name when you leave in the morning," Felix said. "*If* they let you stay the night."

"You haven't got to be mean about it."

Felix scoffed. "I'm not being mean."

Soon-hee sighed and rolled her eyes. "Let's just go home."

"Come over tomorrow. They'd love to see you," Felix insisted.

"When are they leaving?"

"Thursday morning. Back on Tuesday. Sort of sweet, isn't it? Still going on romantic weekends after all these years?"

"Your parents are so sweet it makes me want to die," Oscar said.

Felix reached over and intentionally messed up Oscar's hair. "Come over tomorrow. Promise."

Oscar fixed his hair. "Fine." He stood.

Felix stood too and offered his arm. "Can I walk you to your car?"

Oscar took his arm. "How could I say no to such a gentleman?"

Felix offered his other arm to Soon-hee, which she declined.

She followed Felix and Oscar out of the Bell.

"Promise you'll come over?" Felix asked.

"I said I would."

Felix squeezed him and bid him farewell, then started to walk home. He stopped at a quieter joint for another drink on the way home. He hadn't planned on turning in so early. He wasn't going to sleep anyway, so he might as well be out and about.

He ended up staying to chat with a couple of girls and got home around three in the morning.

Plenty of time to get ready for bed and get enough sleep to be up by eight.

He checked Papa's office to make sure he hadn't fallen asleep in there again. Bibi usually made sure he didn't, but sometimes they fell asleep too.

He found both parents securely in bed.

Oscar came over for lunch.

Papa and Bibi absolutely laid into him with questions, not accusatory or anything, but wanting to know all the details of what he'd been up to since they'd seen him last.

Oscar didn't come over as much as Felix liked. He teased Felix sometimes about still living at home.

Sometimes Felix thought he was jealous of Felix's parents.

He hadn't seen his parents since he'd come home. As far as everyone knew, Charlotte Banks had likely been kidnapped and murdered by some pervert in Nova Scotia. Felix felt sort of bad about that.

Papa wanted to know all about what Oscar did for work.

Felix listened as Oscar made fencing stolen goods through his pawnshop sound like a legitimate enterprise.

The fact that Oscar owned a store impressed Papa.

Sometimes Oscar got really interesting things at the store. Felix had bought Bibi jewelry there a handful of times and hadn't disappointed yet.

"Now Felix says you're living with someone," Bibi asked.

"Not like that," Oscar said. "She's a friend."

"It's just Soon-hee," Felix said.

"Oh, her," Bibi said.

Soon-hee and Oscar had only recently moved in together. Soon-hee had a lot of trouble keeping a roommate and never exactly gave a reason as to why when Felix asked. Finally, she'd moved into the apartment above Oscar's shop.

Oscar looked at Felix. "Oh, her?" Oscar asked.

Felix wiped his hands excessively and didn't look.

"What is it with you two?" Oscar asked.

"I don't know, she doesn't like me," Felix said, which was what he said any time Oscar asked about the obvious tension between them. "Maybe ask her."

"She says the same thing."

"That I don't like her?"

Oscar grinned. "No. That she doesn't like you."

Felix shook his head. "Well, I never did anything to her!" he huffed.

After lunch, Felix walked Oscar back to the shop. He browsed through a few things, didn't buy anything, and went home to finish editing the most recent manuscript he'd been sent.

Editing didn't make for fascinating work for most but finding all those little errors made Felix feel better about the things in life he couldn't fix. Not to mention, he learned a lot. He'd edited articles and texts on hundreds of different arcane and magical topics.

He had three chapters left in the most recent bestiary Finnigan and Schuul had written. His current chapter made updates to the current body of knowledge about werewolves.

No one had put out a scientifically accurate bestiary ever, to the best of Felix's knowledge. The class he'd taken on supernatural creatures in undergrad had used a text from 1533 and had included entries that weren't just inaccurate but outright offensive. Sitting in a lecture hall full of mages that believed vampires had garlic aversions had made for one of Felix's more miserable learning experiences.

He was still the only creature that had ever attended the Reinhart-Queen University of Arcane Magics and Sciences.

Rumor had it one of the students at the Academy had fairy blood, but people made that assumption based entirely on the vivid purple color of the girl's eyes.

He made it through the last chapters of the bestiary and woke up in time to make his parents breakfast.

He did everything he could to get them out of the house and to the train station not just on time but early.

He had plans.

Papa seemed to know as much. "Don't do anything stupid."

"I don't know what you're talking about," Felix said.

Papa's mouth barely changed.

It felt utterly bizarre to have a father that looked the same age as him. Oh, the beard did a little bit to make him look older, as did the circles under his eyes and his mannerisms, but once upon a time, Papa had looked old to Felix.

Now they could be classmates.

He squeezed his father, kissed Bibi's cheek, and made sure they both got on the train.

He waved to them as the train departed.

As soon as he got home, he set to moving the furniture around in his bedroom, pushing the bed and the desk off to the side so he had room for the chalk circle he needed to draw. The whole thing took about two hours to draw, and he spent another hour checking it for errors.

He didn't want to end up dead.

In fact, he wanted exactly the opposite of that.

He wanted to live his life without checking over his shoulders for angelic assassins.

A Community paper had wanted to interview him a few months ago to get the perspective of the only demon to grow up steeped in arcane magic. None of the other magical universities had ever had a demon attend, not even the University of Triviai.

His parents had put their foot down. They'd practically raved for days about how dangerous that would be.

They'd even gotten Lucifer on board, calling him up to see if he could do a better job of frightening Felix into submission.

Of course, they hadn't called it that. They'd called 'talking some sense' into him. The only time Papa ever looked happy to see the Devil was when they'd asked Satan to talk some sense into Felix.

The first time they'd done it, Felix had tried to drop out of school when he'd turned sixteen. They'd ganged up on him for a handful of other things, like trying to move out when he was nineteen or doing a year around in Europe on his own at twenty, all things that he'd been glad enough he hadn't done within a few years. Not that he hadn't wanted to do them, but now he understood how dangerous it could have been for him on his own.

He always folded under pressure from three directions, all his parents staring at him with pure desperation.

This time, though, it had taken more than just a few words of warning.

"I'm not worried about that angel!" Felix had said.

"No, but what about that cult? Did you ever take care of that?" Ira had asked, glancing up at Satan. Ira, the Devil's companion, functioned more as a gossipy, out-of-town uncle than as a fourth parent.

The Devil's eyes had widened.

Ira had frowned, straightening up. "What's that face?"

"We didn't tell him," Bibi had said.

Ira had gasped and covered his mouth. "Oh, darling, no! I'm sorry. I thought you had."

"No," Lucifer had murmured. "He's so young, he shouldn't have to know that."

The argument about the interview set aside, Felix had pressed his parents for information about this cult and learned that they'd killed his mother and tried to kill him, too.

No one had said it, but he figured out soon enough that the cult, Moralists they called themselves, had killed his mother because of him.

He'd take care of them, and the angel, and then he could finally stop worrying about people wanting him dead.

His parents could stop worrying and he could live his life.

He'd written an anonymous tip to the Moralists, he'd figured out the spell to bind this angel, and he'd slit all their miserable throats just like they'd wanted to do to him.

His fingers found the scar the angel had left at their last encounter.

He checked the circle one last time, then stepped inside.

He unclasped the amulet from around his neck and tossed it onto his desk.

He wiped his hands on his trousers.

He wasn't five anymore.

The angel appeared within minutes.

Felix jumped out of the circle.

The angel tried to follow but couldn't move past the chalk. It glared at him.

Felix tried not to laugh, but he hadn't expected the angel to look like this.

Oh, the golden skin and curls he remembered, but he didn't remember the angel dressing like a Greek statue.

Well, Felix amended, if he was dressed like a Greek statue, he'd be wearing nothing. Maybe a cape, they always seemed to have capes.

He had seen one statue, though, of a Classical soldier in a skirt of leather strips and a cuirass and this angel hit the mark.

He covered his mouth, then got to the task at hand. He grabbed his notebook, found the final draft of the spells, and began the incantation.

The angel drew his sword and made a valiant effort to escape the circle, but within minutes, Felix's spell had him on his knees.

He bound the angel to Earth, no more slipping into the in-between places that Heaven and Hell used to move around. He masked the angel, too, so none of his brethren would find him.

Finally, and this was the riskiest part, he darted into the circle and clasped a cuff around the angel's wrist to bind him from using his powers.

It would disappoint Papa to know that Felix had used one of those cuffs, but Felix hadn't seen any other way about it.

He grabbed the gun he'd bought at Oscar's pawn shop.

A few shots to the head, maybe one to the heart, to make sure, and then he'd burn the body.

He checked to make sure the gun had bullets.

Then he checked again.

He cleared his throat.

The angel glanced up.

Felix leveled the gun at the angel. He reminded himself that this *thing* had stabbed him without an ounce of hesitation.

He pressed the back of his hand to his mouth.

The angel watched him.

Felix sighed. He lowered the gun.

He'd figure it out. He just couldn't do it right now. He needed to think.

He set the gun on his desk.

The circle would hold for a while. A few hours, probably.

After an hour, he still needed to think.

He checked the shed, found some rope, and headed back to his room to tie up the angel.

"Put your sword down."

The angel didn't move.

Felix sighed. He twitched his fingers and the sword leapt out of the angel's grip.

That, at least, registered with the angel. He frowned at Felix.

When Felix stepped into the circle, the angel immediately lunged for him. Felix twisted out of his grip and shoved his hand into the angel's face, knocking him out with a quick burst of panicky magic.

He rubbed his hand on his trousers to dispel the funny tingling that lanced through his palm.

Felix tied the angel's wrists, then his legs. He added a gag for good measure.

He found a knife strapped to the angel and tossed that with the sword.

He sat on his bed and tried to think but didn't get past thinking that he'd fucked up and needed help.

The Devil would know what to do.

Felix would call Lucifer.

In a few days.

If he couldn't figure something out on his own by then.

And he always figured something out.

He glanced at the angel, which was staring at him with those orange eyes. Felix wondered if it would be too much to blindfold the angel, or maybe put a pillowcase over his head.

He got up and left the room.

He paced around the house for a while. He made himself a drink, and then made several more.

Eventually, he went back into his room and sat on the floor in front of the angel. He set the bottle of whiskey in front of himself.

The angel sat.

Felix pointed out. "Your skirt's kind of...riding up there." He nodded towards the expanse of shimmering golden thighs exposed by the way the leather strips of his skirt had fallen.

The angel glared. He made no attempt to speak.

Felix tipped a little more whiskey into his glass, just enough to cover the ice he had left. He took a sip, then reached for the gun he'd left on his desk.

He placed it next to the whiskey.

A few minutes later, he checked to make sure the bullets hadn't gone anywhere.

He drained his glass, grabbed the angel's sword, and used it to move his skirt to a less compromising position.

All this left the angel unaffected.

Felix slept uneasily that night. He stashed the sword and the knife under his mattress with his notebook and slept with the gun nearby.

He woke several times and each time found the angel sitting there, just as Felix had left him.

Glaring.

Unmoving.

In the morning, Felix gingerly tugged the gag out of the angel's mouth. "Do you eat?"

The angel stared.

Maybe Felix had been wrong to think of him as glaring; his gaze was cold and murderous, but not angry. "Food?" he clarified.

No answer.

"Come on, sunshine, it's an easy question."

Still nothing.

Felix walked away.

He made himself breakfast and occupied himself with things around the house. He tidied and brought in the mail, he made small talk with the neighbors and tried to read.

He couldn't relax, couldn't clear his head, couldn't think.

He brought a sandwich and set it in front of the angel.

The angel didn't move. Didn't even look at it.

Felix went back downstairs.

He ate his sandwich.

He read over the ritual for summoning his father, then convinced himself he didn't need the Devil's help.

He'd get rid of the angel.

Maybe a gun was just the wrong weapon for him. He'd never even fired one before.

He'd never really done anything to anyone before. Oh, sure, a few fights here and there, but he'd never turned a weapon against another person.

Maybe magic could do it.

There had to be a spell to kill the angel, painless and quick and mess-free.

It would probably be better to kill the bastard than give him to Lucifer.

When he went back upstairs, the angel had eaten the

sandwich, leaving nothing but crumbs on the plate.

The next night, for dinner, Felix brought food to the angel. He set the plate down and then settled his own in front of him.

He'd eaten alone last night, and this morning, and this afternoon.

He'd never eaten alone so many meals in a row.

Bibi and Papa had never gone away without him before. Their vacations had always been family vacations.

He'd called a friend or two, but they all had other plans that evening. After those friends, he didn't have the kinds of friends one could invite out for dinner.

Maybe lunch or a quick coffee, but most of the people he knew were colleagues or acquaintances. Almost all of them mages who would have liked to get their hands on him for an experiment or two, or old classmates who'd grown old and wise enough to be wary of a demon.

He set a fork near the angel. "So."

The angel stared, but this time at the meatloaf Felix had placed in front of him.

Bibi had left it for him.

"So if I let you go, will you hunt me again?" Felix asked.

"You cannot stay in this world."

The angel's voice startled Felix. He'd expected something harsh, masculine, something with bravado and malice. Instead, he sounded factual and calm, and bizarrely soothing.

Felix took a bite of meatloaf. "Why not?"

"You doom it."

Felix frowned. "*I* doom it. That's ridiculous. What have I ever done to doom anything?"

"You are born of the unholy."

"Yeah, and most of us are harmless."

The angel finally lifted his gaze from the meatloaf. "You are the only antichrist among them."

Felix almost laughed. "The what?" He grinned. "The antichrist?"

The angel nodded.

"He makes 'em a little screwy up in Heaven, doesn't he? Fucking antichrist."

The angel looked put off.

"I don't have any plans to destroy the world. Are you going to eat, or what?"

The angel looked at the bindings on his wrists, which linked to the ones around his legs. He couldn't move much, which was, after all, the point. It mustn't have made for easy eating.

Felix scooted closer. He tugged at a few knots and adjusted the ropes so the angel could move easily. "Go for the sword and I'll hog tie you next time."

"You could end the world," the angel said.

"That's stupid."

Felix shook his head. He scooped up a bite of meatloaf but couldn't bring it to his mouth. He tossed the fork back on his plate. "Nonsense."

The angel didn't argue.

"I've never even done anything that bad!"

"It's about what you could do."

"Jesus Christ," Felix huffed. He grabbed his plate and sat at his desk. He shoveled his food and watched the angel out of the corner of his eye.

He did really seem to struggle to eat tied up like that.

Felix needed to get his shit together.

He couldn't keep this angel around.

He stayed up all night reading, trying to find some way to get the angel to leave him alone.

He could always put the amulet back on, move somewhere else, and hope that the angel would never find him again.

Spend the rest of his life hiding, have his parents worrying about him, never really safe.

Maybe he could go to Hell, live with Satan and Ira.

The thought made his skin crawl.

He came back for the angel's plate later and found it all devoured again.

And there was this antichrist business!

He'd have to talk to someone about that. He didn't know how he could make it to twenty-six without knowing if he was the antichrist or not.

Then again, he'd made it to twenty-six without knowing a cult had murdered his mother, or that his mother had tried to kill his father.

He lay in bed for a while but still couldn't sleep.

"Hey," he called.

The angel didn't answer.

He conjured an orb of light and sat up in bed. He scooted to the end.

The angel remained where Felix had tied him.

"What's your name anyway?"

"I don't have one."

Felix wrinkled his nose. "That's sad. Fuck. Daddy didn't love you?" he guessed. "Anyway. Do you uh. Do you use...You know. Bibi uses the bathroom. Do you need to?"

The angel stared at him, his face illuminated and the room nearly pitch-black behind him, like he was right out of some chiaroscuro painting.

God might have made his angels screwy, but He'd also made them beautiful. What business did a murderer have with hair like that! Those wonderful golden curls and he been sent here to kill a baby.

"Well?" Felix demanded.

"I'm a soldier."

"Soldiers piss, too. Been tied up for a while."

The angel's brow wrinkled. He looked unsure of himself. Finally, he nodded.

Felix got out of bed and cut the ties around his feet. "Uh. You know, no funny business. I'll tie you back up."

The angel stood like it hurt to do so.

Felix made sure he had the gun on him as he walked the angel to the bathroom. He closed the door partway for him, leaving it cracked just to make sure he didn't try anything. He looked at the floor, waiting. He peeked in when he'd heard the flush, then the sound of slurping.

The angel had his hands cupped under the faucet, guzzling water like a man dying of thirst.

Felix's stomach did a funny sort of turn.

They walked back to his room in uncomfortable quiet.

He tied the angel's legs again.

JUNE 9, 1940
Sunday

FELIX TRIED again with lunch. He brought the angel a sandwich and a glass of water this time.

He untied his legs.

The angel watched.

"You're kind of a fucking creep, huh, sunshine?" Felix asked, feeling the angel's eyes on the back of his neck. He glanced up.

The angel kept staring.

Felix scooted back and slid the sandwich toward him.

He still had no idea what he was going to do.

They ate.

Felix asked questions sometimes. He didn't get many answers. Finally, he asked, "No manners up there, huh?"

"What?"

"It's not very polite to ignore someone when they're talking to you."

"You keep asking me things I don't know."

"You don't know why God wants me dead?"

"I..." The angel swallowed. "Heaven sent me. Not the Almighty."

Felix raised his eyebrows. "Isn't He the one pulling the

strings?"

The angel didn't answer.

Felix cleared his throat.

"I don't know."

"Well, what do you know?"

"That I'm a soldier. That my mission is to kill the antichrist. That I cannot return home until I do," the angel said. He looked at the cuff on his wrist. "Not that I could now anyway."

Felix opened his mouth but heard something downstairs.

The front door.

He stood. It was too early for his parents to be home, but from his doorway, he called, "Bibi? Papa?"

The voices that called back did not belong to his parents. "Upstairs!" they hissed.

He almost threw up.

The Moralists! And a lot of them, too.

He'd forgotten about them, too absorbed with this stupid angel. The trap he'd so carefully planned utterly set aside for the assassin he couldn't kill.

He scurried back into his room. He grabbed the angel by the arm and pushed him. "Out the window." He rubbed his hand and saw it had gone red across the palm.

He'd worry about that later.

"Why?"

"Go," Felix insisted and shoved him.

The angel clambered out the window.

Felix gave him another shove. He could hear the voices, at least six, coming up the stairs. He ducked out the window and up onto the roof.

Even with his hands bound, the angel managed to follow.

Felix pointed toward a chimney that belonged to an abandoned house down the street. Ramshackle and abandoned since '35, but in some sort of weird status with the bank that prevented it from being demolished.

The angel gave a brief nod and followed behind as Felix scuttled across the roofs.

Felix yanked open the window on the second story of the abandoned house. Plenty of neighborhood kids had snuck in here for their first drink or a session of petting, away from the eyes of parents.

The angel hesitated.

Felix grabbed him by the cuirass. "Get in."

The angel struggled through the window and practically fell. He remained on the floor where he landed.

They waited, silent, breathing hard but trying not to make too much noise until Felix raked his hands through his hair. He swore hideously to himself, then he straightened out his clothes and brushed off the dust he'd gotten from the floor.

"Why?" the angel asked again.

"They would have killed you, too."

The angel frowned.

"You're not human."

"I'm an angel."

"Doesn't matter. You're not human and they don't ask questions."

The angel sighed. He stood in front of Felix, almost like he wanted to square off with him. "Why not let them kill me?"

Felix's eyes widened.

That would have fixed at least one of his problems. He rubbed his face.

They couldn't stay in this building and he couldn't walk a golden man tied up and dressed like a legionnaire around town and home to go unnoticed.

"Listen, can we...Can we sort of do a truce for a minute? Those Moralists, they're not keen on you or me."

The angel said, "They killed your mother."

His throat tightened. He nodded. "So you. You aren't on their side?"

"Heaven sent me."

Felix sighed. "Can we not kill each other right now?"

"You can't kill me."

"And you can't go home if I'm dead," Felix warned. He pointed to the cuff on his wrist. "And good luck getting anyone to take that off you if you do me in. My father's not a mage you want to cross."

"I have to kill you."

"But do you have to do it right now? Or can I untie you and get us to somewhere those nutjobs can't find?"

"To what end?"

"They killed my mother. I don't know anything about her, but I know she didn't deserve to be killed. Can you give me time to at least sort them out? Then you can go back to hunting me or whatever it is you've been doing."

"I've been hunting you," the angel confirmed. "I could hunt you forever."

"So you'll let me deal with them?"

The angel nodded.

Felix untied his hands. As he worked at the knots, he had to rest his hand on the angel's arm somewhat.

The longer it took, the more his hands started to hurt.

He pulled back to see a burn where he'd touched the angel.

He glanced up, then used a pocketknife to cut away the bonds. He'd worry about that later if he lived long enough to worry about it.

He stepped back, his heart pattering, not sure if he trusted this angel to keep his word.

As soon as the angel moved, Felix flinched.

The angel stood and Felix was five again, a knife in his shoulder. The exact taste and smell of the day filled his senses. He wanted to cry.

He wanted his parents.

The angel rubbed his wrists.

Felix could feel his heart throbbing through every inch of his body.

"My knife."

"At home."

"I need it back."

Felix shook his head. "The fewer things you have to stab me with—"

"It could be dangerous if a human were to possess it."

"How dangerous?"

"Depends on the human."

Felix gritted his teeth. "Wonderful."

"I need it."

Felix said, "I'll get it, Christ, but we've got to give them time to clear out. I heard at least six."

"Eight," the angel corrected.

"Fine. Eight. I don't like those odds. Regular humans would be one thing, but Moralists make a living out of killing guys like me." Eight was more than he'd expected to show up to just to take him on. They'd only sent a pair to kill his mother.

He wondered if her killers had come to finish the job. It would have been a nice feather in their cap, better than some stray

Moralist who'd slept with the wrong person.

The wrong monster.

"You have a plan?" the angel asked.

Felix shrugged. "Sort of. We'll lay low for the night."

That would bring them to Monday.

One day to get this fixed before Bibi and Papa came home.

No, he'd telephone and tell them to stay a while longer on vacation. They didn't need to come home to his mess.

Felix gestured for the angel to follow.

"Where are we going?"

"Somewhere safe."

He went straight to Oscar's shop.

Soon-hee sat behind the register and raised an eyebrow at Felix when he came in.

Felix walked right by her.

He went and pawed through the used clothing until he found a pair of trousers and a shirt for the angel. He added a pair of shoes. "Here, get dressed."

"Why?"

"Because you stick out like a sore thumb! Are you going to argue about everything?"

The angel didn't argue anymore. He started to strip.

Felix didn't bother to stop him.

"Hey!" Soon-hee called.

Felix went over to the register.

"What is he doing!" she demanded.

Felix waved a hand. "Never mind. Is Oscar around?"

"He's upstairs."

"Angel!" Felix called. "Sunshine, hey! Upstairs."

The angel came over, half-dressed, his arms cluttered with goods.

"You have to pay for those!"

"Oscars knows I'm good for it!"

"You know we *both* own this place," Soon-hee said. She came around the register to block Felix from going upstairs. "You have to pay for that."

"Honestly!" Felix rifled around in his pockets and found them empty. "I'm good for it!"

She shook her head. "You walk in here like you own the place—"

"I'm sort of in the middle of something here, so can you just *move?*"

"Getting upstairs is part of your plan?" the angel asked.

"Yeah."

The angel moved forward.

Felix threw out his arm to stop him. "Whatever you're going to do, think about it first."

"You said we need to get upstairs," the angel answered, calm and without contempt.

"Preferably without brutalizing the lady," Felix pointed out.

The angel looked over Soon-hee. "I wouldn't have to."

"I'm getting the police. You're trying to steal from us," Soon-hee warned.

Felix grabbed the golden cuirass from the angel. "Fine, fucking *here*, that'll cover it." At that moment, he went from not liking her to hating her guts.

"That's mine," the angel protested.

"It's fine, I'll get it back as soon as I go home and get my wallet."

"And my knife," the angel reminded.

Felix grunted. He pushed past Soon-hee to go upstairs.

The angel followed. "I need that back."

Felix whirled around on the stairs. "I will get it back for you!"

The angel moved onto a lower step.

"I'm going upstairs to talk to my friend. He has a place we can lay low. Tomorrow, I will go home and get my wallet, and your knife, and I will get your...thing. Armor back. Okay?"

The angel licked his lips. He nodded.

Oscar met them at the door to his apartment. "Heard you shouting," he said. He looked past Felix at the angel. "Oh! Is...That's the angel! Felix, what did you do?"

"I need a place to hide."

"From what, the fucker's right here!"

"Moralists."

"Moral...Felix. Moralists! Jesus, your parents go away for ten minutes and you get up to your stupidest idea yet!"

"I didn't come here to get yelled at. Will you help me or not?"

Oscar sighed. "Yeah, let me get dressed."

"And you, too," Felix said over his shoulder to the angel.

Oscar grabbed Felix by the arm and dragged him aside. "That is the angel who stabbed you?"

Felix nodded.

"Is that what you bought a gun for?"

Felix shrugged.

"I thought you'd be fucking around playing Sam Spade, not actually trying to get yourself killed!" Oscar hissed.

"I know!" Felix returned.

"You have the *worst* ideas."

Felix pressed his lips together.

He and Oscar had already had this fight. They'd had it several times.

"Anyway, I pissed off Soon-hee," Felix said.

"You pissed me off, too."

"Do me a favor and don't sell that armor. She made it like I was trying to steal from the shop."

"What? No, I know you're good for it," Oscar said. "Let me get dressed."

Oscar dressed.

Felix sat on the couch and took a minute to breathe.

Oscar came back upstairs with the armor. He held it out to the angel. "Figure this is yours?"

The angel took it.

"I don't know what I ever did to her," Felix said.

"Yeah, well, when you figure it out, let her know, cause I can't get a good answer out of either of you about why my closest friends decided they need to act like a couple of nasty high schoolers instead of adults," Oscar said. "You ready to go?"

Felix nodded.

They followed Oscar out the back and down several increasingly shady streets until he brought them up to the attic apartment of a boarding house.

The apartment had no obvious entrance and required the use of a spell to open.

Oscar used this place to hide hot items, and himself, if he'd made a bad business call. He never went into too many details as to how he'd finally funded the work he'd had done in Triviai, but Felix could make a few guesses.

"Before I go, you want to tell me what's going on?" Oscar asked.

"You'll be mad."

"I'm already mad."

Felix gestured to the couch. He gave a sanitized version of how he'd envisioned this long weekend going, skirting around the fact that he'd lacked the nerve to end the angel.

Oscar absorbed the story, shook his head, and left without saying anything else.

Felix glanced at the angel.

He was just standing there, his armor clasped against his arms. He'd been watching Felix and Oscar.

"What?" Felix demanded.

"You'll get my sword, too. When you go back."

"Is the sword like the knife? Dangerous if someone gets ahold of it."

"No."

"What's the big deal with that knife, anyway?"

"The blade carries a purpose," the angel said.

Felix stopped himself from rubbing his shoulder. He turned away from the angel and paced around the apartment. Kitchenette, bathroom, bedroom, and a hodgepodge of furnishings in the living area.

The kitchenette had a variety of non-perishables and as much as Felix wanted something to eat, he wasn't keen on Vienna sausages at the moment.

He rifled through the drawers, found nothing of interest, and delved into the bedroom. He came back with a book and a pack of cards. To the angel, he said, "Pick one."

The angel frowned. "For what?"

"You planned on just standing there for a day?"

The angel looked around. He eyed the couch. He glanced between the book and the pack of cards. "I couldn't use either of those."

Felix opened his mouth, then closed it, not sure what to say. He tapped his fingers against his lips, eyes narrowed at the angel. "What have you been up to for the past quarter-century?"

"Looking for you."

"And that's it?"

The angel nodded.

"Well, you found me. Maybe pick a new hobby."

"It's my mission," the angel reminded.

Felix tossed the book at him.

The angel caught it, then set it down on the couch. He kept ahold of his armor through the whole thing.

"Oh, what, not a fan of Proust?"

The angel didn't answer.

Felix set himself in front of the coffee table and shuffled the deck of cards, setting up a game of solitaire. He tried to ignore the angel, who stood there, watching him play. After about a quarter-hour, he swept up the cards and glared up at the angel. "What!"

"I don't know what to do."

"Can't help you there."

The angel continued to stand.

"Sit down."

"Why?"

"Because you're making me nervous."

The angel didn't move. He didn't even set down his armor.

"He didn't bother to give you any brains under those curls, did He?" Felix asked. "Would you just sit?"

"Why?"

"Because if you don't, I'm going to put you in the linen closet."

The angel didn't move.

Felix stood and gave him a push toward the couch. "Sit down. Put your stuff down. You can't just stand there for a whole day."

The angel sat. He set his armor beside him. He placed his hands on his knees.

Felix didn't find him any less unsettling when he sat, it turned out. He tried to play another game of solitaire, but couldn't even get the cards set up before he demanded, "Do you have to keep staring at me?"

"How old are you?"

"Twenty-six."

"I've looked for you for twenty-six years. I'm supposed to kill you," the angel said mildly.

"I know."

"Why did you let me find you?"

"Cause I was sick of waiting for you to find me again," Felix said. He went to touch his amulet but realized he didn't have it.

"I couldn't find you. Even when I got back to this city, I couldn't find you anywhere. You could have hidden forever."

"Hiding's not really living." Felix pulled his knees up to his chest. "I'm gonna live a long time, you know, and I don't want to spend the rest of it hiding and looking over my shoulder and hoping you wouldn't find me."

"You let me find you."

"I planned on shooting you," Felix reminded.

"You didn't."

"Obviously."

"Why?"

Felix shook his head. "I don't know." He wished he had.

Or, at least, he wanted to wish he had.

As soon as he pointed that gun at the angel, he'd known he couldn't do it. He couldn't just shoot someone like that, even if the bastard had already stabbed him. Even if he'd had dreams about getting killed like that for years.

"What's it matter to you, anyway?" Felix asked.

"It doesn't. I..." The angel frowned. "I'm...confused."

"Makes two of us." Felix put the cards back in their box. He grabbed the book the angel had set aside and checked the inside cover.

Signed! Oh, Oscar would be mad if he knew Felix had tossed it like that. He returned it to where he found it and rifled through for a book that he knew had no value.

He found an old *Black Mask* and flopped on the bed with it.

He heard nothing from the angel.

After a while, he forgot he was there, absorbed in a story he'd already read. He even remembered the ending, but that didn't matter.

Hunger got the better of him eventually.

He found the angel still sitting there. "Don't you ever sleep?"

"I'm a soldier."

"What's that mean?"

"I can wait."

"Wait for what? You have something better to do?" Felix asked.

"I...I'm supposed to kill you."

"Yeah, later. We talked about this."

Felix took his tin of sausages back to the bedroom and looked around for something else to read. He found a whole stash of dirty pictures. He spent a little while sorting through them, thought he recognized a handful of movie stars, then put them back where he'd found them.

No point in getting excited now.

He sat on the floor and ate the sausages, trying not to think about how badly he'd messed up.

Bibi would be furious.

Papa might faint. He hadn't fainted yet, but he always looked so aghast at the stupid things Felix got up to.

He went back to the living area and found the angel asleep. Or, at least, with his eyes closed. He tossed the empty tin in the garbage and washed his hands.

The angel drew his gaze. He looked utterly perfect. No, not perfect, that wasn't quite it. Serene and innocent.

Beatific.

That was the word.

Felix didn't remember him like that. He remembered as him stern and cold and fucking terrifying.

Felix couldn't help but watch him, almost fascinated that *this* was the threat that had overshadowed every moment of his life. This air-headed statue, a total void of a person, had determined his entire life to this moment.

What would Papa and Bibi have let him do if not for this angel?

Would they even be his parents if the angel hadn't hunted him?

Would the Devil have raised him? That idea bore a lot of thinking about. It would have changed everything.

He needed to talk about someone about this antichrist matter, too. He knew the term from as a vague yet fictional figure from art and history, and from a philosophy class he'd taken as an undergraduate. Nietzsche had written about it, but that definitely didn't have anything to do with Felix.

He reached over and placed his fingertips on the back of the angel's hand. Within a minute, he had to yank them back.

Red and smooth, just like he'd held them to a hot surface.

That didn't happen when he touched Bibi or any of the other Fallen he'd met over the years.

But they were all Fallen.

This angel still belonged to Heaven. Maybe...

Felix didn't like to think about it, but maybe things like him just couldn't touch holy things. He'd never been inside a church now that he thought of it. Bibi certainly wasn't a Christian and Papa had been raised that way but didn't like to talk about religion on a personal level.

As an academic, he could go for hours about world religions and the history of various churches, but as a man, he only said, "It's hard to have faith when you see what prayers go unanswered."

That had to do with the plantation where he'd grown up.

As for Felix, it wasn't that he didn't believe in God. But he believed in lots of gods, not just the one who'd made his father. Bibi had met a lot of deities in their life and spoke about them readily enough. Felix knew they weren't a liar or a teller of tall tales, at least, not when it came to their own life. Discounting other religions made a person ignorant and too easy to surprise, Bibi liked to say, and they had raised Felix on stories of gods, creatures, and monsters from across the world.

Belief was one thing. He certainly didn't worship any of them, especially not God. If the God in Heaven had sent an angel to kill a baby, Felix would sooner spit on Him.

Still.

Something about this angel found him so repellant that his skin blistered just for making contact.

Maybe he was the antichrist.

He poked the angel.

The angel startled awake.

"Just me, sunshine, calm down," Felix soothed when he saw the angel's eyes go wide.

The angel took a breath, then that look of serenity returned.

"What did you mean about me being the antichrist?"

"You are an antichrist."

"An antichrist? So there are more of us?"

"All others died before they could crawl."

Felix breathed, "Fuck." He rubbed his nose. He hated to think of that. Little babies killed by this awful, serene bastard. "You're a habitual baby killer, then?"

The angel shook his head. "Not me. Heaven sent others before. This time, Heaven sent me."

Felix thought he heard a touch of something odd in the angel's voice. Reticence. Or maybe shame. Probably because he'd failed. "So what about these other ones?"

"What about them?"

"Where do we come from?"

"Every so often the Beast spawns a child that could doom the Earth. Marked as you are." The angel nodded toward Felix's arm.

"What, my birthmark?"

The angel nodded.

Felix peeled up his sleeve. Just a pale brown smudge. "My dad knocks up some poor girl, the baby comes out with a birthmark, and then what, some rosy-cheeked cherub comes and stabs it to death?"

"We're not cherubim, we're soldiers."

Felix waved a hand, brushing that protest aside. He didn't care about that. Classifications of angels, demons, undead, and other supernatural creatures got messy. Even the Fallen argued among themselves about what their title meant, or what their title even was.

Malak ha-satan, many called themselves, but some spun it differently.

Bibi said no one was right and no one was wrong, it all depended on where they'd fallen when they'd come to Earth and what languages they'd learned, and when they'd learned them.

In other words, it was a mess.

"But you are baby killers."

"Just...Just those ones," the angel said.

"Those babies," Felix insisted.

The skin around the angel's eyes crinkled. He swallowed. "Yes."

"Alright, just so we have that established," Felix said.

"Heaven demanded it."

Felix rolled his eyes. "Great. Is that the same guy who killed all those babies in Egypt, too?"

"He is the Almighty, you cannot comprehend His will," the angel informed him stonily.

"Not much interested in comprehending why someone wants to kill babies."

The angel scowled.

"Is that why I can't touch you?"

"What?"

Felix placed his hand on the angel's, then drew back once it started to hurt. He turned his palm up to show the reddened skin. "Is that cause you're an angel and I'm a demon?"

The angel grasped Felix's wrist and pulled it closer to study his palm.

Felix tried to yank his hand back when it started to burn. "That *hurts,*" he said when the angel didn't let go.

The angel released him. "I had myself warded against the Beast."

"A spell?" Felix guessed.

The angel nodded.

Felix gingerly inspected the burn around his wrist. It would heal pretty quickly. It also made him feel a little better that it was a spell and not a natural occurrence. He stood up and headed toward the bedroom.

He didn't want to be around the angel anymore.

"There's, uh, there's food in the kitchen," he noted before he closed the bedroom door.

Next time he went out, he found an empty, mangled can of beans and the angel asleep on the couch again.

He'd even laid down this time, curled up on his side like a dead grub.

Felix checked the time. Around two in the morning. As good a time as any to head home and assess the damage.

He found the front door hanging open, the door jamb in rough shape. He examined the damage to the door and sighed.

He should have heard them doing that to the lock.

He should have made sure Papa's security spells were in place. Papa set them every night, he'd shown Felix how to set them, but Felix hadn't worried about it.

That angel had distracted him.

It shouldn't have gone like this.

He carefully pushed open the damaged door and stepped inside, sighing again at himself and the mess he had made.

He closed his bedroom window, retrieved the angel's knife, and packed a change of clothes. He grabbed his wallet, and the gun, and checked to see if the Moralists had taken anything.

They hadn't disturbed a thing but his room and the front door.

They might have been murderous cult members, but at least they weren't burglars.

Downstairs, he found a man, gun drawn, waiting for him. "Police."

He put up his hands. "I, uh. I live here."

The cop pointed a flashlight at his face, then put his gun away. "Felix, right?"

He nodded.

"Detective Tom Kensington. I know your dad."

"Hiram?" Felix asked, just to make sure he wasn't one of the Devil's earthly agents. Not that it really mattered to Felix, but he liked to know who, or what, he was addressing.

"Hiram," the officer confirmed. "You know what happened?"

Felix shook his head. "No, my parents are away, I went to visit a friend. Do you have any idea what happened?"

"No. But we were keeping an eye on the house. Your father's always been...a friend to the station."

Felix knew that. Papa made strategic donations around the city to buy his family a little more tolerance than usually afford people like them. More than once, the University had helped apprehend criminals of the supernatural variety. "Any guesses? Witnesses?"

"No, neighbors heard a disturbance, gave us a call. We looked everything over, doesn't look like they got into much...We still processed the scene and everything, though, don't worry," Kensington assured.

"Thank you. I, uh. I'm gonna go back to my friend's place, I figure." Felix headed toward the door and Kensington followed.

Felix yanked the door shut behind him, slamming it hard enough to make the mangled door and frame stay together, then added the spells he should have before to keep people out.

Kensington took out a card. "We're keeping an eye on the place. Let Mr. Reinhart know that. We'll figure this out."

Felix tucked the business card into his wallet. "I'll make sure he knows."

He headed back to Oscar's safe house.

The angel was still asleep.

Felix jimmied a chair under the bedroom door and curled up on the bed, trying to ignore the musty scent of the duvet.

THE SOUND of the door rattling woke Felix.

Someone slammed their hand against the door. "Wake up!"

He scrambled out of bed and pulled aside the chair. "What, what? What happened?" he demanded of Oscar.

Oscar looked out of breath, his cheeks flushed, and his shirt a little damp. "Your parents are on their way home."

"What? It's...They're not due home until Tuesday."

"The cops called them. I guess they left an address with the neighbors." Oscar grinned. "In case you got up to something."

Felix grunted.

"So they called home and you weren't there, so they called me, and I..."

"Told them."

Oscar shrugged. "Your parents *should* come home! You're in way over your head on this one."

Felix glanced out into the living room.

The angel had resumed standing.

"What time?" Felix asked.

"They said they'd be on the first train home."

"Which is?"

"They'll be in at nine."

Felix rubbed his face. He looked at his watch. Two hours. "Thanks, Oscar."

"What are friends for?"

"I owe you," Felix said. "Oh! And I got my wallet."

"I'm not worried about it, honestly. We'll figure it out when this is done. Okay?"

Felix nodded. "Thanks. Really."

"You're welcome. Really." Oscar glanced over his shoulder. "So, what's the deal with the angel?"

"I don't know, I think we have a truce. Listen, I'm gonna wash up quick. Do you want to come to the station with me?"

"I would, honest, but I got to get back to the shop. I've got...I've got someone coming in. I'll stop by later."

Felix nodded.

Oscar saw himself out.

Felix washed up, put on a clean change of clothes, and headed for the door.

"My knife."

"I have it."

The angel extended his hand.

"I'll give it back when this is done."

The angel took a step forward.

Felix jabbed a finger toward him. "Don't! I'll give it back when I'm fucking...fucking ready for you to try to kill me again. I have to go get my parents. You wait here."

The angel shook his head. "No."

"Excuse me?"

"I go where you go. I won't lose you again."

Felix scowled but didn't argue. He headed out and the angel followed.

At the train station, he paced around while the angel stood.

When he spotted his parents, and they were easy to spot, both of them several inches over six feet tall, he ran to them. He felt like a child, but he threw his arms around them anyway.

Before he could explain or apologize, or possibly even lie, his father pulled away and stepped in front of his spouse and son, a spell on his lips and his hand raised.

"Oh, no, no, Papa, Papa, wait," Felix said, squirming out of Bibi's arms and grabbing his father's arm. "Don't, it's..."

Papa glanced at him.

"We've...We've got a truce."

The angel had followed Felix toward his parents.

"Right?" Felix asked the angel. "Haven't we got a truce?"

The angel nodded. "We have a truce."

Bibi grabbed Felix and hugged him again. "I don't even have it in me to explain how upset I am."

"Listen, come…Come back with us, I'll explain everything."

Papa hadn't lowered his hand.

Felix put himself between Papa and the angel. "Let me explain."

"Oscar explained it sufficiently," Papa said.

"Listen, just, let's get somewhere safe. Let's get out of sight. Okay?"

Eyes still on the angel, Papa nodded.

He brought his parents back to the safe house, which felt a little less safe each time he came and went from it.

The angel loomed in the background as Felix tried to explain his line of reasoning to his parents.

"I showed you a dozen times how to set the spells," Papa said.

"Well, clearly he wasn't thinking straight," Bibi said. "Or at all."

Felix didn't argue. He deserved this. "I just…I thought I could take care of it."

"Take care of what?" Papa asked. "Felix, your intention was really to kill all those people?"

Felix shrugged. "They want me dead. Why shouldn't I kill them first?"

"You're not a murderer," Papa reminded softly.

"I'll learn to be!"

"To what end?" Bibi asked.

"Because I don't want to be afraid anymore. I don't want to *hide* all the time." He looked at the angel, then turned back to his parents. "Did you know? About this antichrist thing?"

His parents exchanged a look.

"Now, Felix," Bibi began.

"The thing is," Papa started.

"You knew!" Felix cried.

"There's nothing *to* know," Bibi said. "You're not the antichrist."

From behind them, the angel said, "He is the antichrist."

"You're not part of this. Go fucking stand around somewhere else!" Felix barked.

The angel looked taken aback. He took several steps away from them.

Felix turned back to his parents. "What's that mean, being the antichrist? I'm supposed to end the world or something?"

"No," Papa said.

"Of course not, you're not going to end the world," Bibi insisted.

"Absolutely not," Papa agreed.

"I don't know, it's serious enough for God to send an assassin after me!"

"You're not going to end the world. Whatever Heaven thinks you are, whatever that mark means, it's just...it's a potential. It's a *choice*. It's something you become, not something you are," Bibi said.

Felix crossed his arms. "You never told me."

"Because there's nothing to tell. That's not who you are," Papa said. "It doesn't matter what anyone else says. You were not put on this Earth to end it."

"No, apparently, he was put here to make bad choices," Bibi murmured.

Felix huffed, but all the indignation went out of him in seconds. He uncrossed his arms and put his hands in his pockets. "What, uh. What does he have to say about it? My dad?"

"It is a potential, not a promise," Bibi answered.

"I'm not...I'm not one of those plans he has, then? Like Papa was?"

Bibi shook their head. "I doubt it. No one can say for sure what he's up to but...Felix, he honestly cares about you. He loves you. You aren't just a pawn."

Felix shrugged.

"I promise," Bibi said.

Felix nodded. He scuffed his shoe against the floor. "Are you really mad?"

Bibi sighed.

Papa threw his arms around Felix. "No, of course not. I'm glad you're still alive. I don't know...Felix, what would I do if something happened to you!"

"I didn't...It wasn't supposed to go like this."

"You really must start thinking about your choices!" Papa insisted.

Felix didn't have an answer. He squeezed his father.

"I swear, this is going to be what kills me," Papa murmured.

"Don't say that!" Felix insisted.

Bibi leaned in and kissed both of them on the tops of their heads. They moved into the kitchen, looking through the cabinets and examining the cans. "Your father and I discussed a few things on the way home. You seem to have..." Bibi looked at the angel. "Neutralized what we thought was the greater threat. That leaves us with the Moralists, until such time that the angel decides he should resume his mission."

"Ah, we don't have to worry about Sunshine over there," Felix assured. He turned to look at the angel. "Right?"

Bibi sighed. "Christ, Felix. You named him?"

"What? I...No. I didn't *name* him. He doesn't have a name."

"I know. None of the new angels have names. They're mass-produced. There're dozens more like him waiting around to take his place."

That sounded grim. Felix hadn't meant 'sunshine' as anything more than a nickname, a borderline misnomer. The angel always looked so...neutral. Empty. He didn't move for hours sometimes.

Bitchy, Felix realized, he was being bitchy, calling such an even, somber creature something like 'sunshine.'

The angel didn't seem to have the social wherewithal to recognize bitchiness.

"It's just...It's not really a name. He's just...you know, all shiny and golden. It just. I couldn't just call him 'hey, you' all the time."

"You spent three years *refusing* to learn Mildred's boyfriend's name," Bibi pointed out.

Even Papa looked disappointed.

"I don't care, it's not his name. Call him whatever you want. It just matters that we have a truce!" To the angel, Felix demanded, "Tell them we have a truce."

"I already told them we have a truce," the angel said.

"Do you have to be difficult?"

"Give me back my knife and I'll show you how difficult I can be."

Felix raised his eyebrows. He put one hand on his hip. "Why don't you try to come get it? For a soldier, I'm not seeing—"

"Felix!" Papa warned.

Felix scowled at his parents and the angel.

"We need to figure out what to do about the humans," Bibi reminded.

"Uh, do you think the police could help?"

"If we knew anything to tell them, I'm sure they could," Papa said.

The angel came closer. "They're well organized?"

They all turned to look at him.

Papa nodded. "They've decided it's their mission to reclaim Earth for humanity. They make a regular nuisance of themselves, especially for those creatures who live outside Community cities. A vampire on his own meets a quick end if he can't keep a low profile. Those of us in cities usually go untouched."

"Safety in numbers," the angel said. "If they're organized, they're watching your house."

"The police are watching our house," Felix said.

"Clear the police out, then your humans will show their faces again. At least eight came into the house, they might have left a few outside as lookouts. What's your goal with them? You planned to kill them. Does that stand?"

"Uh. No," Felix said. He glanced at Papa. "Could we get them to put the Moralists in prison?"

Papa nodded.

"Go home. They'll find you again."

Felix smiled. He couldn't help it. "Not bad, Sunshine."

He immediately wanted to shove the words back into his mouth.

The angel didn't return his smile.

"And then what?" Bibi asked.

"I..." Felix put his hands in his pockets. "I might have a pretty good entrapment spell ready to go."

His parents huffed.

"Where did we go wrong?" Bibi asked.

Felix's cheeks grew hot.

Papa tsked. "Oh, Phaedrus, leave him alone. What bright ideas did you have when you were twenty-six?"

"None. I had absolutely no ideas when I was twenty-six. I lived in a sentient ocean full of other angels, timeless and infinitely joyful. What about you?"

Papa shrugged. "I cut off my hand."

"Ah, yes. Felix, rest assured, you are still at least one step ahead of your father."

"Oh, two, at least," Papa said.

Bibi raised an eyebrow.

"We did get married when I was twenty-six."

Bibi scowled. "You insisted."

Papa grinned at his spouse. He took their hand and kissed the back of it. "I couldn't let you get away."

Felix wrinkled his nose. "Ew."

Bibi kissed Papa. "You know, you ruined a very nice vacation for us, Felix."

"Ew," Felix repeated without any real feeling behind it. Even if he engaged in the socially obligatory protests, he liked seeing his parents still so in love. Decades later and they still saw the whole world in each other.

His parents grinned at each other.

He grinned at them.

The angel remained there, looming and watching, without a smile.

Felix smacked the angel in the chest with the back of his hand. "Lighten up, Sunshine."

"Are you going to keep calling me that?" the angel asked. His voice carried no judgment, no derision or displeasure. Mild, a hint of curiosity.

"Uh. You have something better for me to call you?"

"No."

Felix said, "Anyone for breakfast?"

"At the house. There's nothing here but cans."

"There's a little store down the street, I'll go grab something."

His parents both looked at him.

"I mean, we should eat something, shouldn't we? Before we get started on a whole big thing? Who knows how fast those nuts will show up once we clear the police out?" Felix reasoned. It was sound logic. It showed on both their faces.

Plus, he hadn't had a fresh-cooked meal in days.

"Go, fine. Be careful," Bibi said.

Felix checked his pocket for his wallet. He had the angel's knife stowed in the inner pocket of his jacket.

He didn't like the feel of the knife. It had a funny, buzzing kind of energy, like one of the artifacts the researchers in the university's labs were always messing around with.

He glanced back to see that the angel had followed him out the door. "What's so dangerous about this knife anyway?"

"It has a mission."

"You said that already. I don't know what that means."

A flicker of discomfort showed on the angel's face. "The...the first time I found you."

"Stabbed me."

"Then. When I stabbed you, it should have been enough. It was not. I lent what I could to the blade so that next time my hand would strike true."

"Knife that can't miss. That doesn't sound dangerous so much as handy."

"Divine power is not meant to be handled by humans."

"Then you'll feel a lot better knowing it's in my pocket being handled by no one," Felix said. "And besides, I'm not human."

"That might be worse."

Felix couldn't help but flash a grin. "I couldn't shoot you, I'm not about to stab you," he said.

Stabbing felt much too personal.

And messy.

They didn't talk much after that.

Felix perused the small grocery store. He couldn't cook, but he could follow a list. He wandered through and selected a handful of breakfast basics. Bread, sausage, eggs, butter. An onion for good measure.

It took him a while to find a good onion among the paltry ones on display.

About halfway back from the store, the angel edged closer to him. Quietly, he said, "Someone is following us."

Felix forced himself not to turn around.

"Turn left."

"What, into the alley?"

"Now," the angel said.

They turned into the alley.

Felix set down the bag of groceries safely off to the side.

About two minutes later, a young woman turned down the alley. She paused and started to backpedal.

Sunshine lunged at her.

Felix didn't react, too busy noticing that the young woman was about his age and rather pretty.

He didn't understand why Sunshine had gone after the woman until she started to fight back.

She managed to put up a struggle.

At first, Felix sort of wanted to watch, to see where this would go, but she pulled out a knife and almost made contact. Felix stepped in to help. He grabbed her from behind and pried the knife out of her fingers.

When she started to scream, the angel clamped a hand over her mouth.

It felt weird, the three of them sandwiched together like that. Especially because either the girl or Sunshine smelled nice.

Felix somehow doubted it was the angel.

Sunshine shifted to hold the woman more securely.

Felix stepped back. He looked over the woman's outfit, a blue-and-white number with brown, heeled Oxfords. Perfectly pinned curls framed her face. She didn't look like a cult member; she looked like a schoolteacher. Suddenly, he felt embarrassed. What if they'd gone and accosted some poor, innocent woman?

"You're sure she was following us?" Felix asked.

Sunshine turned his eyes toward the knife by Felix's feet.

Oh. That. He looked back at the woman. "Why were you following us?"

She struggled against Sunshine.

Felix could see the angel tighten his grip, squeezing so hard he dug into the soft flesh of her arm.

At least, it looked awfully soft.

He glanced around and grabbed the groceries. "You can get her back, right?"

"It would be easier if someone hadn't stripped me of my powers."

"Can you do it or not?"

"I can do it."

Felix adjusted the groceries and stomped off.

When the three of them walked inside, Bibi sighed, "Oh, Jesus fucking Christ."

"Phaedrus!" Papa scolded.

"What is that? What are you doing?"

Felix set the groceries down. "She was following us."

Sunshine walked the young woman over to the couch and made quick work of securing her with sundry bindings he found lying around. It looked like a belt and Felix's tie.

Felix appreciated the efficiency, even if he didn't think she needed to be tied up. He approached. "Why were you following us?"

She regarded him warily. She looked over Sunshine, too.

"Go ahead, go...Go away," Felix told Sunshine.

Sunshine narrowed his eyes. "Why?"

"Because no one wants to talk to you, you big dumb bastard," Felix snapped.

"You see the kind of example you set for him!" Papa said to Bibi.

Sunshine frowned. He took a few steps back.

"Actually, come over here," Bibi called to the angel. "You can help me cook. Hiram's absolutely useless in the kitchen."

The angel made a slow, unsure approach.

"I did want to chat, too," Bibi said.

Felix tuned them out.

Bibi wanted to know everything about everyone if it would make for a good story. They couldn't help themself.

Felix sat beside the young woman. "Will you at least tell me your name?" He tried his best to sound amenable and not like a kidnapper. He'd seen the knife in her hand and he still couldn't believe it.

She looked him over again, holding eye contact. She had gorgeous eyes, round and clear and blue as the sky.

Felix almost wanted to look away. It was light enough that the red of his eyes would show through instead of just looking black. Most humans found that color unnerving. A girl who wanted to cleanse the Earth of creatures definitely would.

"My name is Grace." She spoke as if her name was for his ears only.

"I'm Felix."

"I know."

He shouldn't have smiled, but she'd said it almost warmly. "You're, uh. You're a Moralist?"

She nodded but couldn't quite look at him. "My whole family belongs to the order."

Oh, they were an *order* now. Felix held back that thought. "You were following me?"

She nodded. "After you ran away, we needed to find you."

He couldn't help but raise an eyebrow. "Find me?"

She nodded. Her lipstick had gotten smeared in the struggle, the red of it blurring the lines of her mouth. Probably from when Sunshine had put his hand over her mouth.

"You had that knife. You sure you weren't trying to do more than find me?"

"A girl alone ought to be prepared."

"I don't know about that. The girls I know don't carry-knives."

"Do you know a lot of girls?" she asked. Her voice still had that same low tone. It felt like she'd asked him something intimate.

He sort of wanted to squirm in his seat. He looked away from her, not sure how to answer.

He heard Bibi say, "...bringing home strays left and right. I told his father we should have gotten him another cat."

He looked over.

Bibi was talking to Sunshine, whom they'd put in front of the stove. They had the angel stirring something. "And what does his father say?" Bibi cast a pointed look toward Hiram.

"That a cat isn't going to fix anything," Hiram supplied.

"Not going to fix anything. And here we are!"

Felix couldn't help but stand up. "What do you mean, fix anything?"

"Did you ask her where her friends are yet?" Bibi asked.

Felix came around to stand nearer to the kitchenette. The apartment didn't have much room for privacy, but he didn't want to talk about Grace in front of her like that. "It's been ten minutes."

Bibi huffed.

"What do you mean fix things? What's got to be fixed?"

Papa patted his arm. "Nothing."

"Hiram," Bibi said.

"Phaedrus."

"Tell me," Felix insisted.

Bibi shook their head.

"Bibi!" He nearly stomped his foot.

"We worry about you, Felix. Honestly. You...your world is so small. How many friends have you got? What do you do for fun?"

"I...I have friends. And interests."

"You're either out with Oscar or you're in your room reading."

"I like to read! What's wrong with that?"

"At least with Kathleen, you two would go out, see other people."

"Kathleen wanted to get married," Felix reminded.

"Now you're spending your time trying to set your friend up with someone," Bibi continued. "You should be out enjoying life. Doing something."

"The boy likes to read. I don't see the problem with that," Papa noted.

"You don't have any friends, either," Bibi reminded, jabbing a wooden spoon in Papa's direction.

"I have you."

Bibi sighed. To Felix, they said, "I just worry. I worry about how much time you spend alone. That's all. It's not good to be alone all the time."

"Did you want me to marry Kathleen?"

"Absolutely not. But I want you to have friends. More than just Oscar."

"What's wrong with Oscar?"

"Nothing. Oscar's *wonderful*, but someday you're going to wake up and Oscar won't be with us anymore. And I worry what that will be like for you."

Felix hated to think of that. Absolutely refused to think of it. "That's a hundred years away. What a stupid thing to worry about." He turned to walk away, but there was nowhere to go.

He went to the bedroom and flopped onto the bed.

It really was a stupid thing to worry about.

He and Oscar had been friends for two decades at this point. Nothing would change that. Not Soon-hee and whatever her problem was, or Oscar's disastrous taste in men, or anything.

Unless something could.

Sometimes he felt like something had.

They weren't the same kids who'd played checkers and jumped rope. Sometimes he thought Oscar had lived an entire second life while he'd been in Europe and Felix had just stayed behind, stayed in Pickering.

Stayed the same.

He would stay the same forever.

Oscar wouldn't. He'd keep getting older. He'd keep dating, he'd probably find someone he wanted to go steady with.

Felix groaned.

He grabbed a pillow and covered his face. He let out a shout.

This was stupid.

The bedroom door opened.

Papa laid down next to him. He folded his arms on his belly. "Do you want to talk about it?"

"No."

"They always want to talk. Talking helps them. Being around people helps them."

"I know."

"We don't think anything's wrong with you."

Felix sighed.

"I keep saying it's okay to be alone but..." Papa sighed. "You know, I'm not right about everything. I...I didn't have friends growing up. Not really. I had a brother. He was my best friend, or…I thought of him that way. I don't know how he thought of me. Then…then he was gone. I struggled with that. I had people to help, though. Good people."

Felix knew this story. He knew how Papa had grown up.

"I was…I was desperately alone. Desperately. I just." Papa sighed again, long and deep. "I got lucky. Fantastically lucky. Luckier than I *ever* deserved. I fell in love, really ridiculously in love with the first person who showed me romantic affection."

"That's a lot of adjectives, Hiram," Felix said in a perfect imitation of Bibi. He could do their nowhere-and-everywhere accent to a T, better than even Papa who'd known them for longer. A lot of old creatures had funny accents like that, most of them on their fifth or sixth language by now, having left dozens of homes behind.

"It could have gone so much differently. They found me and I wouldn't trade that for the entire world, but it could have been someone else. Someone who wouldn't have been so kind."

"I hope you're not worried about my virtue."

"No. But I am a little worried that you're making puppy eyes at a girl affiliated with a cult that wants to kill you. That killed your mother."

Felix sat up, nearly scandalized. "I was not!"

"What do I know? I never liked girls. Maybe that sweet doe-eyed look doesn't have the same effect when it comes from a comely female face."

"Just because she's pretty doesn't mean my brain is going to stop working."

"I don't know, you almost married Kathleen and she was half as pretty as the girl out there," Papa said.

"I knew you didn't like her!"

Papa shrugged. "It doesn't matter if I like her."

"She could have been your daughter-in-law. You don't want to like your daughter-in-law?"

"I'll like her if you like her. And you didn't like Kathleen enough to marry her."

"Hence not marrying her."

Papa gave his leg a pat. "You do have a modicum of sense about some things."

"I love you, too."

Papa let out a little chuckle. "Besides, you can afford to take your time about these things."

Felix smiled.

Papa smiled back.

The smell of breakfast had flooded the apartment.

"Should we see if Bibi needs help?" Felix asked.

"You go. I'm going to lie down for a bit."

Immediately, Felix felt concerned.

"Oh, stop, stop! I'm fine. We got up early for the train, that's all."

"Promise?"

"I promise."

Felix asked, "You had a nice trip?"

"I'd say it bears revisiting if we could leave you alone for more than ten minutes. Maybe we ought to hire some sort of minder."

Felix rolled his eyes. He rolled out of bed and followed his stomach to the kitchen.

Bibi handed him a plate, set one aside for their husband and themself, then doled out a portion each to Grace and Sunshine.

Grace picked at hers. Maybe all the excitement had put her stomach off.

Sunshine, on the other hand, ravaged his plate. He ate like he'd never had food before.

Felix jabbed a fork toward him. "So do you need to eat or not?"

Sunshine swallowed an enormous mouthful of food. "I'm a soldier."

"What's that mean?"

Sunshine took a smaller bite. He chewed thoughtfully. "It...it means I can wait for a while. Put off sleeping and eating for a while longer. Other things are more important."

"Like staring at me in the middle of the night?"

Sunshine scowled, a petulant little twist of his lips. He shoveled another bite into his mouth.

"You hold your fork like an absolute beast."

Sunshine's scowl deepened.

Felix grinned. He picked up his fork and demonstrated a more civilized grip. "Like so." He delicately pierced a piece of sausage and popped it into his mouth.

Sunshine watched.

"Nothing going on in there, huh?" Felix noted. He took the rest of his food and went to sit beside Grace.

She hadn't eaten much.

"It's not poisoned, promise."

She even smiled. She took a little bite, though she had to balance the plate on her lap and maneuver the fork with her hands tied.

They didn't talk as they ate.

He took her plate when she'd finished. He washed the plates and cooking utensils.

Bibi patted his back.

Sunshine watched.

He was always watching.

Felix almost asked him what he was always staring at.

Instead, he dried his hands and found the deck of cards from before. He set up a game of solitaire on the coffee table. Every so often he glanced up at Grace.

"When you aren't, uh, out catching monsters, what do you get up to?" Felix asked her.

"The same thing as any girl, I imagine."

"What, like knitting, collecting stamps? You go out with your girlfriends?"

"Why wouldn't I?" she asked.

Felix shrugged. Maybe being in a cult didn't preclude her from having a good time. The Devil had said that his mother was funny.

Grace glanced over her shoulder.

Sunshine stood in the kitchen, not doing much.

Bibi had gone to lie down with their husband.

"Your mother..."

Felix's head jerked up.

"Her name was Mercy, wasn't it?"

He nodded. His stomach had worked its way into his throat. He tried to swallow.

"We're a small community. People talk about her."

"Obviously," Felix said. "They killed her."

"No, I don't...I don't mean like that," Grace said. "She...I'm sorry. It must be hard for you to hear about her."

Felix shook his head. "No. No. Tell me. What do people say?"

"Some people aren't kind but...Mercy Specter got out. She got away, at least for a while."

"Got out."

Grace shook her head. "What am I saying? Don't listen to me."

"Well, go ahead."

"I felt for her, you know. Even if she, she made some questionable choices, she never had to die like that."

"Questionable choices like having me?"

Grace shook her head. "No." She smiled. "You were her baby. She must have loved you so much." Grace's smile faltered. She pressed her lips together. She sniffled.

"My, uh. My father said she was funny. Did people have anything else to say about her?"

"They said Mercy had a big heart." A few tears skated down her cheek.

Felix went to sit beside her. He handed her a handkerchief.

She dabbed her eyes. "I'm sorry."

He didn't know what to say.

She looked toward the bathroom. "Do you mind if I freshen up?"

"Oh. Go ahead."

She tried to stand but couldn't with her legs tied.

He knelt to untie them.

She walked into the bathroom and reappeared with her lipstick cleaned up and her hair tidied. "Thank you." She returned to her seat on the couch. She smoothed the skirt of her dress.

The right shade of blue for her eyes.

She handed back his handkerchief.

He tucked it into the inner pocket of his coat.

Her eyes followed his movement.

She smiled at him when he saw her watching.

He stood up. "I. I'm going to get a glass of water. Do you want something?"

"No, thank you."

He grabbed a glass of water and guzzled it.

Sunshine watched him. He looked over at Grace. "You should tie her legs again."

"Should I tie you up, too?"

"You keep telling people we have a truce."

Felix made a face at him. "I. I'll be right outside." He didn't stay to evaluate the look the angel gave him. He sucked in a few slow breaths to calm himself.

He was getting worked up over nothing.

Everything had gone sideways. He ducked back inside after a few minutes.

He smacked Sunshine as he walked by. "Come play cards."

"I don't know how."

"Are you incapable of learning as well as independent

thought?" Felix asked. He stalked over to the table.

Sunshine followed. He sat next to Felix.

Felix wrinkled his nose.

"Tell me about cards."

Felix couldn't tell him to go away, not when he'd just asked him to come over. "Uh. Well. First things first, I guess?"

Sunshine nodded.

"There are four suits. Two red and two black. Clubs, spades, diamonds, hearts." He shuffled through the cards, laying them out so the angel could see the differences.

Once they got through the cards, Felix taught him to play Eights.

The angel caught on in a few games.

Grace watched.

Felix invited her to play.

She accepted.

When Bibi and Papa came out from the bedroom, Sunshine went over to them.

To Bibi, specifically.

The two of them exchanged a few quiet words.

"...seen an angel in two hundred years at least," Bibi said.

Felix went to sit beside Grace again. He couldn't help it. "Will you tell me where the rest of your family is?"

"Oh, no, I..." She blinked several times and pressed her lips together. "They'll be furious! What...What would you even do to them?"

"I don't want to hurt anybody. I just want...I want to live my own life. I want to be safe for once."

"Someone sent us a letter about where you were."

He grimaced. "Listen, if you could just tell me where the rest of them are, I promise, I won't hurt anyone. I want them to go away."

She swallowed.

He watched the line of her throat as she turned away from her.

She smelled nice. She turned back. She kept her voice low when she said, "If I tell you where they are, will you let me go?"

"You'll just warn them."

She shook her head.

"Or you'll bring them to us."

She put her hands over one of his. "I don't want to keep living like this. I don't." She lowered her voice even further, "They use me to trick people. To lure them. I hate it." The whisper of her voice thickened.

He pulled his hand back. He looked over at his parents.

A few tears trailed down her cheeks. Her nose ran.

He offered his handkerchief again.

She took it and dabbed it under her nose, then folded it and wiped her eyes. "I'm sorry. It's just." She pulled in a small breath. "Sometimes I have to do such awful things to get them to come with me."

"Grace, I'm...That's awful. That's...I'm really sorry."

She dabbed at her eyes again. "Do you think this was what your mother ran away from? Sometimes I wish I could...I could just run. I'd never look back. Never."

Felix reached over to undo the ties around her wrists. "Tell me where the others are. Once they're gone, you can go."

"What are you going to do to them?"

"Just. Keep them from hurting people. That's all. They'll be safe," he promised. "You can start over."

She threw her arms around him. She smelled really nice.

His arms settled around her as if by instinct.

She felt more than nice against him. It felt lovely to have her close.

"Felix," Bibi warned from the kitchenette.

He kept his arms around Grace, nothing but the scent of her skin in his nose, the feel of her cheek against his. "It's okay." He rubbed her back.

"You see what I'm talking about?" Bibi asked Sunshine.

Grace tightened her embrace, then slid her hands lower, skating down his ribs. She kissed his cheek.

He wanted to kiss her. It didn't feel right, not with what she'd just said or with his parents so near, but his heart pattered in his chest from a kiss on the cheek.

No one had kissed him in a long time.

He hadn't been on a date since he'd ended it with Kathleen, and she hadn't kissed him for a while before they'd broken up. She'd told him when he made up his mind about marrying her, she'd start kissing him again.

Fair. No one liked getting taken advantage of.

Grace pulled away.

He loosened his arms.

She made a funny sort of motion with her arm as she drew back.

A sharp line burned across his chest.

She bolted, shoving past his parents and twisting out of the angel's grasp when he fumbled after her. She flew out the door, faster than Felix could have guessed, especially in those shoes.

Athletic. Lucifer had described his mother as athletic, too. You'd have to be to hunt monsters.

Not one of the other three followed her, they all moved toward him.

He touched his chest and then understood why they looked so horrified.

She'd cut him across the chest.

He stood and went to the door, shouldering through his parents. He tried to clatter down the stairs after her, but he felt dizzy. He had to stop and grip the railing to stay upright.

Blood loss, probably.

The angel came out to stand beside him. "She took my knife."

Bibi grasped his face in their hands. "Felix, what…Oh, that little…This. *This* is why you need more friends."

"It will heal," he insisted. He pulled out of Bibi's grip.

Bibi grabbed him again, trying to look over the wound in his chest.

"It will heal!" he snapped. "Go see if you can catch her, someone!"

"Felix."

"Fine, I'll go!" He tried to storm down the stairs, his hand tight on the railing.

Sunshine followed him. "She took my knife."

"Yes! She took your *fucking knife*," Felix snarled.

He made it to the bottom of the stairs before he had to stop and breathe.

"It's poisoned."

Felix tried to keep himself upright.

Sunshine peeled back Felix's shirt and eyed the wound.

Felix looked down. Blood flowed freely from the wound. Just a shallow gash, nothing life-threatening. It would heal. "Poison doesn't bother demons as much."

"You are the son of the Beast. This poison is meant to bother you," Sunshine said. Calm and soft, like always. "I applied it when the first blow wasn't mortal. You are lucky she knows nothing of how to use my knife's power, your lungs would be on the floor otherwise."

Felix kept walking. He refused to look at his parents or think about his lungs flopping out of his shattered ribcage. "Figure you can fix it?" he asked the angel.

"Not bound."

"Will it kill me?"

Sunshine nodded.

Felix sank to the ground. He felt awful. "Papa can. He can get the cuff off you. My journal under my mattress."

"I need my knife back."

"I don't have it."

Sunshine crouched next to him. He made an unpleasant snorting noise, then spat directly into the cut across Felix's chest.

Felix took it as a slight. A final act of disrespect.

Then the angel smeared his fingers through the wound, spreading the gob of spit around.

Felix grunted. "What?"

Sunshine grabbed Felix by the arm and lifted him to his feet. He steadied him. "We have an hour, maybe two, before that wears off."

"The spit?"

Sunshine nodded. He glanced at Felix's parents. "I'll see him home. Fix this."

"We'll come," Papa said.

Felix shook his head. "The girl. Try to find her. Please."

"I can fix it," Sunshine insisted.

Bibi put a hand on Papa's shoulder. "Come on, Hiram."

Papa frowned. "I..."

"We're more useful elsewhere before that girl comes back with half a dozen others."

Sunshine pulled Felix back upstairs.

Felix pulled his arm back.

"The bleeding won't stop," Sunshine said.

"It's uh. Angels don't go to Hell without poisoned blades. That poison?"

Sunshine nodded.

"I read about it."

"Then you know you can't fix it without an angel."

Felix wanted to argue, ask questions, but realized he might argue his way out of the rest of his life.

He shut his mouth as the angel wrapped a makeshift bandage around his torso, his hands quick and efficient.

He only burned Felix once.

Felix pulled on a shirt. "The house."

Sunshine nodded.

This time when he reached the bottom of the stairs he felt better. Not great, but less like passing out or losing his breakfast. "So, tell me about this spit thing?"

Sunshine glanced his way.

"I've read a lot about angels, never heard of healing spit."

"Never seen a dog lick his wounds?"

Felix felt stupid. Ten times stupider than he had before, which brought him about to the bottom of the worst intellectual pit he'd ever dug himself into.

"It's like that. But. You know. Divine."

"And you're a soldier," Felix said. "You need better triage than the rest of the bastards up there, huh?"

"You shouldn't have untied her."

Felix flipped him off.

ONCE THEY completed their slow trek back to his house, Felix fished his notebook out from under the mattress. The effort alone made his head throb.

Sunshine reached for his sword.

"Don't!"

"You're not in much of a position to stop me."

Felix scowled.

He'd bled through the bandage.

He felt like shit.

He took the key out from where he'd wedged it in his journal. He pressed the key against the seam in the cuff and it fell off the angel's arm, clattering against the hardwood floor.

Sunshine looked at the cuff, rubbed his wrist, then said, "Take off your shirt."

Felix shrugged out of it. He started to peel away the bandage then wished he hadn't. There was still a lot of blood. The wound had little greenish-black lines threading away from it.

The angel pressed his palm directly against the wound.

Felix couldn't tell if it was working, not really, because in about a minute, the palm against his chest started to burn. It made the blood on his chest smoke. It stank.

He started to squirm.

Sunshine drew his palm back after not much longer.

The dark tendrils around the wound had gone away.

The bleeding slowed. He went to the bathroom to wipe up, careful not to stop it from scabbing over.

He headed back to his room, threw his trousers onto the floor with his bloody shirt, and flopped onto his bed. He shouldn't have. He could probably get the blood out of the trousers, but the shirt was done for.

Sunshine, of course, watched.

Felix didn't care. He took time to breathe. Finally, he pushed himself up. "Why bother?"

"Hmm?"

"Are you supposed to kill me?"

"Your parents made it abundantly clear what would happen to me if you were to die. I don't think it would matter if I wasn't the one who did it."

Felix smirked. "Is that what Bibi was telling you in the kitchen? Didn't figure angels had much in the way of self-preservation."

"I'm not supposed to." Sunshine sounded concerned. "Nothing should matter more than the task at hand."

"Uh-oh, Sunshine. They might take your halo away."

Sunshine blinked. He kept watching Felix.

He looked sort of sad, standing there in mismatched, ill-fitting clothes, holding his sword like he didn't know what to do with it.

Not sad.

Pathetic.

"What else did Bibi tell you?"

"They wanted to know about Heaven."

Felix smiled. He couldn't help it. It took most people a lot of fumbling to figure out what to call Bibi, or to stick to it, at least. Anyone who took to it always provoked a flutter of warmth in Felix.

"I feel like *shit*. You think this is gonna leave a mark?" He glanced down at the cut and the handprint on his chest.

"We need to get my knife."

"Why? What's the big deal with this knife?"

"It has purpose. That woman has purpose, too. She's going back to a whole group of people that have a distinct and unfriendly purpose," Sunshine told him. "I don't know what it will do but it will do something." The evenness in his voice dipped. "It may take them time to learn how to use it but...humans usually find a way to do things they aren't meant to do."

Felix didn't like the sound of it.

Moralists killed people like him, he didn't want that knife to make it any easier for them. He didn't want his stupidity to get anyone else killed.

"My parents are right. I do need more friends." He pushed himself out of bed. He rummaged through his closet.

He pulled on trousers, then waffled between what shirt to wear. He picked his darkest one to avoid ruining anyone more white ones. He had a feeling more shirts would get ruined before this was over.

By the time he finished dressing, he felt almost like himself.

He could have used a bath. A good, long soak.

He glanced at Sunshine. "You remember where the bathroom is? Go ahead if you need it."

Sunshine shook his head. "My knife."

Felix flapped a hand at him. "Then let's go see if they had more luck."

Sunshine nodded and started for the door, sword still in hand.

"You might not want to carry that around with you."

The angel didn't listen.

Before they even left the house, Felix started to think about Grace. How nice she'd smelled and how warm she'd felt against him. Guilt and shame churned together in his stomach. "You want to see a magic trick?"

"No."

"Figured you wouldn't. You're like a block of wood, you know that? He not give you feelings?"

Sunshine glanced his way.

"Makes sense. What use does a solider have for feelings? Must make you all good at stabbing little babies to death."

Sunshine stopped dead and turned toward Felix. "You speak ill of something you know *nothing* about."

"Murdering babies is kind of a good line to draw," Felix pointed out.

The angel took a step toward him. "You cannot set aside the will of Heaven."

Felix scoffed. "Yeah. You can. Two out of my three parents did it."

"I will not fall."

"Talk about priorities." Felix tried to step around him.

Sunshine grabbed his arm. He squeezed tight but said nothing.

Felix shoved him. The slice across his chest twinged and started to ache. "Don't touch me."

Sunshine grabbed him again and dragged him back. "You'll end this world. Every breath you draw brings it closer."

"Hey, look around you, pal. Humans don't need me to end the world. Take a look at some of the shit they're fucking around with in labs right now. Two! Two world wars. You think I did that? You think I started the Depression? Maybe the Spanish flu, maybe that was me." He pushed Sunshine away again. "Hey. Maybe I'm Typhoid Mary. Maybe I'm Hitler. Yeah, I sneak over to Germany every night, draw a little mustache—"

Sunshine pushed him. Not hard, but enough to stop him talking. He walked away.

Felix followed. "You know what, I sunk the Titanic. Yeah, from my father's fucking balls, I had that kind of just pure evil. And the Hindenburg, that was me. Let's see, what else is there? What else? Or did you have a better idea? Cause you know, it's hard, being this *evil*, thinking of all these atrocities."

Sunshine kept walking, head down.

"Or did you just want to take your chance? Huh? This could be it, bud. Your one shot to fulfill that God-given mission of yours."

Sunshine swung his sword. He leveled it at Felix's throat.

"Do it. I dare you. Cleanse the world."

Sunshine didn't move.

Felix shook. He shook all over. "You might as well. That's what all this had to be, right? Some kind of elaborate suicide. Even I'm not dumb enough to do all this and think I'll get out alive."

Sunshine frowned. He even blinked.

"It's gotta be."

The angel stepped back. Even as poorly socialized as he was, he seemed to realize Felix's behavior was abnormal.

Felix pressed forward. "No. Do it." His throat tightened. "What's the fucking point? Living like this? Hiding? Scared all the time. Fucking...fucking alone. Everyone in this town, they know exactly what I am when they see me." He tried not to blink. If he blinked, the tears would spill. He swallowed and tilted his chin up, exposing his throat.

Sunshine stepped back again. He put his sword away. "You don't mean that," he said, for once sounding uncomfortable. Any hunter would be uncomfortable if his prey walked up to him and begged for death.

Even with that silly image in his head, a suicidal deer, Felix couldn't shake the awful churn of feeling within him.

The tears fell anyway. A little whine escaped his throat.

He didn't know what he wanted. He didn't want to die, not really. But he didn't want to live, either. Not like this.

Not clinging on to a childhood friend. He barely gave Oscar room to breathe. Not as a permanent burden to his parents. He'd ruined their only vacation in years, the only time they'd really taken time for themselves in decades.

He wiped his face with his handkerchief. "I don't know. I get irrational when I'm like this. Please don't kill me."

Sunshine looked him over. He searched Felix's face. He pursed his lips, then shook his head. "Maybe your parents caught up with her."

Felix blew his nose then tucked away the handkerchief. "Maybe. The two of them are at least competent."

"You seem competent," Sunshine offered stiltedly.

"Oh, don't start. If you pity me, I really will have to slit my wrists."

Sunshine didn't say anything else.

Felix rambled, talking about nothing and everything to keep himself from dwelling too much on what he'd said, on Grace and Oscar, and his parents, and the enormity of what he'd learned about himself.

Bibi, Papa, and Oscar all stood around in the kitchenette looking like they had a funeral to get to.

"Everyone alright?" Felix asked.

"What about you?" Oscar demanded.

Felix shrugged. "I'm fine."

"Lot of blood for someone who's fine," Oscar pointed out.

Sunshine had left quite a few bloody rags laying around, and no one had picked up Felix's first ruined shirt from where he'd tossed it.

"Ah, no, right as rain," he declared. He flashed them all a smile. He felt a little weak and had a headache, but that seemed normal for the situation. "What about you? What's got you coming by?"

"I said I'd stop by," Oscar reminded.

"Right. Oh. Uh." He glanced around the room and finally noticed Soon-hee sitting on the couch. He waved.

She actually waved back instead of scowling at him.

"I brought lunch," Oscar said.

"You're too good to me, darling," Felix said. He swooped in for a hug and a kiss on the cheek.

He grinned at the room again, feeling sort of jittery.

His parents looked at him. Not stonily, but that quiet, concerned look they had when he got like this. The tilt of Papa's mouth, the crease between Bibi's brows. "He has magic spit, did you know that? Bibi, have you got magic spit?"

"It isn't magic," Sunshine said.

"He's got divine spit. Beatific spit. Uh. Blessed spit," Felix rattled. "Whatever it is. Think of the applications."

His parents looked at each other.

"Maybe you ought to rest for a little while," Papa said.

Bibi added, "It was quite the morning for you."

He waved a hand to brush away their concerns. "No, I'm alright. I already let my nerves get the better of me, you haven't got to worry about that."

Oscar cleared his throat.

"What did you do?" Papa asked.

"I might have tried to goad Sunshine over there into killing me. Whatever warning you gave him worked pretty well, so, uh. Good work with that." He glanced around the room. "Maybe I will go lay down for a bit though."

He made a rather shaky exit to the bedroom. He shed his jacket, set aside his shoes, and lay on the bed, hands folded over his stomach.

It had been an exciting few days. He hadn't gotten a solid four hours of sleep since before Papa and Bibi had left.

As a rule, he didn't care for naps but now seemed an appropriate time.

With how heavy his eyes felt, he didn't think he had much say in the matter.

He woke a while later and stretched out the kink in his back. He wandered out to find the others, Sunshine excluded, chattering eagerly with each other over the remains of lunch.

Sunshine stood off to the side, looming, uncomfortable.

He looked like someone had parked a statue in the living room.

"We put a plate aside for you. Come sit, I'll warm it up," Bibi said.

Felix went over. He sat between Oscar and his father.

Oscar elbowed him. "Oh, no, really, make yourself

comfortable."

Felix clucked his tongue. "Now, I assume you didn't manage to catch up with our Moralist friend?"

"No," Bibi said.

"Should we head home? See if they'll show up there?" he proposed. He glanced at Sunshine.

He looked surprised that Felix had referenced him. "They might."

"You have another idea?"

"Can you defend yourself at home better?" Sunshine asked.

Papa said, "Certainly."

"You should go there. This...these people. They don't like anything that's not human?"

"I swear if you bring up that knife..." Felix huffed.

Bibi said, "It is rather a liability to have a Heaven-forged weapon in the hands of a mortal."

"Alright. How about this? Papa, you and Bibi can go home. Shore up defenses there. Tell the police to hang back. Sunshine and I will see if we can figure out where this girl's gotten to. Oscar and Soon-hee, well, you two just keep being pretty." He winked at Oscar.

Oscar pinched him.

Soon-hee scowled.

Apparently, she still didn't like him. No pleasing some people.

"Agreed?" he asked.

Several people chorused their disagreement. Papa and Bibi wanted him to go home, Oscar didn't think Felix should be out looking for the girl who'd sliced him, and the angel just repeated that he needed his knife back.

It took some convincing, but Felix got his way in the end, though it took him longer to talk them into things than it did to finish his lunch.

Felix might be a good mage, but no one was better than Papa. Bibi wanted to come with Felix to keep an eye on him and he did his best to kindly point out that they were almost useless in a fight.

"Unless they're going to start writing strongly worded letters," Felix added. He grinned.

"Don't you smirk at me like that," they warned.

"Sunshine and I can handle it."

"Like you handled all of this?" Bibi asked.

Papa put his hand on Bibi's arm. "I'll need help at home."

Bibi shook their head. "You're a fantastic mage, Hiram, you

don't need my help to cast a spell."

"No, but someone with two hands might do better at putting the front door back together."

"I can help with that," Oscar offered.

Bibi played with a lock of long, fawn hair. "Why don't you come look at it and I'll decide if fixing a door exceeds my thousands of years of experience with material objects?"

Oscar blushed.

Bibi stood. They touched Papa on the shoulder. "Let's go."

Papa stood.

"You too, Mr. Banks. I think we'll need a new lock, and you may actually prove useful to me in that situation," Bibi said.

Oscar bounced up, eager to help. "I might even have something original to the era. When was the house built? About eighteen hundred, right?"

Bibi nodded.

"I have a few things that might just be perfect."

Bibi swept out, their long jacket flaring dramatically.

Oscar followed right on their heels.

Papa patted Felix on the head and followed.

Soon-hee watched them leave. She gathered up the plates they'd left behind.

"I can get them," Felix said.

She set the plates down with a rattle. "Fine." She made for the door.

He followed her. "Hey."

She rounded on him. "Excuse me?"

"Why don't you like me?" he asked.

"Do I need a reason?"

He reconsidered. "I guess not, no, but I do think you need a pretty good reason to be so nasty."

Her jaw dropped. She angled her head dangerously. "Nice, coming from you. I don't think I've heard you say a kind thing about anyone in three years."

Felix puts his hands on his hips. He didn't know what to say to that.

"Every man Oscar likes and you've got something rude to say about him. Three years and you shred apart anyone he dates," she said.

"Well, I don't want him dating some scumbag who's not going to treat him right."

"And there's another thing," Soon-hee said. "You talk about Oscar like...like he needs you watching out for him. He's not a kid. Or some girl you need to protect. Just because you knew him when—"

"Don't go there with me," Felix warned.

"At first, I thought you were just ignorant. A lot of people are. They're cruel because they don't know any better, and then I heard more and more about your family, and I realized that it's not ignorance. You're just mean and overbearing."

He swallowed. He shouldn't have gotten into this. "Does Oscar think I treat him like a girl?"

"No. Oscar thinks you're funny."

To hide his smile, he turned away and gathered up the plates. He brought them over to the sink. He said, "Uh, listen. Sunshine and I really ought to go find—"

"Go."

Felix kept his lips pressed together until he'd gotten on his shoes and his jacket and out the door. Once out of earshot, he dissolved into giggles.

Sunshine eyed him.

"I am funny," he told the angel.

"We need to find—"

"You ever hear the joke about the angel who wouldn't stop talking about his fucking knife?" Felix asked.

Sunshine walked away.

"It's really funny, I promise. The angel walks into a bar, and he tells the bartender, 'I need to find my knife' and the bartender says, 'Have you checked up your ass cause you act like you've got something worse than a stick up there?' and the angel says—"

"It's not up my ass because an idiot let some woman run away with it."

"Then you do normally keep it up your ass?" Felix asked.

The angel glared.

"You could have gone after her. Got your knife, let me die."

"If you die and I can't get off this planet, I want to at least be able to get a running start."

Felix grinned. He fell into step next to Sunshine. "What exactly did Bibi threaten you with?"

Sunshine shook his head.

"Hmm. Anyway. Since it's not up your ass, where do you think we should look? You're walking with the confident stride of a man who knows where he's going."

Sunshine didn't answer.

"Maybe it is up your ass. I could check for you." Felix immediately couldn't believe himself.

Instead of looking scandalized or open to the prospect, Sunshine narrowed his eyes at Felix, confused and maybe curious.

"Forget I said anything," Felix said. "Where are we headed?"

"She went this way."

"And you know because…?"

Sunshine didn't answer for a while. He looked contemplative. He sighed. "I can…I can sort of feel where it is. With that thing off my wrist, I can tell where the knife's been."

"Like a scent hound."

They walked for a long time, in a straight line whenever they could. The angel sometimes passed through buildings, pushing through a crowded bar to the back exit to avoid deviating from his path.

Sunshine walked ceaselessly, even and steady, without a word to Felix or a glance in his direction.

Then he stopped.

He looked around.

"Penny for your thoughts?" Felix offered.

"It's moving faster now."

He started walking again.

Felix grabbed his arm. "Hey, hang on a second."

"You waste too much time."

"If it's going faster, we aren't going to catch up with it by walking," Felix pointed out.

"It will stop eventually."

"And you're not gonna stop walking, are you?"

Felix could imagine him walking for days on end, maybe pausing to sleep or eat when he absolutely had to.

"It's how I looked for you. Every inch of this city."

"And you didn't find me until I took my amulet off."

Sunshine blinked slowly, thoughtfully.

Felix wanted to say owlishly but that might have just been because of the color of his eyes.

"Unless you want to spend the next twenty-six years walking around…? Let's give my way a shot."

Sunshine shook his head. His eyes scrunched up.

"Uh."

The angel pressed his lips into a thin line. His chin wobbled.

"What, what is that?" Felix asked.

Sunshine gripped his curls and looked at the ground. "I don't understand."

"Ummmmm." Felix struggled with empathy at the best of times, and he hadn't been at his best lately. "About what?"

"Why would you help me?"

Felix shrugged. "I don't know. We've got a truce. Maybe, uh." It sounded stupid even as he thought it, but he said, "Maybe when this is over instead of killing me you can pop back up to Heaven and let them know I'm not planning to end the world. I feel like not ending the world for twenty-six years is pretty good odds."

Sunshine rubbed his face.

"More likely, I'll just run like hell, grab my amulet, and find a new place to live. But it's worth a shot. Come on, come to the university. I think I have an idea." Felix took a few steps. He waited for the angel to follow.

Sunshine came to walk next to him.

Felix brought him up to Papa's office, fished out the right spell book, and dug around for a map of Pickering.

"So, my theory is that since you and the knife are connected, we can use that to figure out where it is. I just need a little bit of you and a map. I used to use this spell to..."

"To what?"

"My cat would get outside sometimes, get stuck up a tree or something."

"Oh."

Felix shrugged. "Bit of something that came from her and I could find right where she was. So." He reached for a crystal candy bowl Papa kept on his desk and dumped out the candies into a drawer.

Sunshine offered his arm, palm up, and started to tug up his sleeve.

"Oh, no, no," Felix assured. "Just spit."

Sunshine spat into the bowl.

Felix worked the spell and added a dribble of ink, just for visibility. He poured the spit on to the map and watched it snake through the city streets then shoot out in a long, straight line out of the city.

It pooled at the edge of the map, threatening to spill over.

"What's that mean?"

"She's out of the city."

Sunshine grit his teeth so hard Felix could hear it. He turned toward the door.

"Don't you want to know where she's going?"

"She's off the map."

"I have more maps. Of bigger areas. We might even have a map of all of Canada. Maybe even the whole world."

Sunshine scowled at him.

"Besides, that line? That's following the train tracks. We know she's on a train going east. I might know where she's headed. These Moralists, I think they tend to live in isolated communities. Their own little towns. Uh, like the Amish."

"And you know where the town is?"

"No. But Bibi might. Or they might know who to call to find out."

Sunshine nodded. "You think that's the town she's from?"

Felix shook his head. "She's American, for sure. Canadian Moralists tend to keep to themselves more, defensive more than offensive."

"You know a lot about them."

"I had to do my research. I had to find out which ones killed my mother. I'm not delusional enough to try to take on the whole lot of them." He leaned against the desk. "You know who killed her?"

"She was dead when I got there."

Felix's eyes went wide. He'd meant the question rhetorically.

"You. You saw her?"

The angel seemed to realize his misstep. He nodded.

Felix couldn't breathe for a second. Lucifer wouldn't talk about it, not really. He thought of Felix as a child and probably would for a thousand years. That and the Devil must have felt some guilt over her demise. Felix didn't know if her death had been swift and humane, if they'd tried to get information from her, if she had fought back. "Was..." He stopped himself from asking.

He wanted to know his mother. He didn't want his current parents any less, but he thought about her. He only knew what Lucifer had shared and they hadn't known each other well at all. They hadn't been serious lovers, just a fling. He knew more about Georg than he did about his mother. He wanted to know about her, but he didn't want one of the only things he knew about her to be how her corpse had looked.

"Who killed her?" the angel asked.

"Her father and her brother."

"I. I'm sorry."

"You didn't do it."

"I wouldn't have," Sunshine said. "She wasn't my mission. She was only human." He went quiet for some time, then said, "I thought these people wanted Earth for humans. Killing humans seems an...inefficient way to go about it."

Felix sighed. He straightened up.

"And that is not...that is not the function of parenthood."

"Yeah, well, I guess uptight pro-human cults don't take well to their members taking the Devil to bed." He headed out the door.

Sunshine followed. "Surely the Beast forced her. They must have understood that."

Felix shot him a look. "That's not something you say to people."

"What isn't?"

"That their dad raped their mom."

"It happens all the time."

"No one likes to think that's how they got here," Felix told him. "And he didn't. By the way."

"According to the Beast."

"According to everyone," Felix snapped.

Sunshine didn't argue.

Felix stomped down the stairs out of the university.

"She could have had other children," Sunshine continued.

Felix stopped to look at him. "What?"

"The point of procreating...one beastly child would not have stopped her from having human children, untainted, continuing her bloodline. Your grandfather was foolish."

As he tried to think of something to say, he stared at the angel, dimly aware that his mouth was open. He could think of nothing, though, his mind frantically blank.

"You are not so foul that you would contaminate others," Sunshine said.

"Thanks," Felix said only to have something to say.

The angel nodded curtly.

Felix resumed walking, temporarily forgetting his destination for a few seconds and heading the wrong way. He turned back the right way, his head down as he walked perhaps the most familiar path of his life, his thoughts and what the angel had said tumbling around each other endlessly.

JUNE 12, 1940
Wednesday

BIBI HAD fixed the door, Papa had warded the house, and Sunshine had loomed awkwardly in the living room through all of it.

Felix, for his part, had located the town to which Grace, or whoever had the knife now, had fled. He'd confirmed its Moralist tendencies and plotted out the best way to get there. He had a bag packed and he'd talked his parents into staying home in case the other Moralists hadn't fled town like Grace.

He hadn't been able to talk Sunshine into staying behind, not that he'd given it his best effort, or had ever thought he really could.

He had found his amulet and slipped into his bag just in case things got hairy between them.

Someone, probably Bibi, had found Sunshine a proper suit, one that matched and fit him reasonably well. He wore his sword across his back and looked like an absolute madman because of it.

His parents warned Felix at least fifteen times to be careful.

Sunshine got no such warnings, although both Bibi and Papa did make extended eye contact with the angel.

It had amused Felix to watch him squirm under their gaze.

Now, they sat on the train.

Felix read.

Sunshine watched him read. Sometimes he looked out the window.

"I'm not that interesting," Felix told him without looking up when he felt the angel's eyes on him again.

They'd sat right next to each other which made being watched all the more unnerving.

Sunshine seemed to realize he'd made Felix uncomfortable. An odd expression flitted across his face, then he asked, "What are you reading?"

"The Shadow." Number one-ninety-nine, to be exact. Felix hoped he'd be around to see the two hundredth, which was due out in a few days. He'd read every single one for the past nine years. "The Scent of Death." He showed Sunshine the cover.

"What's it about?"

Felix handed it over to him. He'd read it already and had packed a few other books for the ride.

Sunshine shook his head. "I can't read."

"Can't read," Felix repeated. He shook his head, then went back to his book. "Magic spit but he can't read."

Sunshine kept watching him.

Felix sighed. He flipped back to the first page. "Chapter one. Quest of Gold," he began. He glanced up to see if Sunshine noticed.

He wasn't just watching Felix now. He was paying attention to him. His face had lost a little of that carved-in-marble emptiness.

Felix kept reading.

Sunshine kept listening.

A little while after lunch, the train stopped.

Felix glanced out the window but saw no station.

Porters came around and told the passengers they had to clear some debris off the rails.

"Nothing to worry about, sirs," one porter assured them.

Sunshine stood up.

The porter looked worried and stepped back. "I'm sorry, sir, it shouldn't be a problem."

Felix stood. He said, "Thank you," pressed a tip into the porter's hand, then waved him on. He asked Sunshine, "What are you doing?"

"The train stopped. We should start walking."

"The train will start again."

Sunshine eyed him.

"The train will start again. Delays happen. Haven't you ever been on a train?"

"No."

That answer didn't surprise Felix. "Well. I've been on trains and I can assure you, we'll still get there faster than if we walked."

He didn't sit.

Felix tugged on his arm. "Sit down."

"I have to—"

Felix pinched him.

"Use the bathroom," Sunshine finished.

Felix couldn't tell if he'd meant to say that all along.

The angel walked away.

Felix waited a moment, then got up too. He slipped over a few rows and hunkered down low in the seat.

The woman next to whom he had sat gave him a look.

He pressed a finger to his lips.

She ruffled her newspaper and turned her nose up but didn't say anything.

A few minutes later, he heard someone come into the train car. He peeked over to see the expression on the angel's face when he came back to an empty seat.

Panic, anger, and betrayal all flashed over Sunshine's face. He looked around, furtive at first, but then openly scanning the other passengers of the car.

Felix ducked back down. He covered his mouth with his hand.

"Honestly, young man," the woman next to him said.

He shook his head at her. His sides ached from the effort of staying quiet.

A shadow fell over him.

He glanced up and tried not to smile.

Sunshine grabbed him by the arm.

"Ow! Hey, ow, ouch!" Felix protested.

The angel dragged him in close. "You cannot hide from me."

Felix pressed his lips together but lost the fight and smiled. "It was just a joke."

"What?"

"You know, it...it was funny," Felix insisted, still smiling.

"It is not funny."

Felix peeled Sunshine's fingers off his arms. Thankfully, the angel let go of him before Felix's fingers started to blister. "Believe it or not, you don't strike me as someone with a great sense of humor."

"Maybe you just aren't funny."

Felix returned to his seat and thumbed back to the page on which he'd left off reading. He opened the book but stayed quiet.

Sunshine loomed for a while but eventually sat back down. He said, "Aren't you going to keep reading?"

"I am reading," Felix answered though he hadn't done more than skim the page and wait.

"I mean."

Felix glanced up. Bibi had done this all the time to him as a child, usually to get him to stop interrupting. He wondered if it worked on angels.

After a pause, Sunshine said, "But read it out loud."

Not a request, not even a please thrown it, but Felix took it. He started to read.

They slept on the train and in the morning arrived at a small train station, where they hired a car to take them closer to Purity Springs.

Felix found the name of the town atrocious. "Borderline unforgivable," he said to Sunshine.

Sunshine eyed the town around them as Felix handed over a sheaf of cash to the driver. He pointed to a factory with a mural of a bubbling spring painted on the side. "That's a spring though."

"Of course, it's a spring, it would be weird to name it Purity Springs if they didn't have a spring."

"It could have been...like jumps. Hops. Springs."

Felix squinted at him and figured he understood what Sunshine meant. "A verb?"

Sunshine nodded. "I think so."

"Oh, he *thinks* so. That's exciting for you. How's it feel?"

Sunshine opened his mouth to answer, then shook his head.

"That one thought has got to be lonely rattling around in there. Maybe try getting it some friends," Felix advised. When Sunshine didn't answer, Felix asked, "Do you know where we're going?"

"To find—"

"More specifically than that."

"No. I'll...I'll walk."

"Alright, well, let's try this on for size: how about you let me talk to a few people? This is a pretty small town by the look of it. It might be easier to ask."

Sunshine stopped and put out an arm to stop Felix, too. "Doesn't the whole town belong to that group? The ones that want you dead?"

"Like I said, Canadians aren't as bloodthirsty."

"Still, this could be dangerous."

"Oh, that just occurred to you right now?" Felix asked. "Like, right this moment you thought, gee going to a town full of cult members, one of whom has already done someone bodily harm, *could* be dangerous."

Sunshine looked at him.

Felix wanted to smack him, do something to get that blank look off his face. "What exactly did my parents say they'd do to you if I died?"

Sunshine shrunk in on himself. "They'll send me to the Pit."

Felix grinned his best wicked grin. "Oh, Dad would *love* that."

Sunshine shuffled uneasily, looking smaller than Felix for once. They stood about the same height, but the angel had quite a few pounds on him and from what Felix had seen, it was all muscle.

Felix kept grinning at him. "Well. Tables have sort of turned, haven't they! Good thing you brought your sword." He set off toward the town.

The angel followed miserably behind.

Felix scanned the buildings they walked past and noticed not just a restaurant, but a malted shop. From what he'd read and heard about Moralists, he'd pictured this place looking more like a colonial village, not a quaint little town.

He stepped inside, the angel on his heels, and approached the counter.

The youth behind the counter approached. He looked a little cagey, but cagey was a warmer welcome than Felix expected here. "What can I do for you?"

"I just got into town. I was hoping you could point me in the right direction."

The youth nodded right away and said, "You're probably looking for the spa, huh? That's down at the end of town, Fulcote Street." The youth leaned a little closer and dropped his voice to share, "Though, nothing personal, but I don't know how Mr. DeVries will take to you, he's old-fashioned like that."

"Oh."

"Figured it might be better to hear it from a friendly face, hm?"

"Sure, sure, of course." Felix couldn't quite tell if the youth meant what he said, or if the town had figured out a politer way of asking creatures to leave.

"Sorry you came all the way out here," the youth said.

"I, uh. I actually didn't know you all had a spa out here."

"Sure. Purity Springs!" He pointed over his shoulder to a painting of a spring, similar to the one they'd seen outside. "Only reason folks ever come here is for the spa."

"What if I said I was looking for someone? Another traveler."

The youth shook his head. "Lots of people come through."

"Fair enough. How about a place to stay?" Felix asked.

"There's plenty. Most of them are on Ulman Street. Up Main a little more, right at the pharmacy."

"Thanks." Felix backed away from the counter and gestured for Sunshine to come along.

"Hey, uh....!"

Felix glanced back.

"Take care," the youth said, his face a little too serious.

A quick walk took them on to Ulman Street, which boasted plenty of hotels, a few inns, and a boarding house.

Felix didn't think this town had more than four or five thousand people, so the youth must have been right about the spa at least. He couldn't think of any other reason for that many hotels.

"It is sort of scenic," Felix said.

Sunshine looked around. "She's not over here."

"I swear, when we get this knife back, I'm fixing to pitch it into a volcano. Go up that side of the street and ask around for Grace in there."

"No."

Felix sighed. "Do you have to argue about everything?"

"Why would anyone tell us where she is?"

"Some people like to help. Just go in, stay you're looking for a friend, that you were supposed to meet up here." Felix walked away. He made it about two steps before he could tell the angel was right behind him. "Stop following me."

The angel didn't answer.

Felix stopped and turned around. "Stop following me."

Sunshine stopped just shy of walking into him. "We're not splitting up."

"No one is going to tell us where this young lady is if *two men* are looking for her. Even if they don't know what we are, would you point a girl out to a pair like us?"

"We're not splitting up."

Felix rubbed his face.

"I spent twenty-six years looking for you."

"And now you know where I live."

"I knew where you went to school, too. I watched that school for two weeks once I found my way back and I didn't see you even once. I walked your city *twice* and never saw you. We're not splitting up."

Felix explained, "You didn't see me because my father made me an amulet to hide me. I'm not hiding anymore."

"It's in your bag."

Felix glanced down at his bag.

"I couldn't figure out where you kept putting that book or what I kept tripping over. I kicked it about six times."

"What if I promise?"

"You are the child of the Beast—"

Felix let out a hideous groan, throwing his head back. He shoved his bag into the angel's arms. "Fine. You take it. Go ask around in those hotels."

Sunshine clasped the bag to his chest.

Felix gave him a push. "Go. Fuck."

No one in any of the lodgings had seen Grace. Felix had made sure to only ask other visitors since most of the staff and clerks at the hotels and inns seemed to recognize him for what he was. Some gave him the same mild warning as the youth at the malted shop; others watched him.

One man had even laid a gun on the reception desk as Felix had neared it.

He'd cleared out of that hotel pretty quick.

He went back outside to wait for the angel. After a bit, he saw Sunshine step outside moving at a strange pace.

Sunshine picked up from a scurry into a run when someone followed him out of the hotel. He came over to Felix, grabbed his arm, and said, "Go. We should go."

Felix jogged along with him.

The man from the hotel ran about halfway down the road toward them, then stopped, shouting a variety of warnings about what would happen if Sunshine came back.

Once they'd gotten far enough away, Felix slowed down and asked, "What did you do?"

"What you told me to do!"

Felix raised his eyebrows. "Repeat to me what you said."

"I'm in search of a thief with—"

"Okay, alright. No, that...that makes sense." Felix nodded. He couldn't blame the angel, not really. He put a hand on his hip. "How many did you go to?"

"Four. I had two left."

"Alright, well, no one in any of mine had seen her. And, you know. Maybe we had the wrong idea here. I mean, the people who live here, they're Moralists. And she's a Moralist. She probably wouldn't stay in a hotel for spa tourists."

Sunshine said nothing.

Felix tilted his head. Something about the angel seemed off. He had his hands clasped behind his back and his eyes toward the ground. "What?"

Sunshine shook his head. "What next?"

Felix shrugged. "What's your gut say?"

Sunshine's face shifted from blank to crunched, back to blank within a second. He clenched his jaw. He didn't answer.

"What's wrong?"

Sunshine shook his head. "What's next?"

Felix shrugged. He had a tart 'you messed this one up' sort of reply on his tongue but kept it to himself. He had no real reason to. Papa had tried to raise him with decent manners and for a while, Felix had tried to keep his crueler bouts of wit to himself, but in the end, sarcasm had won out.

Poor breeding, maybe, or years of watching Bibi snipe away at the people who gave them funny looks, or just wanting people to leave him alone without having to singe off their eyebrows to accomplish it.

"Let's give your way a shot. Maybe I'll think of something. Nothing like a walk to clear your head." He raised his eyebrows, flashed a smile, and headed off.

Sunshine fell into step behind him.

Felix turned and walked backward. "You've got to stop walking behind me."

"Why?"

"Because it's creepy."

Sunshine came to walk beside him.

Felix pivoted forward. "Not to mention, you're the one who knows where we're going." He plucked his bag out of Sunshine's hand. "So, Mr. Sunshine, tell me about yourself while we walk. We've traveled such a long, long way together and yet I feel like I hardly know you at all. You must contain such mysteries." He might have laid on the Southern belle a little thick, judging by the look Sunshine gave him. He didn't drop it, though. "Oh, come now, sugar, I know we got off on the wrong foot, but can't we put that ugliness behind us? Aren't we friends now? Or, at least," and here he fluttered his eyelashes dramatically, "couldn't we be?"

"Why...why are you talking like that? Are you making fun of me?"

Felix shrugged. He dropped the accent. "Not of you. Of sort of the whole situation. Doesn't it whiff faintly of insanity?"

"Why?"

"I mean, it's...silly. This whole thing! I'm the son of a mage, a fallen angel, He Himself and his mortal lover, but this pursued by Heaven's finest warrior thing is a bit much to swallow even for me."

"I'm not Heaven's finest warrior."

"Oh, but you're so glittery and gold, that's got to be some sort of mark of quality," Felix assured.

The angel shook his head. "There are fifty-nine more exactly like me."

Felix didn't know quite what to say.

"The others who were sent, they at least found their targets."

Felix elbowed him. "Is it such a bad thing that you didn't?"

Sunshine only sighed.

"I'm not saying we'll be friends when this is all said and done, but we can work something out. Unless..." A funny feeling squirmed in his stomach, not entirely unfamiliar. "Unless you want to kill me."

Sunshine didn't answer.

Felix didn't press him. He didn't really want to know the answer. He didn't like the idea of someone personally wanting him dead. "Really, though, tell me about yourself," Felix said.

Sunshine stayed quiet.

Felix elbowed him. "You're being rude again."

"I don't know what to tell you."

Felix didn't know how to lead him to an answer. With anyone else, he could have asked about books or films or music, or even fashion or food, or thrown in a bit of gossip. This poor bastard, though...Felix didn't think he knew enough about himself to tell anyone anything.

They walked northward for a while, neither speaking.

"Beautiful day," Felix noted.

The sky stretched above them, clear blue and dotted with puffs of clouds.

Sunshine glanced up. He nodded.

"Would be a nice day for a swim." He could have at least used a cold drink, though he didn't doubt the half-dozen spring water murals around town had aided that thought.

Sunshine nodded.

"You know how to swim?" Felix asked.

"In principle."

Felix thought about a few things he'd thought he'd understood in principle and a lopsided smile crawled across his face. Nothing worked out the way it seemed like it would in principle. He kept his mouth shut about that, though. "You don't swim up there?" He cast his eyes skyward. "Bibi says it's like an ocean."

"The ocean does not swim in itself."

"Oh, that's almost poetic, Sunshine. The ocean does not swim in itself. Did you come up with that?"

Sunshine nodded.

"Apollonian, truly, He made you."

Sunshine sort of smiled at him. It was a weird, aborted expression that quickly turned back into looking ahead of himself. He straightened his shoulders and quickened his pace.

Felix strolled behind, hands in his pockets, feeling like he'd accomplished something.

Sunshine kept up that proud, high-headed walk.

Felix gave him a few minutes then caught up with him and fell into step beside him.

They walked to the very end of town, on and on, until they turned onto Fulcote Street.

Felix elbowed Sunshine and pointed to the street sign.

Sunshine glanced at it.

Felix raised his eyebrows expectantly then remembered he'd spent hours reading to Sunshine on the train. He said, "Fulcote Street. That spa's up here."

"We should turn back."

"Hmm?"

"We were explicitly warned away from this place," Sunshine reminded.

"I've spent a lot of my life being explicitly warned not to do things and yet I've done them and stand here before you," Felix said. He continued down the street.

Sunshine grabbed the back of his coat and dragged him back. "Your parents worry about you."

Felix wiggled out of his grip, slapping the angel's hand away. "Of course, they do, I'm irrational."

"You don't think this might be one of those times."

"I'm irrational *and* stubborn." He moved a few steps forward.

The angel grabbed his arm this time.

"You're very grabby."

"You don't listen."

Felix fluttered his eyelashes. "Why don't you try asking nice, Sunshine?"

Sunshine frowned.

"Normally I'd say I don't mind but given that you warded yourself against my profound unholiness, I'd prefer to avoid any further burns."

Sunshine's eyes crinkled a hair at the corners. "It hurts through your clothes?"

"Well. Not yet. But I don't want to find out. Come on. Let's go snoop around the spa. If it doesn't work out, well, you've got a sword and great motivation to keep me alive," Felix pointed out.

"I'm not in the business of killing humans."

"No, just inhuman babies." Felix set off down the street.

Sunshine didn't stop him this time. He did catch up and tell Felix, "I've never killed anyone."

"But you could."

"I would rather not. There are other ways to render people harmless."

"Well, then I'll rely upon you to do that."

At the end of the street, they found a decent number of people exiting the spa. Felix asked them a few questions about how they'd liked the spa before he headed inside. A menu of services hung in the foyer. The building had the distinct smell of an aged building, some combination of wet stone, old wood, and the leavings of all the people who had stayed within its walls. Every spill and smoked cigarette, every meal its kitchens had seen.

It sort of smelled like home, except Bibi and Papa didn't smoke.

"What do you think? Would you like to take the waters?" he asked.

"I think it's here. Or very nearby."

Felix nodded, then headed further into the building. He stepped inside the lobby and saw no one. A small sign on the welcome desk stated staff would be back soon. He hurried through the building and exited to sprawling grounds on the other side.

The building sat above several acres of land ringed in forest and dotted here and there with spa amenities. Ladies' and gentlemen's bathhouses, a few gardens, the area where the spring itself bubbled up from the earth, a large pond, all connected by a series of paths lined with flowers and shrubs.

On the far end of the grounds sat several small houses, not quite nice enough for guests, and with all those hotels in town, Felix didn't think many people stayed on the spa grounds.

He pointed them out to Sunshine. "Those might be housing for the staff."

They headed down the stairs, passing a few other vacationers.

Felix made sure to smile and greet them, using manners that would make Papa proud. Otherwise, people were likely to contact staff about a strange-looking young man skulking around the spa. On his own, he likely could have kept a low profile, but Sunshine's attitude, appearance, and sword made him much more noticeable.

In the sunlight, his skin practically shimmered.

Felix couldn't help but say, "I bet if you got undressed and stood in the garden, you could pass for a statue."

"Why would I do that?"

"For laughs."

"I don't think anyone would laugh."

"I would," Felix said. "You want to give swimming a try? The pond looks gorgeous."

Sunshine didn't answer.

"Well, you know, if we find Grace, we'll definitely have other things to do, likely in a very immediate way. It is *lovely* here."

Sunshine stayed quiet.

Felix heaved a sigh.

Sunshine eyed him.

Felix smiled.

Sunshine looked away.

Felix poked him in the side. "I'm gonna get you to laugh with me one of these days."

Sunshine walked faster, giving up following the path and making a direct line toward the small houses.

Felix danced over the plants to follow. "People are going to notice…"

"It's close."

Felix made a face at Sunshine's back and followed him.

They poked around the outside of the houses after Sunshine tried the doors and found them locked.

Felix allowed Sunshine to circle the houses twice, trying all the windows, until finally, the angel raised a foot as though he meant to kick down the door. At that point, Felix said, "I can actually open that."

"Then do it."

The first spell he tried didn't work, but that was a spell for kids, one best used on those totally unversed in magic. The second one made it past the enchantment on the door. Moralists hated magic and supernatural creatures too much to delve any deeper than shallow protective charms.

He swung the door open with a flourish.

Sunshine didn't exactly push past him, but he came close. He tore through the house with apparently no concern for whether people would know he'd been there.

Felix stayed out of his way. He tucked a few things into his pockets, interesting items Sunshine had pushed off shelves or turned out of drawers. He stayed right behind the angel, keeping a close eye on him.

Sunshine yanked open a drawer.

Felix saw that green-silver glint of the blade and shoved Sunshine out of the way to get to it.

The angel stumbled.

Felix snatched the knife and darted out of the room and out of the house. He picked up a full out run once he made it out of the house.

He darted into the woods, at the same time trying to root around in his bag for his amulet. With one hand, he managed to find the chain of the amulet and slip it over his head. Once he did that, he dropped his bag and kept running until he found a fallen tree where he could hide himself away.

He didn't have time to craft a spell, nor did he have one tucked away for a moment like this. Instead of drawing on arcane magic, he dredged up everything from the well within himself and shoved it into the knife.

It was artless and imprecise. Messy. Everything people feared about innate magic.

The blade crumbled into dust. The handle shattered.

Felix dropped it to cover his eyes but felt the handle shards embed themselves in his arm.

He could hear the angel shouting, about ten yards away, and then let out an odd grunting whine.

"Specter!" the angel roared.

Felix curled in tighter on himself. He wondered how long he could stay in the woods, how long the angel would look for him here.

He could probably sneak out. He'd never had a problem making himself light-footed. He'd liked to sneak up on Jangles sometimes.

And out of his room.

The crashes of Sunshine through the forest came closer.

"Specter!" he called again.

He did this for some time then abruptly went quiet, which unnerved Felix too much to move.

The angel wouldn't have given up so fast.

Felix burrowed deeper against the tree.

After about fifteen minutes, or perhaps an entire century, he heard footsteps again. Almost silent and sometimes accompanied by the sound of something he couldn't quite identify. Some kind of rustling.

Then he saw the angel.

He forced himself not to move, not to make a sound.

He even held his breath.

If Felix had good hearing, how well could a full-blooded angel hear? He could probably hear Felix's heartbeat.

He tried to comfort himself. Surely the Devil had stronger powers than a mere soldier, one of many copies.

Sunshine moved close enough for Felix to grab. He had a long stick in one hand and used it to methodically poke around everywhere that could serve as a hiding place.

Felix would have to run again.

The stick nearly made contact with his shoe.

Then Sunshine jabbed him hard, right in the chest.

All his breath escaped in one ragged wheeze.

Sunshine pounced before Felix could stand and flee. He locked himself around Felix and then they were wrestling on the ground, sticks and leaves finding their ways into unpleasant places.

Felix grasped for his magic, but he couldn't hold it, he couldn't think, he couldn't do anything except try to scramble away, kicking and writhing. Pointless little flashes of power escaped him here and there, singeing a leaf, snapping a twig, doing nothing to the angel.

Sunshine pinned him, his hands ripping at Felix's clothes. His face had twisted into a sneer, and he had an odd, unfocused look in his eyes. Finally, his fingers closed around Felix's throat.

A desperate sob escaped Felix. He reached again for his magic, tried to think of any spell. He had power called up but clogged his senses as badly as his panic, making it nearly as useless. He shoved his hand against the angel's face, trying to push him away. His hand started to burn, hotter and hotter until he couldn't hold it anymore. "Get off, get off," he begged and then, awfully, started to sob, "Please please let me go *please Sunshine.*"

The angel yanked his hand back.

The chain around his neck pinched him as it broke.

Sunshine's eyes came back into focus and he stared down at Felix, still pinning him with his weight and legs alone.

Felix kept trying to twist away. Again, horribly, he said, "*Please.*"

"My knife."

"Let me go, let me go." He'd never been so scared in all his life and he had no idea why. He'd been in fights and he'd never felt like this. Even when he'd gotten his ass handed to him, he'd never been afraid. Now he couldn't even think, he couldn't do anything but squirm and cry and beg.

His hand hurt, really hurt, and he couldn't breathe.

Sunshine swung his leg over Felix and knelt beside him in the dirt.

Felix scrambled away but ended up backed against a bramble. He almost turned and tried to crawl through it, but he put his wounded hand down hard on a stick and yowled.

"I won't hurt you," Sunshine said, his voice so soft that the words slid right through Felix's brain.

He kept trying to crawl through the tangle of sticks and saplings. His clothes snagged and he could barely move.

Sunshine said, "I won't hurt you."

A keen escaped Felix. He'd never been so ashamed of himself in all his life. He didn't do this. He was brave and clever and stubborn; he *wasn't* afraid of anything, especially not angels.

Sunshine grabbed him and hauled him out of the bramble. He

set Felix on the ground but kept his grip on Felix's arms. "I won't hurt you." This time his voice came clear, insistent but also warm and soothing.

Felix met his eyes.

Sunshine gazed back, absolutely exuding warmth and stability.

Felix swallowed.

Slowly, he settled.

He could breathe.

He could think.

He stopped crying.

Sunshine let him go.

The warmth faded, leaving a weird hollowness in Felix.

Sunshine sat back, his legs crisscrossed with his hands on his thighs.

"What the fuck?" Felix asked.

"You were in a panic. It happens sometimes to soldiers, too. One...one of the things I can do is calm that," Sunshine explained.

"And the rest of it?" Felix demanded.

Sunshine raised his eyebrows.

"Well!"

"You stole my knife. And ran. And hid. And...what did you do to it?"

"I broke it."

Sunshine nodded. He touched his hand to his abdomen. "I felt it. Like a punch. I thought..."

"I'd attacked you?"

"I don't know. I just...I looked for you for twenty-six years. I..." Sunshine licked his lips. He looked down at his lap. "I'd never find you again."

Felix wiped his face on his sleeve, though he didn't feel any cleaner for it. His hand hurt like a son of a bitch. He shrugged off his jacket and picked out the handle shards that had burrowed into his arm.

Sunshine watched.

"With the knife? You know I had to, right?" Felix said.

"You didn't have to."

"How could I have something like that on Earth? You said it was dangerous for mortals to wield and, you know, I'm not exactly keen for *you* to get something like that back, either."

"You could have said something," Sunshine pointed out.

"You don't listen." Felix examined his hand instead of looking at Sunshine.

Sunshine held out the amulet to him.

Felix didn't take it. He stood, brushed himself off as well as he could, then put on his jacket. "Let's go find my bag."

Sunshine pointed to where he'd dropped it.

Felix took back the amulet and stowed it in the bag again. "Where do we go from here, Sunshine?"

"I don't know. The woman no longer has my knife. Perhaps we should return to your home and see if the other members of her sect are still in your city."

"And, uh." Felix didn't know how to ask. He didn't even know what exactly he wanted to ask. "When you said you won't hurt me...Is that...is that just for now or...?"

"I don't know."

Felix nodded. He started walking out of the woods.

Finding a way out didn't take much effort. He'd left a pretty good trail when he'd barged through here on the way in.

No wonder Sunshine had been able to find him.

One more half-baked, dumb idea that should have gotten him killed.

They set off across the lawn and Felix said, "I really could go for a swim."

He heard Sunshine stumble behind him. He glanced back to find Sunshine kneeling on the ground and trying to push himself up. He had a smear of something across one cheek.

"Run," the angel said.

A dozen people emerged from various points around the ground.

Felix flicked a conjured glass dart in their direction and winged one person in the thigh. Another projectile came hurtling toward him and clipped him in the shoulder. He stooped to try and pull Sunshine along.

A sickly sweet, almost rotten smell gagged him.

Another clod of something hit him in the chest and splattered up onto his face.

It reeked of rotten flowers.

Felix went weak all over. He tried to stand, tried to drag Sunshine, but he fell face-first into the grass instead.

IT WAS bright.

It hurt his eyes even closed.

He tried to raise a hand to ward off the light but couldn't move. His arms were bound tight behind his back.

He squinted, tried to look around, but all he could do in the end was turn his face as far from the light as he could.

From beyond the light, a voice demanded, "Why did you come here?"

"I can't see anything," he said.

"Answer."

"I can't even think!" Felix protested. "With the light like that."

The hard toe of a boot collided with his shin.

He yelped.

"Why are you here, beast?" the same voice pressed. It was a man's voice, probably an older man. Older, but not elderly, still vital and apparently not happy at all to meet Felix.

Felix thought of a smart answer, one meant to piss off his captor, but he choked it back, thinking of Papa's missing hand, the scar beneath his eye, the scars on Bibi's body still there even after a hundred years.

He knew his strengths.

He was not a physical sort of person.

"A woman took an artifact from…from my traveling

companion," Felix said, his eyes still squeezed shut as hard as he could get them, his face shrugged into his shoulder. "I told him we'd get it back."

He pulled up his magic but found it nowhere. His pulse spiked.

"What artifact?"

Felix hesitated.

They'd had the knife already, hidden it, they must have figured out something about it.

"Just a knife."

The owner of the voice slapped something thin and hard across his leg.

A switch. He'd been goddamn switched.

Felix hissed and squirmed. He insisted, "It's a knife, I don't know anything more about it!"

"What did you do with it?"

"Got rid of it."

"Where is it?" the voice demanded.

"It's gone. It's shattered," Felix said.

In a rush of air and sound, the owner of the voice toppled his chair over. It skittered back a foot, finally giving him respite from the searing light. His eyes were watering. He tried to curl in on himself, tried to pull up a little defensive magic, but again, he felt nothing.

The switch bit into his arm again.

"Where is it!"

"I destroyed it!" Felix hollered back, finally able to see his captor. A medium sized man, gray-haired and broad-faced. Unremarkable. Hazel eyes and a neat, plain suit. "It's gone, you fucking madman."

The man growled. He spat on Felix.

Something about the glob of wet slime on his face bothered Felix more than the blows. "Untie me, coward, and I'll show you exactly what I did to it."

"Silence."

"Fuck you!"

The switch slapped against his thigh this time. "Silence."

It hurt, really seared something fierce to be hit like that, but more than anything it made his blood boil. He wasn't some naughty child.

"Fuck you! Fuck you, do you know who I am!" Felix shouted

back, knowing how spoiled he sounded as he said it. "I'm a prince of hell—"

"Hell has a thousand so-called princes," the man said. "You are as common as a whore's bastard. It means nothing. You will die like every other monster."

"People know I'm here—"

"Good," the man said. "They will die when they come to look for you."

Felix tried to kick himself away, tried to think of something else to threaten, but the only thing he could think of was, "Fuck you," again.

The man grabbed onto his ankle and dragged him back. He took something out of his pocket and shoved it into Felix's face.

He tried to turn away, that same sickly, rotten smell flooding his senses. He could even taste it.

He struggled, but not for long.

FELIX WOKE in the dark.

It was wet here, and warm, and the air had a mineral tang to it.

His hand still hurt, which told him he hadn't been out for too long. A burn like that would take a day or two to heal at least. He flexed his fingers and thought this might take a week or so to fully get better.

He tried to conjure light but couldn't pull his magic out of his body. It was like trying to force a marble through cheesecloth and he thought if he pulled too hard he'd hurt himself.

He checked his wrists but found no cuff.

He felt around and found bars that, when he touched them, made his back teeth ache.

"Sunshine?"

Something moved.

Nearby, too.

He blinked a few times and could make out a vague shape in the corner. He nudged it with his foot.

The shape grunted and swatted at him.

"That you, Sunshine?"

"Yes."

Felix grinned, despite himself. He went to sit beside him. He didn't know if he was glad to find the angel or just glad he wasn't sharing a cell with a stranger. "How do you feel?"

"My head hurts. I feel sick to my stomach. And I'm thirsty."

"Yeah, I was thinking I felt hungover, too." His tongue stuck to the roof of his mouth. "What…What happened?"

"You fainted."

"So did you," Felix pointed out.

"No. It took four of them to subdue me," Sunshine said. After a few seconds, he added, "Then I fainted."

"Ah."

"Were you questioned?" the angel asked.

Felix nodded, remembered the darkness, and said, "Yes. You?"

"Yes."

"And what did you tell them?" Felix asked.

"That the antichrist destroyed my blade," Sunshine said. "Did you tell them something different?"

"No. You told them I was the antichrist?"

"It seems to be knowledge to everyone but you," Sunshine said.

"Mmm," Felix said. His parents had not told him many things. A lot of them weren't things that should be told to a child, and he didn't blame them for never bringing it up. They still thought of him as a child.

He deserved it.

He acted like a child.

Look where it had gotten him.

He was lucky he hadn't ended up in a situation like this sooner.

The angel quieted for a moment. He drew in a breath, then asked, "Why subdue us? What's the purpose of holding us here?"

Felix rubbed his nose. "Uh."

"What?"

"So. Moralists kind of like to burn people at the stake."

"What?"

"Yeah. Like. As a ritual. A symbolic way to demonstrate their cleansing of the inhuman from the Earth," Felix explained. "I don't think they've done it lately. Too showy. But…you know. Burning the antichrist might really be the feather in their cap," Felix mused. "That's a guess. Hopefully a wild one."

"Do you make a lot of wild guesses?"

"Usually, I make calculatedly unreasonable ones."

"I don't know what that means," Sunshine said.

Felix gave pulling up magic another shot. It produced the same uncomfortable pressure. "What about, Sunshine? Can you use your magic?"

"Angels don't do magic."

Felix scoffed. "Can you tap into your well of divine grace and mercy?"

Sunshine made a disgruntled noise and Felix thought, if he could have seen his face, he would have been scowling. He said, "No. It's...it's stuck."

"Alright, well."

"Well?" Sunshine asked.

"Well, I think we're fucked. Do you have your sword?"

"No."

Felix stood and made a careful examination of the area. Most details he discerned by touch since he couldn't see more than an inch or so in front of his face, and that was only shadow against darkness.

Stone at their back, dirt beneath their feet, and bars on the other four sides. He could feel the bars above him. If he'd been much taller, he would have hit his head standing up. "About ten paces by six paces," he told Sunshine.

He could fit his arm between the bars up to his elbow even if doing so made it feel like his bones would vibrate out of his skin.

He returned to crouch next to Sunshine. Sitting had made the seat of his trousers damp.

Every so often something would drip from the ceiling.

"Any ideas?" he asked after listening to the drips and echoes.

"I hear water."

Felix listened.

A drop of liquid against the surface of a larger pool. Still water. Larger than a puddle.

He felt around and found a pebble and flicked it toward the water.

It plunked into the water.

"I think we're in a cave. Probably one that feeds the spring," Felix guessed.

Sunshine sighed. He hadn't moved. He hadn't explored the cell at all or made any guesses as to their situation.

Felix settled back and seated himself, resigned to having wet trousers. He didn't hear anything but water and their bodies, so he felt safe saying, "They probably don't plan to leave us here to starve. And they can't see in the dark. That means they'll come for us eventually, and they'll come with light. We can make a move then."

Sunshine didn't answer.

Felix poked him. "Just checking to see if you're still alive."

"I'm fine," came the angel's answer through gritted teeth.

"We'll be okay, Sunshine," Felix promised and tried to sound like he meant it.

"Why are you like this?" The question didn't come snappishly, but with a grave sort of wonder tinged with desperation.

"Like what?" Felix asked.

"You..." A strangled sound of frustration came from the angel. "Why do you act like this?"

"I." Felix sighed. "I don't know. I guess...I probably have something to prove. Famous parents and all that."

"What are you proving by treating me this way?"

Felix hadn't expected that question. He didn't know exactly what the angel meant by that. He didn't think he'd treated the angel any particular way. "I only meant I act a little irresponsible sometimes. That I show off. I don't think I've done anything to you. I mean. Other than the kidnapping thing but that...All of this. I got in over my head. It wasn't a misunderstanding, Sunshine, but I'm. I couldn't kill you. Or anyone, probably. I only wanted to stop looking over my shoulder all the time."

Sunshine sighed.

"It was stupid of me to think I could stand against Heaven. I. This isn't how I pictured it. Dying. Burnt at the stake was not high on my list of ways to go. I probably would have been better off if you'd finished the job when I was little. That would have been quick, at least. Right?"

"No."

Felix glanced toward the sound of his voice.

Sunshine seemed to realize he'd misspoken. "I didn't...I wouldn't have made it painful, not more than it had to be. But...but don't talk like that. Don't talk about dying. Or me killing you."

Felix felt around in the dark. His fingers brushed against the side of Sunshine's leg.

Sunshine leaned his leg into Felix's touch.

It felt bizarre, sitting in the dark, silent, with the backs of his fingers against the angel's thigh. But he left his hand there. He stayed quiet.

They both did.

Sunshine made a sound, an aborted sniffle that he swallowed.

"We'll get out of here."

The angel grabbed his hand. "I don't want to kill you."

Felix held on. "I don't want to kill you either."

"I don't...I can't go home but I can't do this either. I can't." His voice sounded thick.

Felix took his hand back because he couldn't bear the burning any longer. His palm still hurt from before. He fumbled to put his hand on Sunshine's back. "You'll figure something out."

Sunshine curled in on himself. He didn't cry or sob, not exactly, but he shook and sniffled.

With no idea what else to do, Felix gave the angel's back a rub. "I guess it is your turn to feel bad for yourself."

After a few more sniffles, Sunshine scooted away from Felix. He cleared his throat, then stood.

Felix could hear him pace around the cell. He wished he could see him so he could at least try to read his expression. "My parents would be *furious* if they could see us now..." he mused.

The sound of Sunshine pacing stopped. His shoes scraped against the ground, but Felix couldn't tell if he'd turned toward or away from him. "Are you going to tell them?" he asked, his voice wavering a little.

"Oh, well...Well, they wouldn't be mad at *you*," Felix said. "They know I'm...well, just a little bit impossible."

"They said to keep you safe. This...this isn't safe."

"Come sit down."

"We need to find a way out."

"There isn't a way out."

"You don't know everything," Sunshine snapped.

Felix made a face and settled back. He really couldn't see anything. "Sunshine, come sit down. We won't get out of here until they take us out. No use in wasting energy like that."

"I can't do nothing."

"Sometimes there's nothing to do, Sunshine."

The angel kept pacing.

Felix sighed. He forced himself to stand and made his way over to Sunshine. He felt around and grabbed Sunshine by the shoulders. He gave a bit of a squeeze, then turned the angel around so he wouldn't be speaking to the back of his head.

"What are you doing?"

"There's nothing we can do, Sunshine. We just have to wait. Didn't you wait in front of my school for two weeks?"

"God graced me with patience."

"So be patient, hmm? Come sit."

Sunshine sighed. "Your school wasn't in a pitch-black cave."

"That would have been an awful place for a school." Felix gave his shoulders a gentle shake. "Come sit down." He pulled at Sunshine, who resisted at first.

Then Sunshine shrugged Felix's hands off. He pushed past Felix with a huff.

Felix heard him sit and went to sit next to him. Not too close, of course. He found himself sort of wanting to be close to the angel. He knew enough about himself to know he got attached easily.

More easily than he should have, really.

He'd probably learned it from his parents, all three of them.

He wondered how differently his mother would have raised him. He almost leaned against Sunshine. He managed not to do that but couldn't manage to stop himself from chattering. "So, I really did mean it. Tell me about yourself. I mean, you've met my parents and seen my house, all I've done is get your spit in my wounds."

"I don't know what to tell you."

"Well, where do you rest that lovely head of curls at night?" Felix asked.

Sunshine stayed quiet for several long seconds. "Wherever seems safe."

A soft, "Oh," slipped out of Felix's mouth. What could he say to that? "Every night?"

"As long as I've been here."

"That's horrible."

"It's my fault."

"How's that?" Felix asked.

"It shouldn't have taken this long. If I hadn't failed so miserably in this..." Sunshine stopped. He sighed. "I should be home already."

"I don't think it's such a miserable failure."

"I fail at everything."

"Oh, no, I don't think so," Felix offered awkwardly.

Sunshine went quiet for a while. When he did speak again, he sounded unsure of what he wanted to say. "What...what about your, uh. Your home. Your parents. They...they care about you."

Felix made a face, pained by the sheer awkwardness of the angel's attempt. Still, he'd tried. Felix wanted to encourage that. "Yeah, they're swell. I lucked out with the two of them. Especially with Papa. He's no fan of my father and, well, most mages think of creatures like me as lab animals more than people. It could have gone awfully sideways especially considering how old he is."

"He looks young."

"Ah, that's a story for a different time," Felix said, then realized they had nowhere to be and little else to talk about at present. "Actually, do you want to know how they met?"

"Yes?" the angel said.

"Alright. Well. I guess..." Felix thought about the best way to tell the story and eventually had to say, "So Papa was born on a plantation. As an owner, not a slave, obviously." Then he cringed at himself. Plenty of people had been born into slavery on plantations and could have passed for white. "Well. Maybe not so obviously, but anyway, the point is, his father owned it and he was going to own it too. The land and the people. Do you follow?"

"No."

"Where did I lose you?"

"A plantation is...is a big farm, right?" Sunshine asked. "And the slaves were from...Africa? I think I remember that much but...time moves differently in Heaven, and I'll admit that the soldiers don't always pay attention to what happens here. It's not within our scope."

"Well, it's about to be. So, yeah, a plantation is a cash crop estate and the slaves were Africans, or their descendants, for the most part. They were brutal places, those plantations," Felix said and continued with the history lesson.

He had a lot to draw on, from his father's accounts to the journals his niece had kept about what she remembered and what her mother and grandmother had told her, as well as her reports of the Civil War.

She had convinced Papa to return to Fall's Hill with her and use the long-abandoned plantation to benefit the Union war effort, but more importantly, to give refuge to the black bodies caught in the crossfire of the war, runaways and freedmen alike.

When the war had ended, they had returned home to their families, leaving the plantation in the hands of those who could continue their efforts toward equity. As far as he knew, Papa still sent them money for their cause, but the group had left the plantation and moved into a building in Thomasville when a fairly severe haunting had started up.

It took about two hours to get to the part where Papa and Bibi met, but Sunshine listened the whole time and Felix didn't get the feeling he was just being polite. Felix didn't think Sunshine knew how to be polite, even if he wanted to.

He wrapped up saying, "And then about a year later, they got married. Or, you know, to the best of their legal ability, they bound themselves to each other. They had had a very nice ceremony, though. I would have *loved* to see that or at least a photograph. Bibi still has their outfit packed away upstairs. It is absolutely the most gorgeous embroidery I've ever seen..."

The sound of distant footsteps caught his ear.

He reached out and shushed Sunshine even though the angel hadn't made a peep.

A speck of light bobbed in the distance.

The two of them sat in silence, unmoving, while the light moved closer and closer.

Soon enough, Felix could pick out the figure of a woman carrying a storm lantern and a paper bag.

Part of him thought it might be Grace. He didn't want to see her and couldn't stop replaying how easily she'd fooled him. His heart pattered at the thought of seeing her, then his stomach flipped when the woman came close enough for him to see that it wasn't her.

This woman had her hair twisted into a chignon and wore a plain black dress. It almost looked like a uniform or at least part of one.

As she stood just in front of the bars, the darkness of her complexion showed itself to be more than the result of shadows. She had dark brown skin and even, full features that walked the line between the prettiness of youth and the elegance of womanhood.

She set down the lantern and the paper bag.

Felix moved.

She stepped back and warned, "Don't try anything funny."

"Ma'am, I wouldn't dream of it," he assured.

She raised an eyebrow.

He smiled. "It's just that we've been down here for a while. We weren't sure what...what, uh, the big plan was for us."

"I just work here," she said.

"Well. My name's Felix. This is Sunshine."

Sunshine didn't move.

Felix elbowed him.

"Hello," Sunshine said.

She picked up the lantern and peered at them, leaning closer to the bars. "Marceline Roy."

"You work at the spa?"

She nodded.

"And does that usually involve checking on prisoners?"

"It usually involves doing laundry. The folks in this town...Some of the older ones, they're superstitious about a lot of things. Mr. DeVries said he had a pair of monsters down here, that they caught you tearing apart the staff housing," she said. She looked over Felix and Sunshine again. "I guess that makes you the monsters."

"Funnily enough, I'm the monster, but it was my friend Sunshine who trashed the house and he's not a monster at all."

"You're both pretty normal looking, whatever you are."

Felix stood up and came closer to the bars. He smiled again. "You'd be surprised how normal most monsters look."

She rolled her eyes. "Let me guess: you're a vampire."

He laughed. "No, but I get that a lot."

"This is unwise," Sunshine said from behind him.

Felix startled. He hadn't noticed the angel stand up, too busy talking to Marceline. "Sorry?"

"The last time you made advances towards a female from this cult, she wounded and poisoned you," Sunshine reminded coldly.

Felix's eyes widened. He glanced toward Marceline. "It's not particularly polite to call women 'females', first off. And I'm not making advances." To Marceline said, "Not that...Not that I wouldn't...Not make advances, that's...I was raised better than that, you know, but not that I wouldn't be interested in..." He sighed. He waved a hand at Sunshine. "Look at you, making me put my foot in my mouth. I absolutely can't take you anywhere."

"We're in a cage," Sunshine said.

Felix turned away from Sunshine and addressed Marceline, "I have to apologize. We've been having a *week* and my manners aren't at their best."

"Mr. DeVries would lose his mind if he knew I was talking to you. I'm only supposed to bring that down," she said with a glance toward the paper bag she'd set down.

"I sympathize entirely with that. Can I just ask one more thing?"

She nodded.

"Are you a Moralist or do you only work for them?"

"My family worked for the DeVries family since before they had to pay us."

"Ah. I see. So your loyalties lie with them?"

"That's more than one question." She bent to pick up the lantern.

Desperate, Felix stepped forward.

She moved back.

"Please. I'm begging you, if you can let us out of here, I'll give you anything within my power to give you."

"I'll lose my job."

"I think they're going to kill us, Ms. Roy," Felix implored. "If you're worried about money, I'll give you however much you want. I'll find you a new job. My family's well connected, and we have money, and I'm actually begging you."

Discomfort flitted over her face. She studied Felix, really looked him over.

"They killed my mother just for having me."

"What are you?"

He pressed his lips together as he gathered his nerve. He never knew what to say to a question like that and given the revelation of his status as an antichrist, he had no idea what to say.

"He is the son of the Beast," Sunshine answered for him.

Marceline turned her eyes toward him. "And what are you?"

"I am an angel."

She shook her head. "No, that's..."

"Look at me and know that the Almighty made me and that I came to Earth to do the will of Heaven," he said, his voice serene.

Felix wanted to touch him. He wanted to wrap his arms around the angel and sink into the warmth of his presence. A voice like that could never lie.

The smallest of smiles graced the angel's face.

Marceline's face softened. "You really are, aren't you?"

"We implore you: help us."

She looked back at Felix. "If he's...If he really is what you said..." She left the question unasked.

"Those who move to destroy him move without knowledge of what they seek to end. The Beast may have sired him, but his fate is not written. We cannot condemn him for what he has not done and may never do."

A few tears dribbled down Marceline's cheeks.

Felix understood.

It was Sunshine's voice and that smile. He was doing something. This had to be another of his powers.

"I have to go," Marceline whispered. "The dishes, I have to go get the dishes done..." She sounded lost. She backed away from the bars.

Felix watched the light of her lantern fade. He groped around for the bag she'd left. Within, he found a thermos of water and a few pieces of bread. He found his way back to the wall, brushing against Sunshine as he went.

"She'll be back," Sunshine said.

Felix felt for his hand, then pressed three slices of bread into it. Just plain white bread, no butter or jam, or a piece of cheese in between. "You think so?"

"It takes humans time to process such an experience. She'll be back."

"I hope so." Felix took a sip of water, then passed that to Sunshine too. "Did you mean that? About my fate not being written."

"Yes."

Felix took an overlarge bite of bread and tried not to think about what Sunshine had said or what would happen if Marceline didn't take a shine to their cause. "You know, this sort of thing happens to the Hardy Boys all the time."

"Who are the Hardy Boys?"

"Oh, it's this book series," Felix said and went on a rambling description of the novels. He talked for what felt like an hour at least before he said, "You've got to be sick to death of listening to me talk by now! I don't ever let you get a word in edgewise, do I?"

"I like listening to you talk."

For once, Felix appreciated the lack of light. His face had flushed hot.

"I've never had anyone to explain things to me."

"Oh, well, we're a family of chatterboxes, between the three of us we could probably explain just about anything."

Sunshine passed the thermos back. "Tell me about your family."

"I told you about them."

"Only the beginning. Tell me the rest."

Felix thought back. "Oh, well, I was talking about the wedding, wasn't I?"

"Yes."

He started back up telling Sunshine about his parents but ended up delving into more about the Academy for Young Learners and the Reinhart-Queen University of Arcane Magics and Sciences, and the subjects he'd studied there.

"So a master's degree, that means you know everything about it?"

Felix laughed. "No, not even close. Even with a doctorate, I wouldn't know everything about magic."

"Why do you study human methods of magic? The Beast's children do such things innately."

"I don't know, why do people learn a second language?" Felix asked.

"I don't know."

"It was rhetorical. That means you don't have to answer it."

"How do you tell the difference?" Sunshine asked.

Felix thought, then finally admitted, "I don't know. You'll have to ask Bibi."

"That one does fascinate me."

"Hmm?"

"It makes sense that a human would find himself drawn to one of the Fallen. Even untied from Heaven as they are, the Fallen were still created by the Almighty, touched by divinity. But for an angel, even a fallen one, to...to marry. To have a child. A family," Sunshine mused.

"It happens a lot."

"Life in this realm is empty. Cold and harsh compared to home. How could an angel turn away from the Almighty for a life here? How can any fleshly pleasure compare to Heaven?"

Felix tittered. "You can ask Bibi that too, but no promises on how they'll take it."

"I don't think any answer could make me understand."

Felix capped the thermos and set it aside for later. "Maybe...you know, maybe wandering Earth in an endless, unattached pursuit of your prey hasn't given you the best perspective of what life here is like. Give sleeping in a bed a chance before you tell the entire realm to get bent."

"I never thought I'd come across one of the Fallen and if I did, I thought I'd pity them. But they look so happy. I feel empty when I see that."

Felix didn't know what to say. He understood what Sunshine meant. He understood the loneliness of not belonging, but at least he had somewhere he belonged. No matter what happened or what he did, he could always go home. Sunshine might never have that. Felix couldn't imagine him staying on Earth, but Sunshine made it sound like he couldn't return to Heaven while Felix still breathed.

"We could fake it," Felix proposed.

"Fake what?"

"My death."

"No. There are no lies in Heaven. We are all one thing and the Almighty can see every part of us. He would know my deception."

"Oh."

They sat in silence for a while until Sunshine asked, "How does the book end?"

"Hmm?"

"The Shadow."

"Oh, I can't tell you! You have to wait for me to read it," Felix insisted. He hoped he sounded optimistic instead of delusional.

"What if we can't get your bag back?"

Felix snorted. It was a funny concern to have but a sensible one. "Well, it's probably with your sword and I figure you're gonna be as stubborn about that as you were about your knife."

Sunshine said nothing.

"I can't see you scowling in the dark."

"I'm not scowling."

"That's a first."

Sunshine made a disgruntled sound.

"*Now* you're scowling," Felix said.

Sunshine pushed him, not hard at all.

Felix nudged him back.

FELIX HAD dozed off, more out of boredom than tiredness. He didn't exactly rest peacefully, either, too uncomfortable and nervous, not to mention damp.

"Felix, wake up," Sunshine's voice came soft and warm to his ears.

Immediately, Felix said, "Who gave you permission to use my Christian name? It is Mr. Specter if you must speak to me."

"I..."

Felix pushed himself up from the ground and brushed the film of dirt from his cheek.

"I only wanted to tell you I think Marceline is coming back." Sunshine sounded worried.

"It was just a joke," Felix assured. "If I were going to insist on formalities, I'd make you call me Your Highness. I am a prince, after all." As he spoke, he scanned the darkness and located the same orange light as last time. "I do hate to meet someone under these circumstances. I must look a fright."

He could smell himself, not just that he was unwashed, but that he'd crawled through the woods and slept in the dirt. The remains of whatever they'd thrown at him still clung to his shirt, dried into a crust that smelled of rotten leaves and dead flowers.

"I'm going to bathe for an entire day when this is over."

"That seems excessive."

"Someday I'll get you to grasp the concept of hyperbole," Felix said.

"Which is?"

Felix sighed. He had to start keeping his catty comments to himself, it was like picking on a five-year-old. "Hyperbole is a literary device used to indicate extreme exaggeration."

"Thank you."

Felix glanced toward the sound of his voice. He sounded so sincere. "You know, you've got to start telling me off when I get mean like that."

"Far be it from me to correct Your Highness's manners."

Felix snorted.

Marceline, and the lantern light revealed it was her, had come close enough that he could wave. She carried with her Felix's bag and Sunshine's sword. "They're inviting people from all over to watch you burn. I...I couldn't. Even if you are what you say you are, I couldn't let anyone go through that. Mrs. DeVries wanted me to plan a menu for two hundred." She looked at Sunshine, reverence and a small amount of guilt on her face. "And I wouldn't be a very good Christian if I left you down here, would I?"

"Thank you for coming back," Sunshine said.

She set down the lantern and the other things she'd brought. "The...the only thing is if I do this—and I will! But when I do, I can't stay here. I don't exactly have the means to get myself anywhere else."

"Anywhere it is that you need to go, we'll get you there," Felix assured.

She nodded. She took a key out of her pocket, her hands unsteady, and unlocked the cage.

Felix thought he might throw up. After everything that had happened, it felt impossible that a stranger would help them. He hoped most people would do the same in Marceline's shoes, but he'd started to worry that he could depend on anyone to do the right thing. He'd read enough about the horrible things people could do to each other, the things they'd let other people do, and he kept waiting for Marceline to change her mind.

Their lives might not be worth her job.

She swung the door open.

Felix nearly bounced out of the cage. His first instinct was to hug Marceline but given how little they knew each other and how dirty he was, he settled on saying, "I owe you my life."

"Nobody deserves to die like that."

Sunshine fastened his sword across his back. He moved toward the way Marceline had come in.

"No, not that way," she said. "That comes out right up by the house and it's so busy they'll see us for sure. It's like they're planning a wedding. We need to go in deeper to get out."

Felix stared toward the way she'd come.

Who was up there?

Grace, surely, and that awful man who'd knocked him around, and dozens of others who'd do the same to him or worse.

Still.

He was a prince of Hell. He knew magics of many kinds. He had, temporarily, an angel on his side. He was the antichrist, apparently, too, and what that had in store, he had no idea. He was a powerful being by all accounts.

He had all that and here he was, filthy and totally dependent on the goodwill of a stranger.

He had invited his mother's killers to his home and now the only people he really had in the world were cleaning up that mess for him.

Hopefully.

Hopefully, he hadn't gotten them killed too.

He shoved that thought down.

"I hate the sound of that," Felix murmured. He picked up his bag as well as the other one she'd brought. He tamped down all the discomfort stirring in him. He had to. Otherwise, he'd weep in front of these strangers, in this dark, horrible place.

The bag she'd brought was light. It must have held her belongings. He couldn't imagine she owned much.

"I can carry that," she said and reached for it.

"Gracious, what kind of gentleman would I be if I let my savior carry her own bags?" he asked.

She blinked a few times. "Uh. Then it's this way."

Marceline led them deeper into a cave.

Felix wished he could see, then realized he could cast again. Without thinking about it for more than a second, he dropped back a step, threw up his arms, and conjured as much light as he could. He sent up an orb up toward the ceiling and watched it fill the cavern with a reaching silver glow.

Stalactites hung from the ceiling and the light gave their slick surfaces a sheen. The water below them glittered darkly and stretched out past what his light illuminated.

"Oh, isn't it beautiful, Sunshine?" Felix asked.

"It looks wet."

"Yes, thank you for that." He turned back to Marceline and found her with her mouth covered and her eyes wide. His light reflected in her eyes.

"What is that?" she whispered.

"Oh, just a bit of magic. I can, I can get rid of it," he said. He forgot how people outside the Community reacted to magic. He'd scared a child to tears once trying to show her a trick.

"You made that."

"Sorry."

"You made that," she repeated.

He nodded. He reached up and tugged the light back down, making it smaller and dimmer. "I'm sorry, I didn't mean to startle you, Ms. Roy."

"No, it's lovely."

He looked at the orb in his hand. He glanced up at Marceline and gave her a bashful smile.

"We should keep moving," Sunshine said.

"Of course," Marceline said. She turned back but did look over her shoulder once as she started walking.

"Is...?" Felix began.

Marceline looked back.

"There was a girl. A young woman. Her name was Grace."

"Oh." Marceline's voice came flat. "Her."

"She's still here?"

Marceline confirmed, "She's staying with the DeVries."

"I didn't like her either," Sunshine offered freely from behind Felix's shoulder.

Marceline made a sound that might have been a suppressed giggle.

"I don't think she was exactly at her best," Felix said.

Sunshine sighed.

"Well!" Felix said but didn't have anything to follow up with.

"She a friend of yours?" Marceline asked.

"No, not...Not by a long shot, I figure. We actually came here to get something from her," Felix said, "Something she stole."

"My knife," Sunshine said as if on cue.

"That was your knife? Mr. DeVries had Jonathan hide it from her."

"It should not have been in mortal hands," Sunshine agreed.

"Oh, I don't know if that's what he thought, but he didn't like the idea of someone like her having it. I guess they have ranks, you know, the Moralists. He made that knife seem special, like only the higher-ups should have it. I didn't see much to fuss about."

"It was poisoned," Felix said.

"Makes sense why he fussed about it, then," Marceline said.

"But..." Felix didn't want to ask, not with Sunshine listening. "How did Grace seem?"

Marceline didn't answer for a bit. "Maybe you don't really want to know."

"I'd appreciate it if you'd share."

Slowly, she revealed, "She seemed excited for them...to do what they were going to do to you. She didn't have a lot of nice things to say about you. Or your mother. And some of the things she came up with...She didn't exactly seem in her right mind."

Felix's stomach flipped and his body went cold. Then he flushed all over. Of course, it had all been an act, she'd sliced him the first chance she'd had.

"A mortal shouldn't carry a weapon with Heavenly purpose," Sunshine explained. "Things of divine making sway mortal hearts too easily. Humanity will always reach for a higher being."

Marceline said, "Toward the Lord."

"Not always," Sunshine offered easily. "Many gods have held the hearts of man, and some men's hearts are held by things of this Earth."

"Many gods?"

"I know little of the others, they do not often visit Heaven and when they do, the Almighty meets them on the Citadel, from which angels have long been barred," Sunshine explained.

"Sunshine, don't scare her," Felix tried to scold. His voice came out raspy and broken, like the angel had scared him. It wasn't hearing about Heaven, he knew all about that. It was Grace and the rest of these Moralists. He'd been stupid. Hopeful. He swallowed, waited until he knew his voice would be even, and asked, "So where are you headed after this, Ms. Roy?"

"My aunt and uncle live in Toronto."

"Oh, so we're headed in the same direction. It'll be nice to have someone to talk to for a change. Sunshine isn't much for conversation. Have you been to Toronto before?"

"A few times when I was younger. Before my father passed

away."

"Oh, I'm sorry."

"It was a while ago."

"Still, I'd be devastated if anything happened to my parents. Um, your aunt and uncle, you're close with them?" he asked.

"Close enough. I have a cousin about the same age as I am, she might need a roommate. She might be able to help me find a job."

He felt the need to say, "I understand what a risk you've taken to help us, to the best of my ability to understand. I meant it when I said I'd repay you."

"Thank you."

They walked for about an hour more before anyone else spoke. Felix had taken his conjured light and moved ahead of the other two. The cave only moved in one direction, so he didn't worry about getting lost.

Behind him, he heard Marceline speaking with Sunshine. They kept their voices low, and Felix tried not to listen in when he realized they were talking about Heaven and God again. He'd long since taken his stance on those things and knew that angels, or at least the Fallen, didn't always like to discuss them either.

Sunshine didn't sound upset, more nostalgic, which didn't surprise Felix. Sunshine hadn't chosen to leave Heaven. Felix probably sounded the same way when he talked about the easy comfort of his childhood. He didn't have the same sort of adult complications that other people his age had, and he still missed how simple things had seemed when he'd been small enough to sit on Bibi's lap.

Although, he reflected, both his parents were so tall he probably could still fit.

Someday he'd have to move out and get a job that required more than his evenings and weekends. He might even settle down.

Maybe.

Kathleen had gotten so set on a wedding and he'd almost entertained the idea until she'd mentioned children, too. A wedding could have been nice. He liked a party.

Children, if he had them, were decades away, not just a few years. He really didn't consider himself the fatherly sort. He liked children and didn't mind having them around, but he didn't feel that urge to have one of his own.

He'd be a good uncle, he figured.

In the end, it wasn't fair to Kathleen. She wouldn't stay young forever and she was a decent mage, but that didn't mean she'd be able to cope with raising demon children or having the Devil as an in-law. She'd still gotten funny about Bibi and she'd known them for years; she'd never been able to quite wrap her head around the idea that Bibi wasn't his mother. She'd understood it in a biological sense but never that Bibi wasn't trying to be a woman.

Eventually, they'd just stopped discussing it. He'd never introduced her to Lucifer.

Anyone he married would need to accept his parents, all three of them, and that Felix wasn't human.

He didn't know where that left him.

Obviously, he wouldn't likely marry another demon. He'd met some that had to count back four or more generations before they reached the Devil, but still, he felt funny about it. He knew people married cousins, or distant cousins, but he didn't know if that would suit him.

Vampires, fairies, and the Fallen would at least live as long as he did. Witches, werewolves, and mages would know enough about the supernatural community that they wouldn't think him a lunatic.

Then again, he considered the various factions and prejudices that lived even within the Community. Witches didn't like demons, vampires had terrible reputations, werewolves tended to stick together, and mages hovered on the outskirts, more interested scientifically than romantically in the supernatural.

It didn't matter.

Papa might have gotten married when he was twenty-six, but Bibi had been hundreds of years old the first time they'd gotten married.

He had time.

He went back to eavesdropping on Marceline and Sunshine.

He got sick of that, too, and dropped back to walk between them. He looped an arm through Sunshine's arm and would have done the same to Marceline if he'd known her a little better. "Darling, really, you haven't got to bore the poor lady to death."

Sunshine frowned.

Felix grinned.

Sunshine extracted his arm from Felix's grip. "She asked."

"I asked," Marceline said.

"And has he entertained you? I've been trying to get him to say something worthwhile for days."

"It's illuminating," Marceline said.

Felix raised an eyebrow. He elbowed Sunshine. "Illuminating. Maybe I'm not the only one who's a sucker for a pretty face."

Sunshine scowled.

Felix widened his smile. He'd missed seeing the angel scowl like that. Or, at least, seeing him scowl was better than assuming he was scowling. Some of his scowls looked more severe than others and Felix liked having that to go by.

This scowl didn't look all that severe. Maybe he didn't have a lot of practice with other expressions. Judging by what Sunshine had said about his life on Earth so far, a scowl had probably done him a lot of good. If Felix had been out looking for food or a place to sleep, he would have avoided someone with a scowl and a sword like Sunshine's.

A small part of Felix thought Sunshine could almost be a person with a little more practice.

He didn't doubt that Sunshine would revoke a lot of the stances he'd taken during their brief captivity. People said a lot of things they didn't mean when they thought they were about to die.

He didn't want to think about that, and he didn't want to talk about Heaven. "Ms. Roy, tell me about yourself."

"I don't figure there's much to tell, Mister..."

"Oh, no, Felix is just fine. And I'm so sure there is at least one thing to tell. We've gotten through names and employment, let's move onto hopes and dreams."

"I..."

Felix smiled. "Sunshine was telling me that his dream was to become a circus acrobat."

"I didn't say that," Sunshine said.

"And I told him I've always wanted to go to the moon."

"You didn't say that."

Felix sighed.

Marceline giggled.

"What have you always wanted to do?" Felix asked.

"I've always wanted to ride a horse."

"Hmm?"

"Mr. and Mrs. DeVries keep horses and I always thought they looked so beautiful."

"Hmm, horses. That's a start. What else?"

"What do you mean?"

Felix said, "I can't be the only person who dreams of other things, can I?"

"Why dream about something you can't ever have?" Marceline asked.

"That absolutely breaks my heart, Ms. Roy," Felix said.

She dropped her eyes and didn't say anything.

Felix waited a while for her to say anything, but she stayed quiet. Finally, he couldn't take it and said, "I meant that. I wasn't trying to be unkind."

"I'm sorry. I didn't mean to make you think that's how I felt."

"I just...I really do hate that this world makes people feel like they can't have dreams. Everyone should have a dream, even if it's just..."

"Riding a horse?" Marceline guessed.

"I suppose it isn't my place to tell your dreams aren't big enough," Felix admitted. To Sunshine, he said, "And I shouldn't have told you that you could never be an acrobat. Any circus would be lucky to have you."

"I never said—"

"Darling! Please, I'm only teasing, no need to get yourself worked up," Felix scolded gently.

Marceline glanced between them.

Felix wished he hadn't said anything and then wished he hadn't felt ashamed of what Marceline might have assumed. He hated that fake explanations and excuses ran through his head. He especially hated that he had thought to blame his parents for his behavior.

His parents had tried so hard to keep that sort of shame out of his life, but the world hadn't made it easy for them.

He rubbed his nose and moved ahead of the other two.

He needed to get out of this cave.

He needed to go home.

He clenched his teeth and kept himself quiet, but he couldn't keep his eyes dry. He stayed far enough ahead of the others that they couldn't see him wiping his face.

It took about two hours to walk through the cave.

Felix didn't realize they'd gotten close to the entrance until he felt leaves and sticks under his shoes.

It was dark outside, and they'd come out in the middle of the woods. The leaves created a canopy thick enough to obscure the moon and stars.

He made his light a little brighter and held it up.

"Ms. Roy, please don't take this as me not having faith in you, but I don't see much of a path to follow among these trees," Felix said.

"I know the way to town."

Felix looked around again.

"You're a city boy, aren't you?" she asked.

He blushed. "It's a small city."

She stepped in front of him and easily found her way to a small trail footpath that was little more than a swath of cleared leaves. "It's about twenty minutes to town."

"I'm going to suggest you for the Order of Merit," Felix told her.

"You really do like to tease people, don't you?" she asked.

"It should be taken as a gesture of affection," he said.

Once in town, she brought them around back to one of the hotels. She rapped on the door and a man in his thirties answered.

"Is Sam working?"

"Sure is."

"Do you think you can send him out to talk for a minute?"

"He's busy, Marceline."

"It's important," she said.

"He'll come out to talk at the end of his shift. I don't know what you're doing up in the middle of the night either."

Her face stayed neutral. "Do you think we could come in then? Seeing how it's the middle of the night."

The man sighed. "As long as you stay out of the way."

He brought them to a back room off the hotel kitchen. It looked like a changing room of sorts. Everyone in the kitchen had worn a uniform.

Felix found the bathroom and did his best to clean up. He thought about changing his clothes but putting clean clothes on his still mostly dirty body didn't make sense. He felt a little better with his face and hands washed, at least. He'd scrub up better on the train.

He stretched out on one of the benches and used his bag as a pillow. "So. What's the story with Sam?" he asked Marceline.

"I'm hoping he'll give us a ride to the train station," she said.

"Ah." He folded his hands over his stomach and closed his eyes. "I'm not going to sleep."

After about two hours, a man the same age as Felix and Marceline came into the room.

"Mr. Wallace said you were looking for me?"

"I need a ride, Sam," Marceline told him.

He frowned. "A ride where?"

"To the train station."

Sam's eyes went wide and his lips parted. He pulled in a breath. "Why?"

Felix had a funny feeling he was about to witness something uncomfortable. A break-up or a family farewell. He sat up and tried to make himself a better part of the background.

"Because I'm leaving. And you're the only one I can ask."

Sam shook his head. "You can't go."

"Sam, I'm going. You don't have a say in that. You only have a say in whether you drive me to the train station or not."

Sam looked at Sunshine and Felix. "Marceline, can we talk somewhere private?"

"Sunshine and I can wait outside. Find us when you're ready," Felix said. He tugged on Sunshine's sleeve.

They stood around quietly outside.

Felix nudged a garbage bag with his shoe. He sighed and rolled his shoulders and paced around.

"What happened to being patient?" Sunshine asked.

"Sunshine," Felix scolded, "Don't expect me to take my own advice."

Sunshine shook his head.

Felix fished his wallet out of his bag and went to count how much he had left. He slipped his fingers inside and found it empty. "Uh-oh."

"What?"

He dropped to his knees to see what else had been taken. He couldn't find his amulet.

"What?" Sunshine asked.

"They went through my bag." He'd packed light at least, so there hadn't been much to take, but not having any cash certainly put a damper on his situation.

He checked every part of the bag to see if he'd missed anything.

He found a few dollars folded and tucked into one of his books. Not much help there.

He ran his fingers along the bottom of the bag and found a small set of stitches in the corner. The thread had almost exactly the same color as the fabric. He hadn't put them there, but the bag had belonged to Bibi first. He felt around the stitches, then tore the fabric when he felt something in the lining of the bag.

"What are you doing?" Sunshine asked.

Felix pulled out a leather wallet. He peeked inside then gasped.

"What?" Sunshine demanded.

Felix stood, took Sunshine's hand, and tipped out dozens of loose gems, rings, and earrings. He grinned and let out a manic giggle. He pulled his hand back. "Bibi used to be a bit of a thief."

He remembered Bibi buying this bag, though, which meant 'used to' was a lot more recent than Felix had thought.

The gems didn't exactly solve his problem, but they made things easier.

"Do you think this town had a pawn shop? Or...do you think you can buy a train ticket with jewelry?"

"I don't know."

Felix opened the wallet and held it out to Sunshine, who carefully tipped everything back into the mouth. He snapped it shut and slipped it back into the bag. "Maybe Marceline can give us an idea. She seems like she's got a good head on her shoulders."

"You shouldn't entangle yourself with anyone right now."

"Oh, Sunshine, I haven't entangled myself with anyone! Not that I'd be hugely averse to the idea of a little entangling if the right parties were interested." He flicked his eyes over Sunshine and gave him a smile.

Sunshine frowned.

Felix cleared his throat and smoothed out his jacket. He didn't know why he kept flirting with the angel. He didn't even like him that much as a person, so he definitely didn't have any interest in him as a bedmate.

He'd been single for a while. That had to be it. After Kathleen, he hadn't wanted to date and now that the idea tickled his fancy every so often, he wasn't sure how to get back in the water.

That actually made a lot of sense. He was practicing. Clearly, he needed it, based on how poorly he'd read things with Grace. The angel made a perfect target because he'd never know if Felix said something stupid.

"What's it matter to you, anyway?" Felix asked.

"Hmm?"

"If I was interested in Marceline in a romantic sense. What difference does it make to you?"

"The last woman you made advances toward nearly killed you."

"I don't think Marceline's got the same sort of agenda as Grace did. She's not a member of a cult, first of all, and if she *did* want me dead, she probably would have left me in that cage to be burned alive," Felix pointed out. "And I'm *not* flirting with her. I'm being polite. You should try it sometime."

"It looks like flirting to me."

"And what do you know! Just because a man is nice to a woman doesn't mean he's making advances."

"Is that what that means?" Marceline asked.

Felix spun around. "I'm so sorry, Ms. Roy—"

"You might as well call me Marceline." She crossed her arms loosely over her chest.

"So. Is your friend willing to help us?"

"No."

"Oh." He put his hands on his hips. He glanced at Sunshine. "No?"

"It was an emphatic one to be sure," she said.

"Well. That's not such an enormous setback. He has a car?"

"If you want to call it that."

"Even better. Is he still inside?"

She nodded.

Felix stepped around her and went back into the kitchen. He found Sam tying his shoes on the bench where Felix had lain early. "I'd like to make you a proposition."

Sam glanced up. "I'm sorry, sir, I—"

"I want to buy your car."

Sam frowned. "Sir?"

"I need to get out of this town. Urgently. I'm willing to give you much more than it's worth. What do you drive?"

"A, uh. I'm not sure I follow, mister, I'm really sorry."

"Sam, right? It's not a hard concept. I want to buy your car. What do you drive?" Felix said.

"It's, uh. It's a Ford."

"Dare I ask what model?"

"It's a twenty-eight Model A. Uh, been in the family for a while."

"If you're intent on having it returned, then I would like to rent your car," Felix said. He dropped the bag, took a knee, and fished out the wallet of gems. He poured a dozen into his palm. "I see at least six diamonds here and not piddly little ones, either. You could buy probably two new cars. Buy your own hotel."

Sam stared at him like this was some kind of trick. He shook his head. "It's not about the money. I can't let her throw her life away like this. She has a good job up at the spa, and they treat her good enough–”

“Who is she to you? Is she your girl? Or a relative?” Felix guessed.

“Her brother’s my best friend. He asked me to look after her when he left for the service.”

“I can appreciate that. I’d want someone to watch after my family, too, but here’s the thing. Ms. Roy has already made her choice. You are not keeping her safe by keeping her in town. She and I are already in danger. We need to leave as soon as possible.”

Sam still had his eyes on the diamonds. “I’m worried about her. She...she’s talking about *angels*, mister.”

Felix took a calculated gamble. He put away the gems. “So, you don’t believe in God?”

“I–”

“We’ll find our own way, then. I hope when you need help, someone helps you.” He turned and went back outside.

“Well?” Sunshine asked.

“Give it a minute.”

It actually took two minutes, by Felix’s count, for Sam to come back outside. He looked distraught and Felix almost felt bad about that.

To Marceline, he said, “You’re serious.”

“They’re up to something I can’t be a part of at the spa. I can’t,” she said.

“Fine. Fine. I’ll drive you. But you gotta promise to call as soon as you can.”

“Course I will, Sam.”

He nodded, ran his hand over his curls, then said, “It’s parked at the house.”

Sam turned away and Felix heard Marceline mutter something about having told him that before and him needing to listen the first time.

“Some people won’t listen unless it comes from a figure of authority,” Felix commiserated, then read Marceline’s face and realized he’d come off as arrogant. He hastened to add, “Or a perceived authority figure. I do usually look the part better than this. But when you think someone can make trouble for you, you just tend to listen a little better.”

“Did you tell Sam you’d make trouble for him?” Marceline asked delicately.

"I tried to buy his car. I think that got his attention a little better than threats."

"Oh, that thing is a piece of junk. You don't want to buy it."

"I'd buy a whole train if it would get me home. If I could summon a Pegasus to fly home on, I'd do that too."

Marceline chuckled. "I wouldn't mind seeing that!"

"Sadly, it outstrips my abilities, but I am good for more than just nightlights."

"Are you telling me people there are who can?"

"I mean...I'd hate to put that idea in a mage's head. Who knows what they would do to two or three dozen horses on their way to a Pegasus? I still don't know how you grow up surrounded by Moralists and not know about magic, though."

"Like I said, the older folks are superstitious but other than that, they don't talk much about what they believe. They have meeting houses that they all go to on Sundays, I figured they must be sort of like Quakers or Mennonites. Calling each other Elder So-and-so, or Sister, or Brother..." She shrugged. "An old man tells you to watch out for witches, you think he's a little paranoid."

Felix nodded. He'd made the luddite association with Moralists for some reason too but having outdated ideas about the place of the supernatural community didn't translate into being old-fashioned about everything. All that aside, Purity Springs did seem like a nice enough town. He searched for something to say and could only come up with, "Marceline Roy, that's French, isn't it?"

"Yes."

"Specter is Dutch, I think. Which, if it is, I'd like to have a word with someone because if I'm going to be Dutch of all things, then I'd like to be a little taller." He caught her looking him over. "Not exactly a strapping specimen of European virility," he agreed.

"Oh, I'm...I'm not staring. Or, I don't mean to."

"No, no, it's...I'm a little funny-looking. I come from a funny-looking family. We're used to being looked at. The important part is learning which looks are harmless and which ones will cause trouble," Felix said.

He'd never said that out loud to anyone. It sounded casual in his head, but aloud it sounded grim.

"You're not funny-looking."

He flashed her a smile. "Sure I am. At least once a year I get asked if I'm albino, which I am not, if you were wondering. Which is not nearly so bad as Bibi being asked why they're green...or any number of other things."

"Green?"

He nodded.

"That's got to be...startling."

Felix shrugged. He couldn't attest to that, having grown up with Bibi. He called, "Sunshine!"

The angel stopped walking and turned around. He didn't answer but fixed his eyes on Felix's face, waiting.

"Were you startled by Bibi being green?"

"No."

"Really?"

"Angels come in many colors outside the human spectrum," he answered and fell into step beside Felix and Marceline. "Those who did not fall speak still of Phaedrus."

"Really?"

"The Almighty made no new angel of stories, only notaries. Phaedrus is missed. I never thought I'd meet them, let alone like this."

"Hang on, who's Phaedrus?" Marceline asked.

"Oh, sorry, Phaedrus is Bibi. Bibi is what I call them," he said.

At his age, he really shouldn't have been calling his parents Bibi and Papa; he should have left that behind in his childhood. He couldn't imagine looking at Papa and calling him 'father' or 'sir' like some people called their fathers. He didn't know what on Earth he would call Bibi either.

"So, another angel?" Marceline guessed.

Felix opened his mouth to explain, but before he could, Sunshine launched into a clinical description of the Fall. It sounded like something between a text and a battle report. It was also the most Sunshine had talked since they'd met, so Felix kept his mouth shut.

It made Felix realize what a terrible enemy he would have had.

And might still have, he recognized. He put his hands in his pockets and tried not to think about that, especially now that he had no amulet to hide him. He didn't like knowing that he couldn't hold his own in a fight against Sunshine, either.

He didn't think the angel was more powerful than him, it was that he scared Felix just about shitless. Maybe the angel had made him afraid, just like he'd made him calm down. Fear had its significant power and if the angel could control that, he would win against Felix every time.

Felix didn't think so, but he didn't like thinking that fear had come from inside himself.

He dropped back and walked behind the other three. Sam had taken the lead and glanced back every so often, uncomfortable and nervous. Who wouldn't be, in his situation? Sunshine and Marceline looked relaxed with each other, talking like new acquaintances, yes, but ones who'd met under much more normal circumstances than they had.

Felix lagged further and further behind.

He had nothing to say and never knew what to do with himself when he ran out of words. His defaults tended towards nastiness and flirtation, neither of which would get him anywhere good with the trio in front of him.

He wanted to go home.

He glanced up.

The moon had inched closer to full since the last time he'd looked at it. By the time the Moralists had readied themselves to burn him, a full moon might have been his last sight. Probably symbolic or something.

He stood and looked up at the sky for a while. He could see more stars here than he could in Pickering.

Hell had one star and that was less than thirty years old. His father had made it for his companion.

The air had a nighttime warmth to it, cooler than the blazing heat of the day, but still warm enough that he wanted to shuck off his jacket, maybe take a cool bath.

"What are you doing?"

Felix turned to see Sunshine had stopped walking with Marceline and come back to stand beside him. He hadn't even noticed him come over. "Looking."

Sunshine looked up. "They look happier here."

Felix tilted his head.

Still staring up, his head tipped back, Sunshine said, "You can see more of them. They don't look so lonely."

Felix almost told him stars don't get lonely, but he figured Sunshine already knew that. And he was right, the stars did look happier here. Brighter and clearer. He watched Sunshine watch the sky. He had to tear his eyes away and forced himself to say, "We should catch up."

Marceline and Sam had gotten pretty far ahead of them.

Sunshine waited for Felix to take the first step, then walked alongside him.

"Heaven really still talks about Bibi?"

"Yes."

"You should let them know."

"Why?"

Felix shrugged. "The Fallen don't ever get to talk to angels or hear about Heaven, not more than once or twice a century. It must be nice to know people still think about you at home. That you're missed."

"How many years has it been since they fell?"

"No one knows. The Fall scattered them all over the world, and some of them through time. I guess that's what happens when you fall out of a timeless dimension. For some, it has been a millennium, or two, or three...or more. I know Bibi lived in Egypt, in a temple of Thoth for a while."

"They must have incredible strength," Sunshine pronounced.

"They can pick up me and Papa at the same time, so you're right on that account," Felix said. "Useless in a fight, though."

Sunshine opened his mouth and turned toward him to correct him. He scanned Felix's face, closed his mouth, and scowled.

Felix smiled. "Bibi *is* an absolute marvel. You should tell them that, too."

Sunshine arched an eyebrow.

They caught up with Sam and Marceline.

Felix looked over the car and couldn't see why Sam hadn't wanted to trade it for a handful of diamonds. He put their bags in the trunk, held open the door for Marceline, and then opened the door for Sunshine too because he was looking at the door handle like it might bite him.

As they rattled down the road, jostling each other in the confines of the backseat, Felix became aware of how much he and Sunshine smelled.

He wanted to apologize to the others.

AN OLDER woman traveling alone took pity on Felix when she saw him trying to haggle with the clerk who was unwilling to take gems for tickets. She bought one of the rings Felix had for a hundred dollars and a pair of earrings for fifty.

She and Felix made their way through the exchange with the knowledge that she had picked out the least valuable items there and offered about half of what they were worth. However, doing so left her without much in her wallet.

"I do need enough to get me into town," she told him.

"Oh, no, ma'am, you've just about saved my life," he said. "Thank you."

"Do be safe, young man. I'm not sure what kind of predicament you're in..." She looked him over. She could recognize that his suit, though soiled and tattered, had once been one of quality.

He leaned in and whispered, "Would you believe if I said I was a runaway prince? Not the heir apparent, of course, but somewhat in line for the throne."

"I very well might."

He nodded toward Sunshine. "My minder isn't thrilled about this at all. I tried to shake him but he's persistent."

She looked at Sunshine, who did fit the part of disgruntled bodyguard rather well. "Next time, try to make your way with a little more cash on hand."

He laughed. "Duly noted, if I survive the hiding my father gives me when they catch me."

"Good luck, young man."

"A thousand thank yous." He tucked the cash into his wallet and tried not to think about how much his hand hurt. He gave a bow and a smile, then returned to his companions.

"You're a con man," Marceline accused lightly.

"No. I'm a liar and only a half-hearted one at that. I didn't con her out of anything. She paid me a hundred dollars for a two-karat sapphire. If anything, I've been conned."

"Is it enough?" Sunshine asked.

"To get us to Pickering," Felix confirmed. "Marceline, you may need to tolerate a stop there if it doesn't trouble you too much."

"Not at all."

Half an hour later, he had hunkered down in a seat, his bag clutched against his chest. He nodded off almost immediately and when he woke a few hours later, he found his companions asleep as well.

He poked Sunshine in the shoulder.

"Hnng?" Sunshine peeked open one eye.

"I'll be right back."

"Mmm."

He returned feeling marginally cleaner. He'd scrubbed up to the absolute best of his ability and changed his clothes. He thought about trying to wash his hair but settled for combing it.

Even if he didn't feel squeaky clean, at least he looked better.

He nudged Sunshine when he got back.

"What?" the angel grunted.

"I'm back."

Sunshine huffed and folded his arms tighter across his chest. He squeezed his eyes shut like he could force himself back to sleep. A few minutes later, he opened his eyes and sighed at Felix.

"Well! You always get worked up when I go anywhere."

Sunshine sighed again. He rubbed his eyes.

"You look sort of awful."

"I'm *tired*. I haven't slept a whole night through in...well. How many days has it been?"

"That's your fault. I told you to sleep," Felix told him.

"How could I sleep?"

Felix sighed. He crossed his arms. "Are we going to do this

back and forth? You did this to me, and I did that to you and so on. It's going to get old fast."

"We don't have to."

"Good. I'd rather just...put it behind us. You can go put a good word in for me upstairs and we can go our separate ways."

Sunshine gave him a long, serious look.

"What?"

Sunshine swallowed. "You still haven't untethered me from this realm."

"Oh, well. I will. We haven't had much in the way of time."

Sunshine nodded.

"I've got the spell at home. Don't worry." Felix slumped in his seat. "Go back to sleep."

"No, I'm awake now. The bathroom...?" He glanced around.

Felix pointed, then nestled further down into his seat.

A day later, he paused in front of the front door to his home to examine the new lock and doorknob. A little more ornate than what they'd had before.

"Is something wrong?" Sunshine asked.

"They changed the lock." He looked at the key in his hand, then stowed it and rapped on the door. It felt almost profane, knocking on his own door.

Bibi pulled open the door like they thought they might need to kill whoever might be on the other side. "Oh, thank Christ, it's you. I thought it was another one of those *insane* cult members. Don't even get me *started*..." Bibi noticed Marceline. "Felix, sometimes I think you are *trying* to kill your father. Is that another one?"

"No, this is Ms. Marceline Roy, I owe her my life as well as a train ticket, at the very least," Felix said.

"Ms. Roy, please, come in. I do have to apologize, the house is in a bit of a state but well, if you've had the misfortune to fall in with my son, then you must recognize that he is an absolute sower of chaos."

Felix frowned.

Marceline said, "Thank you very much."

"Could have at least *called*, Felix, to tell me we had a guest," Bibi said, and asked Marceline, "Surely, you'll stay for the night? I'm sure whatever you've been up to has been harrowing."

"Oh, I don't want to impose, mmm..."

"Doctor," Felix supplied quietly.

"Doctor, I don't want to be a nuisance," Marceline said.

"Ridiculous. Have a seat. I'll get a room ready," Bibi insisted.

"Where's Papa?"

"At the police station." Bibi looked at Sunshine. "You, too, come in and close the door."

Sunshine obeyed but didn't move more than a few feet inside the house.

Bibi put a hand on Felix's shoulder and guided him upstairs. "I trust things are resolved with that knife?"

"I hope so."

"Hope is not sufficient at this point."

"I destroyed it."

Bibi raised an eyebrow.

"I didn't know what else to do."

"And the angel tolerated that?"

"You just about scared the piss out of him, Bibi. Telling him you'd send him to Hell!"

Bibi smiled. "It worked, then? What about that woman?"

"I didn't see her. But either she'll come try to find me, or she won't. Without the knife, she's not any more of a threat I had hanging over my head than before."

Felix readied one guestroom while Bibi did the other. By the time he finished, Bibi had already gone back downstairs and put out a few refreshments and Felix had a new appreciation for Papa having to do everything with one hand.

Bibi asked what had happened.

Before Felix could intervene, Sunshine began a detailed and too accurate description of the trouble they'd gotten into. Unable to think of any other way to stop him, Felix sent out a bit of power and tipped a glass of water onto Sunshine's lap.

Bibi narrowed their eyes at Felix.

"Oh, gee, Sunshine, let's get you a towel," Felix said. "And you know what? I bet we could use a bath...not, not together but uh. You know. You smell."

Sunshine stared at him.

"I wasn't going to say anything but..." Felix shrugged and made a sympathetic face. "It's pretty bad."

"You smell."

Felix stood and said, "The bath is this way."

"I could smell you a mile downwind," Sunshine said as he followed Felix upstairs.

"Bibi, maybe you could get Marceline settled?" Felix suggested.

He walked Sunshine to the bathroom and nodded toward the tub. "Are you familiar with such a contraption?"

"I don't think it will be hard to figure out."

Felix snorted. "Right. Anyway. Soap, towels, hamper." He pointed as he named them. "Help..."

Sunshine had started to strip.

Felix thought to correct him but then reconsidered that embarrassment about being undressed in front of other people was not exactly something the angel needed. He'd be back in Heaven soon enough.

Besides, unless he was hiding extra eyes or the face of a lion somewhere, it wasn't anything Felix hadn't seen before.

Instead of staring, he made himself useful and started to run a bath.

Sunshine put a foot in without checking the water and immediately danced back, a hiss of pain coming through his teeth. "It's *hot*."

"Of course, it is, you dumb bastard, it's *steaming*."

Sunshine scowled at Felix, then at the water.

Felix adjusted the taps and checked the temperature. "You think you can figure it out from here?"

"Yes."

He didn't sound sure. "Something else you understand in principle?" Felix guessed.

"I know what a bath is." He got into the tub, then started washing himself like he had something to prove.

Felix hesitated, then backed out of the room. He closed the door and found Bibi waiting for him, leaning in the doorway of their bedroom. He startled, then put a hand to his chest. "Don't scare me like that."

"What don't you want me to know?"

"Uh...if I don't want you to know, why would I tell you?" he asked.

Bibi fixed their eyes on his.

Felix moved a little closer. He rubbed the back of his neck. "It...I mean, it all *just* happened. I'd like to get Marceline squared away, have a bath, and sleep in my own bed for a night. I'm tired."

"The angel seemed ready enough to talk."

"I'd also rather have you hear it from me instead of someone with the social wherewithal of a brick."

"I don't know, he seems a little looser than he was before you left. I only had to tell him to sit down once," Bibi noted. They looked toward the bathroom door. "What will happen when your father comes home and tells him that the Moralists are taken care of? Will your truce be over?"

Felix's stomach flipflopped. He shrugged. "Can we talk about this later?"

"Mmm."

He threw his arms around Bibi. "Please," he insisted softly.

Bibi rubbed his back. "Of course."

He squeezed harder.

Bibi squeezed him back.

Felix stayed in Bibi's embrace long enough that he could hear their heartbeat. It reminded him of being a little boy again. "Are the Moralists taken care of?"

"Your little trap worked like a charm. I think your father made a few adjustments, but you know he can't let sleeping dogs lie. The trickiest part was getting them to the police station."

"And they'll go to prison?"

"Of course. They're only human and they did break in armed to the teeth. It's a pretty easy case."

A little tension slid out of him. He sighed into Bibi's chest. "Can I have a *croque monsieur* for lunch?"

Bibi kissed his hair. "Of course."

"I love you."

"I love you too, darling."

After a bath and a nap, Felix gave his parents a partly true, carefully edited version of what happened. He didn't want to lie to them, not really, but he also didn't want them to know he'd had a nervous breakdown in the woods. He suspected the story he got from his parents had similar omissions, especially given that some of the furniture in the living room looked the worse for wear than it had when he'd left.

Sunshine focused more on devouring three sandwiches than he did on Felix's story, so he didn't contradict anything Felix said. He also didn't seem to notice that all the other Moralists who'd come to Pickering had made their way into the custody of the police.

Papa and Bibi didn't like what had happened, but they were glad to wash their hands of the whole mess.

Sunshine followed Bibi around the kitchen to help clean up, hurrying to obey their every direction.

"Papa, watch out, you might have competition," Felix teased.

Papa snorted.

Bibi shook their head and rolled their eyes. "Felix, don't be rude."

Sunshine looked openly scandalized. He turned his big orange eyes to Bibi and said, "I would never dare...!"

Bibi patted Sunshine's shoulder. "You'll learn to ignore him when he gets like that. Here, dry the dishes."

Sunshine took the dishtowel like it offered salvation, like he could find solace in dry plates and those alone.

Once they'd eaten and squared everything away, Felix retrieved his jacket.

The angel had gone upstairs. Felix suspected he'd fallen asleep, which was fine. Felix didn't need the angel lurking around for what he planned next.

"Where could you be headed?" Bibi asked.

Felix didn't know what to say. "Just out."

"Out," Papa repeated.

"Yes."

"Out where?" his parents asked together.

Felix shrugged. "I have a few things to take care of."

"What further mess could you have possibly made, Felix?" Bibi asked.

"It's..." Felix looked at his shoes then dragged his eyes back up. He squared his shoulders which, narrow as he was, mustn't have had much of an effect at all. "I want to see them. The Moralists."

"Haven't you had enough of them?" Papa demanded, his voice unusually raised. "You've put yourself in such enormous danger—"

"They're in jail, aren't they? They're only human. They can't hurt me through the bars."

"What could you *want* with them, dearest?" Bibi asked.

"My mother...her...her family killed her. It was them I contacted. It was...I. I want to see them," Felix forced himself to say. "I have to see them."

"No," Papa said.

"Papa."

"No, Felix, you are not to see those people. They are dangerous," Papa continued.

"They killed her. I want to know if they're here. If they came to kill me too. I have to know."

"You don't," Papa said.

"I'm going."

"I forbid it. Do not go there."

Bibi murmured, "Hiram."

"You forbid it?" Felix demanded, not able to wrap his head around that. "You forbid it. I'm twenty-six, I'm not a little boy. You can't forbid me from doing anything."

"You are a child, Felix, and you *act* like a child. And more than that, I am your father, and I am telling you not to go," Papa said, all the normal honeyed warmth of that Deep South accent bled out of his voice.

"Then stop me," Felix spat. He turned and slammed the door behind him as he left.

He heard his father call after him, but he didn't stop.

Adrenaline and spite carried him all the way to the Pickering jail. He was somewhat well known there, due to Oscar's habit of needing to be bailed out.

Once inside the building, his resolve softened.

Did he want to do this?

He approached the officer on duty and subtly slid over a few bills, making his request to see the prisoners as mild and polite as possible. Felix had done this before, come here for information before. His parents didn't know, of course, or at least, he hoped they didn't.

The officer took the money.

They always did.

Felix thought it would be easy to spot the Moralists, but he couldn't pick them out. There were plenty of other roughs and drunks in the cells tonight.

He spotted a familiar face, though, in one cell and paused before it.

He couldn't place it.

Someone he'd seen around the Bell maybe.

The man looked up. He had dark eyes, deep green like pine needles, and a hank of gray-and-white hair hung in his eyes until he slicked it back.

It was not Felix's face exactly. Too broad and too old, the features at once too strong and too soft. He had a somewhat careworn look about him, like a grandfather who'd worked hard all his life, or had fallen on hard times lately.

Like a grandfather.

Felix stared at him.

The man rose.

He was tall and broad shouldered. His wasn't battered, exactly, but he had a scrape on his jaw and tears in his clothes. Suspenders dangled from the waist of his trousers.

"My name—" Felix began.

"You have no name."

He flinched from the voice. It wasn't rough or unkind. It was an unpleasant statement delivered mildly. "My name is Felix Specter," he finished, doing his best to keep the shake out of his voice.

"No. It isn't. You have no name. Especially not that one."

"It's what my mother named me."

The man shook his head again.

"Your daughter."

The man shook his head again.

"The one you killed," Felix said, too loud, his voice bouncing off the walls.

People had gone quiet to watch their exchange. More interesting than watching someone sleep off a rough night or barf up their dinner.

"I had no daughter to kill," the man said. "Not by the time you had finished with her."

"Me? All I did was be born, I didn't have time to do anything else."

"It never should have come to pass," the man said.

"I..." He didn't know what to say. He didn't know what he had wanted. To see his mother's kin because he could never see her, maybe, or to see the person who'd ended her life and ended the life that Felix should have lived.

He never would have traded his parents for his mother. Never. And there was no way he ever could have had them both. But if Mercy Specter had to be dead, it would have at least been nice to know about her. To have seen her face even once.

Not some extrapolation he had from his father's descriptions and his own features.

"What was she like?" Felix asked. "That's...that's it."

The man didn't answer.

"Please."

He shook his head.

Felix reached through the bars and grabbed his shirt.

The man grabbed his wrist, crushing it with all his strength.

Felix took hold of the man's arm with his other hand, digging his fingers in and sending enough magic into him to numb his legs, to loosen his grip, to bring him to his knees. It was unchecked, undirected power, wielded without any purpose but to dominate, to press this man into compliance, to feel better because now he felt so small and stupid and weak. "All I want is to know about my mother."

"Monsters don't have mothers. Monsters don't have names," the man growled, his hand still holding Felix's wrist hard, but no longer hard enough to hurt.

Felix crouched in front of the cell, grasping hard onto the man like he could make him say something nice about the daughter he'd killed. "Just tell me."

The man sat up a little straighter. He gripped Felix's arm as if to steady himself. "You don't have a mother. You don't have a name. You are a monster. Even your face is the beast's face."

Something bubbled up in him, some surge of frustration and hurt and shame. He gave the man a shove with a shout, hard enough to send him falling back.

He stormed out, shaking, not thinking.

"Everything alright in there?" the officer asked.

"I found out what I needed to."

"You didn't make a mess, I trust."

"No," Felix answered shortly.

He walked out of the station.

He couldn't go home. He couldn't stay here.

He wouldn't go see Oscar.

He sat on the bench outside the jail.

Someone came to sit beside him.

He didn't bother to look up.

Someone sat on his other side and a tingle of fear ran down his spine.

Were there others that hadn't been captured?

He looked around.

Papa sat on his left, the Devil on his right.

He gritted his teeth and lifted his chin, not ready to be told off. He sniffled, though, and couldn't look at Papa.

He faced Lucifer. "What are you here for? Are you taking them to Hell?"

"No," Lucifer asked. "Their souls will be mine soon enough and I don't want them any sooner than that."

"Well then?" Felix demanded.

"Well," Lucifer asked. "I have been informed of your escapades of late, little one."

"I'm not little!" he snapped.

"You are very little," Lucifer said. "I could swaddle you like a babe and carry you in my claws if I wanted."

Felix scowled.

"And you are my youngest," Lucifer said. "Likely...Likely my last. Although I thought that a few hundred years ago, too..." He trailed off then cleared his throat. "But I must ask, are you well? Should I be concerned?"

"I'm fine."

"Because I am concerned."

"I'm not going to do anything. I'm not...I'm not going to *be* the antichrist or hurt anyone or...light the house on fire and torture little animals," Felix said.

Lucifer looked at Papa. "Reinhart, are these the things you've been saying to my son?"

"No! He reads these dreadful novels," Papa said, "Such grim things."

"I am not concerned about what you will do, Felix, I am concerned about your wellbeing," Lucifer clarified.

"We all are," Papa added.

"Well, don't bother with that. It's done. I've learned my lesson."

"Felix," Papa said. It wasn't scolding or reproachful, but it sounded sad. He put his hand on Felix's arm.

"I know!" Felix said. He stood up, pulling away from them. "I know. I was stupid and I almost got us all killed. I know it was bad because you bothered to call *him*, too, and that means I royally fucked up."

The language had Papa looking openly shocked, like he'd never heard such bad language before.

Lucifer's face didn't change.

"Where's Bibi? Don't the three of you like to gang up on me for these things?"

"Bibi is waiting at home," Papa said, "In case you changed your mind." He stood slowly. "I wish you had. I wish...I wish you hadn't heard whatever those people said to you. I wish you didn't feel like you needed to do this."

Felix swallowed.

His father didn't approach.

Lucifer asked, "Are you happy here?"

"I'm fucking miserable."

Papa looked like he wanted to cry.

"I brought you to your parents because they could give you what I could not," Lucifer said. "Your mother wanted you to grow up on Earth. I wanted you to be safe. But...but you're older now, Felix, and you can make your own choices. If you want to leave Earth, my home is always yours."

Papa and the Devil both stared at him.

He took half a step back, then glanced back at the road. "You're sending me away?" he asked Papa.

"No!" Papa insisted immediately. He wrapped his arms around Felix.

Felix took several steps back.

At that, Lucifer got into the mix and said, "The road, perhaps, is not the best place to have this conversation," as he pulled Felix out of the road like he was scooping up a stray kitten.

"We aren't *sending you* anywhere," Papa said. "We would never send you away, Felix, but...But we're worried about you, honey. We want you to be happy, that's all."

"I wouldn't be happy in Hell."

"You've been to Hell only as a baby," Lucifer pointed out.

"Yes, well, the realm of torture and brimstone doesn't exactly sound appealing. What would I even do there? Torture people? Get tortured? Is this some kind of, of...reform school?"

"Hell is more than torture and it is *not* on fire," Lucifer assured. "Visit if you'd like. Whenever you like. The choice is yours."

"I don't *want to go*," Felix insisted, not quite able to believe that he was on the verge of tears again, about to be sent away from home, no closer to freedom or knowing about his mother than he had been when this had started. "Papa, what did Bibi say? Do they want me to go, too?"

"We aren't sending you away."

Felix looked at Lucifer.

"It would be a choice, little love," Lucifer said. "And one you clearly have no interest in." The Devil put a hand on Felix's cheek. "I offered only because you seem so unhappy."

Felix had never thought of himself as unhappy.

But, then again, happy people didn't do the things he'd done.

"I'm sorry," he said.

"You aren't in trouble," Papa said. "Maybe...maybe we should just go home."

Felix nodded.

Lucifer kissed the top of Felix's head. "I am always here should you need me."

"I know."

"I mean it."

"I know, Dad."

Lucifer smiled at that. He touched Felix's face again. "Maybe you could come visit some time."

"I'll think about it."

The Devil nodded and then was gone.

Papa and Felix looked at each other.

"Papa, I—"

"Please, come home," Papa said.

Felix folded himself against his father's chest. "I really am sorry."

"I'm not angry."

He sniffled. "I love you."

"I love you, too, Felix. I will always love you. No matter how many murderous cults you lead into my house," Papa said.

Felix held in a chuckle. "It's Bibi's house."

Papa tightened his arms. "Speaking of Bibi..."

"We should get home," Felix agreed.

IN THE morning, Felix brought Marceline to the train station and sent her on her way with a packed lunch and a check for more than enough money to help her set up a new life in Toronto. She'd given her aunt and uncle a call and found out that her cousin could use a roommate. He waved to her from the platform and made her promise to call when she got settled in.

"Maybe you can come visit," she'd said.

He'd told her, "I'd like that."

Once the train pulled away, Felix said to Sunshine, "That felt a little too easy."

"I don't understand."

"Doesn't it feel like something should go wrong? Everything has gone ten kinds of sideways lately."

"Oh."

Felix looked the angel over. He couldn't shake the feeling something bad would happen soon. He knew, logically, that Sunshine had many reasons to fill that role, but found himself hoping that it wouldn't come from him. He swallowed and looked around the platform. He started walking. "Let's head back. I can, I'll unbind you and you can...You can go up there and tell them they haven't got to worry about me."

Sunshine didn't say anything. He walked a few steps behind

Felix and didn't look quite so upright as usual.

A nervous chuckle escaped. "If you're going to try to kill me, you could have the decency to give me a heads up and let me get a running start."

"I'm not going to kill you."

"But...?"

Sunshine stayed quiet.

"But?" he asked more insistently.

Sunshine shook his head. "I don't know. Something's..." He sighed. "Something's wrong. I don't know what to say or how to say it."

"Oh."

"I don't have an answer for you. I'm sorry."

Felix shrugged. "Where will you go?"

Sunshine's head jerked up, his eyes wide.

When he wasn't scowling, he didn't look so much like a statue, and with his eyes wide like that, he very nearly looked like a person. A lost, confused, and possibly frightened person. Felix caught himself feeling bad for him.

"I don't know," he breathed.

"You'll figure it out," Felix assured.

He shook his head. "I won't. I don't...I don't know *anything*. I don't know what to do, or, or where to go!"

Felix knew Sunshine had nowhere else to go, literally. Without killing Felix, he had no purpose on this earth and Felix didn't figure he could go out and pick up a job. He opened his mouth and intended to offer to put up Sunshine at a boarding house for a week or two while he thought things out, but what he said was, "Come back to the house."

"Even I know that isn't right," the angel said, his voice coming out like it was stuck in his throat.

Felix raised an eyebrow.

"My presence is an imposition and a threat."

"You looked for me for twenty-six years," Felix reminded. "I didn't think you'd pass up an opportunity to keep an eye on me like this." He really couldn't believe himself.

"I shouldn't."

"Well, you could *at least* be a gentleman and walk me home," Felix said.

The angel nodded.

Once home, Felix reminded Sunshine he had to come get his

things, and then he offered him lunch, and then came up with enough distractions to keep Sunshine busy until Papa and Bibi came home.

He turned the job of distracting Sunshine over to Bibi, who without being asked gave the angel a handful of tasks to help get dinner ready.

By nightfall, they'd decided Sunshine would spend the night.

When Felix peeked in the guestroom to check on him, he found Sunshine asleep face down, sprawled out like he'd collapsed.

The next morning, Felix slipped out before Sunshine woke up. He hadn't moved much in the night.

Felix headed down to Oscar's store. He waved to Soon-hee, who sat in her usual spot behind the counter.

She narrowed her eyes at him.

He thought about saying something nasty. "Is Oscar upstairs?"

"Oscar's out."

"Will he be back soon?"

"I don't know."

Felix scuffed his shoe against the floor. "I'll give it a few minutes." He wandered around to browse the various wares. Most of it didn't spark much interest, but sometimes he'd find something good. People tended to pawn interesting things in a town like Pickering.

He had parked himself in front of a glass display case containing various weaponry, his eyes sliding over the knives when someone clapped a hand on his shoulder.

He didn't jump. "Hi, Oscar."

"I'll sneak up on you someday."

"Not likely."

Oscar slung an arm around his shoulders and looked at the knives, too. "If you couldn't shoot him, you probably can't stab him."

"I'm not going to stab him."

"He's probably in the wind by now anyway."

"No, he's...He's in the guestroom."

Oscar shook his head. "You are something else."

Felix pointed. "How much for that one?"

Oscar opened the case and showed Felix the price tag.

Felix took it, examined it, and said, "I'll take it."

"I don't know, your parents gave me an earful about selling you that gun."

Felix rolled his eyes. He went over to Soon-hee and placed the knife on the counter in front of her.

Oscar followed him over. "I really feel bad about selling you that! Honestly, if I had any idea what you were going to get yourself into, I would have—"

"Told my parents? Aren't we a little old for that?"

"But you could have died."

Felix handed over a few bills to Soon-hee, who wordlessly sorted out his change. He smiled and said, "Thanks."

"You want me to wrap that?" she asked.

"Please."

Oscar sighed. He put his hand on Felix's arm. "Please tell me you aren't planning anything like last time."

"I promise."

Oscar didn't look convinced.

"Let's go out on Friday. Are you still on about that singer at the Bell?"

Oscar huffed. "He's seeing some waitress now."

"Have you recovered yet?"

Oscar gave him a dirty look. "What happened to sympathy?"

"I ran out four or five singers ago."

Oscar gave him a shove.

Felix nudged him back. "Let's go out Friday. I need to do something normal again."

Soon-hee handed the wrapped knife over. "I'm busy on Friday."

"Oh? What's happening on Friday?" Felix asked.

"That's during the day," Oscar told her. "We can go out at night."

"What's happening during the day?"

"Soon-hee's got a doctor's appointment," Oscar informed him dismissively.

Her cheeks turned bright red. "Oscar!"

"What! It's not anything bad," Oscar said. "Christ, and of all the people in the world, Felix doesn't care."

"A woman's business at the doctor is still private," Soon-hee insisted.

Oscar rolled his eyes. "It's just an exam," he told Felix. "She's just hysterical about it because she doesn't like you. You told at least four different people you had a doctor's appointment the other day."

"Ah, yeah, but Oscar, that's her business to tell people, not yours," Felix said. "Anyway, I didn't come over just to piss people off."

"What did you need?"

Felix shrugged. "I don't know. I wanted to see you. Friendly faces have been lacking in my life of late."

"You reap what you sow," Soon-hee offered tartly.

He didn't exactly know why but that made his eyes go misty. He cleared his throat and rubbed his nose hard enough to banish the feeling. He told Oscar, "So now that you're done with Phillips, I have a friend from the university I'd like you to meet."

"Oh, Felix, I don't know about that."

"You never let me set you up with anyone, not once!" Felix pouted. "He's absolutely lovely and he's so sweet and I just know you two would hit it off."

"If he's so great, why don't you go out with him?" Oscar grumbled.

Felix ignored that. "Friday night! You'll be there."

"I don't know."

"Promise," Felix insisted. "His name is Jacob."

"Fine."

Felix grinned. He threw his arms around Oscar. "Ugh, I'm so excited! You never let me set you up!"

"Because you always try to set me up with people I'd never date."

Felix tried to set Oscar up with people who would like him and treat him well instead of the people he seemed to prefer, but he kept that to himself. He gave Oscar a squeeze then stepped back. "Eight o'clock, at the Bell. Promise."

"I promise."

Felix grinned and told Soon-hee, "You should come, too. Jacob goes for both so you know, if Oscar's too stupid to like him, you might be able to swoop in."

She didn't look at all pleased with the suggestion.

Felix shrugged.

He stopped by the University on the way home and found Jacob in the laboratory working on his thesis. It took less effort to talk him into the venture than it did Oscar, especially since he and Oscar had actually met a few years ago. He'd asked a few questions about Oscar and his stutter had flared up when Felix had teased him about liking Oscar. Felix had found that endearing as anything and wondered if he'd ever made someone stutter just talking about him.

Felix had felt relatively safe asking if Jacob had an interest in men because even if he didn't, he at least wouldn't have taken offense to the question. Felix had overheard Jacob defending Papa from the less open-minded University students a few times.

He stopped by Papa's office before he left, reminded him to eat lunch, and then headed home.

He found Sunshine sitting on the stoop.

"Hi there."

Sunshine looked up. "The door's locked."

Felix sat next to him. He handed over the wrapped knife and watched as Sunshine unwrapped it.

He stared at the blade.

"I felt bad about ruining your other one. You seemed awfully attached to it. I know it's not the same but..." He shrugged. He'd done his best to pick out one about the same size and weight as the knife he'd destroyed.

Sunshine turned the knife over in his hands a few times.

Felix shrugged. "I don't know."

Sunshine let out a long breath. "I can't tell Heaven that I believe you're harmless."

His stomach flipped. "Um. Oh."

"They'll only think that I've spent too long away. Lost my mind or fallen or gotten tricked. If I go back, they'll send someone else and they'll think you're dangerous enough to warp my mind."

"Oh."

"I'm sorry. I know that's what you wanted."

"So, what will you do, then?"

"I don't know," Sunshine admitted.

Felix sighed. He looked the angel over. "You can stay. Here, I mean. With us. Until you know what you want to do."

Sunshine shook his head. "I couldn't. Even a few days have felt like...like I'm an invader. Or a spy."

"Are you?"

"No. I don't think so."

"Then you shouldn't feel that way," Felix told him.

"How should I feel?"

The first answer he thought of made him smile, but he gave a kinder one, "You should feel like our guest."

"Even I know you don't keep an assassin as a guest," Sunshine pointed out.

"But you aren't an assassin anymore, are you?"

"I don't know what I am."

Felix used his thigh to nudge Sunshine's leg. "My parents are under the impression I need more friends."

"We can't be friends."

That felt like someone had dug a spoon into his insides and tried to scoop out his guts. He swallowed.

"I tried to kill you."

"Well, sure, but I tried to kill you, too. Let's, um. Let's just chalk it up to being pawns in the cosmic family issues between my dad and your maker."

Doubtful, Sunshine asked, "You could do that?"

"I think so. Could you?"

"I think so."

Felix smiled.

Sunshine looked away.

Felix nudged his leg again.

Sunshine nudged back.

"I'm going out on Friday. You should come along. You're going to have to learn to be a person if you're going to stay on Earth."

"Maybe."

"It'll be fun. Or at least, it will be educational."

Sunshine sighed. "Phaedrus does keep saying I have a lot to learn. They asked me to open eggs today..."

"Crack."

"What?"

"You crack eggs. You don't open them."

"Well, I'm not good at it, whatever it's called."

Felix said, "Ah, you'll get there, Sunshine. I believe in you. Most people do learn how to crack an egg within a reasonable number of attempts."

Sunshine didn't answer.

Felix figured he didn't know what else to say.

They sat in silence for a while, watching the people on the street pass by.

Felix waved to his neighbors.

Bibi came home to find them still on the stoop. "What are you doing out here?"

"You locked Sunshine out when you left."

"Gracious, I'm sorry. Don't you have your keys, Felix?"

"It's a nice day."

Bibi looked up at the sky. "It is." They held a small cardboard box in their hands. It had holes in the sides.

"What's that?"

"Oh. Yes. Well." Bibi cleared their throat. They handed over the box.

Felix could hear the scrape of tiny claws and he took off the lid.

A brown tabby kitten sat within. It blinked up at him then mewed.

"We did talk about getting you another cat before any of this started," Bibi said, "And Yvonne's cat had a litter a few months ago. I was set, actually, to go get one as soon as we got back from our trip, but I had to push it back a little. Anyway, that's the runt of the litter, all that was left, which really is sort of perfect for you, isn't it?"

He pretended to take offense. "Are you calling me a runt?"

"Well, you haven't managed to get to six feet yet and with a father like yours, you really should be taller."

Felix picked up the kitten and set the box aside. He showed it to Sunshine. "What should we name him?" He doublechecked to confirm the sex.

Sunshine stared at the kitten like he'd never seen one before.

The kitten gnawed on his thumb.

A few names rolled through his mind, but he didn't like any of them. He looked up at Bibi. "Sunshine says he's going to stay with us for a while longer."

"Does he now?"

Sunshine scowled at Felix. "I didn't—"

"Of course, you're welcome to stay," Bibi said.

"So you can tell Papa?" Felix asked.

Bibi put their hands on their waist.

"Oh, you know how he gets!" Felix whined. "He's so...protective."

"With good reason, given your behavior recently."

"But you'll tell him."

"I'll speak to your father."

Felix grinned.

"I suppose an angel is not the worst thing you could have brought home," Bibi muttered as they fished out the keys. "You have a whole pile of mail waiting upstairs for you, my love, you ought to tend to that."

Felix kept the kitten cradled against his chest as he followed Bibi inside.

"Will your father be upset if I stay?" Sunshine asked quietly.

"He'll act upset, but Bibi can talk him into anything."

"And it is my house," Bibi reminded. "Felix, go take care of your mail. Sunshine, I could use you down here."

The attempt at separating them was so obvious that Felix almost pointed it out. He thought better of it.

Before he went upstairs, he kissed Bibi's cheek and thanked them for the kitten.

Sunshine came upstairs later with his arms full of clothes. Old things of Bibi's, likely, since Papa was too narrow for anything of his to fit the angel.

Felix brought the kitten and went to sit on the bed as Sunshine sorted through his hand-me-downs. He recognized a lot of them as the plainer garments of Bibi's from the past few decades. They would do fine until Sunshine got his own wardrobe, though they'd probably need to be hemmed.

The kitten chased the bottoms of Sunshine's pants as he moved around the room.

"You know, we don't have to keep calling you Sunshine. You could pick a real name."

"It doesn't make any difference."

"You should name the cat, then. Since you didn't get to pick out your own name."

Sunshine looked down at the cat. "How do you name a cat?"

"Based on appearance or personality, or uh, other cats you've heard of."

Sunshine picked up the kitten and studied it. "He's brown. Should we name him after something brown?"

"Sure."

"Dirt is brown. Uh. Trees. Wood." Sunshine glanced at Felix.

Felix tried to hide his grimace.

"He has stripes."

"Yeah, he does."

"Can...can we name him Stripe?"

"Better than Dirt."

Sunshine sighed. "I don't know."

"Well, give it some time."

At dinner, Sunshine watched the kitten devour its plateful of food and make snorting noises as it went. He named the cat Piglet, which Felix actually liked.

Sunshine seemed proud of himself for figuring it out.

More than he pitied the angel, Felix kind of looked forward to having him around. Pickering didn't have a good crop of new and interesting people coming into town. Most interesting people left as soon as they earned their degree at the University and got a job elsewhere, Felix had found.

It would be refreshing, too, to take Sunshine around and show him the ropes.

After a few weeks, even Papa admitted Sunshine made a nice addition to the household. Once he relaxed, the angel turned out to have an even temper.

One day, when he thought Felix couldn't hear, Papa pointed out, "Felix really needs someone with your temperament, you know. He gets so worked up about things sometimes. I do worry about his nerves...But it almost makes me feel better that you've been going out with him. He really would get into trouble sometimes."

Felix had decided to give the angel a few months to acclimate before he started getting Sunshine in trouble, too.

About the Author

Dan is an author and educator who has lived in Connecticut for their entire life. They received a degree in education and later wrote their Master's thesis on representation of women in same-sex relationships in contemporary Spanish literature and cinema.